Strawberry Kisses

By Marianne Rice

Book 2 in the Rocky Harbor Series

Also by Marianne Rice

A Well Paired Novel
At First Blush
Where There's Hope
What Makes Us Stronger
Here With You
Finding Our Way Back
Something More
All of You

A Wilton Hills Christmas
Marshmallows & Mistletoe
Cocoa & Carols
Peppermints & Packages

Band of Sisters
Ten Million Fireflies

Rocky Harbor
Staying Grounded
Strawberry Kisses
Wounded Love
Playful Hearts

The McKay-Tucker Men
False Start
False Hope
False Impressions

The Wilde Sisters
Sweet on You
Then Came You
Wilde for You

Standalone
Smoke & Pearls

Dedication

For Rick. Thanks for giving me lots of entertaining big brother stories to share with my children: vitamin and butter sandwiches, banana guns, paper routes, chestnuts roasting over an open fire, spankings and wooden spoons, mullets and leather pants. Even though you had cooties when we were little, you're still my favorite brother.

CHAPTER ONE

"**I** don't have a good feeling about this." Rachael Riley clasped her shaking hand around her throat and swallowed. Her knees shook as she tapped her Nikes on the floorboard of her sister's old Toyota.

"Dude. Man up. This is just what the doctor ordered. You need to kick some ass."

Rachael bit her tongue and calmed her breathing. She and her sister were as opposite as could be. While Lucy's punk rocker sense of style had toned down over the past year, her attitude still reflected her wild side.

Lucy had only been part of the family for six years, adopted at seventeen, and by then Rachael had moved across the country to live with her boyfriend. If she'd only known how that would turn out.

Since returning to Rocky Harbor, Maine and reclaiming her life, Rachael had slowly gotten to know her eclectic sister. Before Lucy, Rachael was the youngest of the five children the Rileys had adopted, and the only girl. While Rachael had the benefit of being raised by the loving family since she was eight, Lucy had come into their lives as a hardened, abused, and druggy teenager. They'd hardly been sisters, much less friends for very long. And even then, their conversations were usually limited to food and weather.

And now here they were, sitting together outside The Warehouse. How the heck did she let Lucy talk her into this hair-brained idea?

"Maggie didn't say I needed to kick some ass," Rachael mumbled as she opened the car door. Therapy with her soon-to-be sister-in-law had really helped Rachael get through and process the past years—heck, the past few decades of her life—but taking self-defense classes had never come up in their sessions. This was all Lucy's idea.

Lucy rounded the hood and draped an arm around Rachael's shoulder. "Maggie agreed the class was a good idea. Think of this as a sister bonding thing."

"This isn't exactly what I had in mind. What happened to talking over coffee and a bagel?"

"Everything is always about food with you. Come on." Lucy tugged her arm, pulling Rachael toward the ominous gray and green steel structure.

If it wasn't for the sign in the parking lot indicating the boxing ring, self-defense and karate classes, one would think it was a warehouse storing...stuff.

"Can't we just go for a run or something?"

"You do look like you're dressed more for that than a kung-foo class. Thank God Maggie got you out of that dreadful wardrobe you used to hide behind. This suits you much better."

Rachael glanced down at her running shorts and the silly shirt Graham got her. *Obey the Cook* flared across her chest. When she fled California she'd left all her belongings behind. Dylan had controlled every aspect of her life, from what she ate to what she wore and where she went. He wanted a thin, plastic, tanned bimbo on his arm to show off. When she returned to Maine she borrowed some of her mom's old skirts and loose T-shirts, not caring how she looked. Hiding behind her long hair and baggy clothes, she had felt safer.

She glanced at Lucy's get up. Tight black spandex shorts and a Depeche Mode tank top that looked like it had been around for a few decades. "You're wearing running gear too."

"Yeah. But I don't look cute."

"I don't look cute."

Lucy snorted, opening the door for her. "I hear the instructor is hot. Like *I want to lick the sweat off your abs* hot."

"That's disgusting." Rachael scowled as she walked inside. She'd made headway in the past year. Her ex was still in jail, and would be for a few more months, and she detailed out a plan to start her own business, *Kids in the Kitchen*. Mingling with adults made her edgy, but Rachael loved to cook, and kids were cute. Men, on the other hand, intimidated her.

And she hated Dylan for that. Never again would she allow another human being to control her. She wasn't a weak-minded idiot, but living with his abuse for five years turned her into someone she wasn't. Her mother and brothers, God bless them, had been patiently trying to help Rachael crawl out of her shell, and with the help of Maggie, she was one step closer. Having a therapist marry into their family was kismet.

All the Riley kids had issues, none wanting to talk about them. But when Doreen Riley adopted them, she loved, nurtured, and raised them, giving each teen all the love in her heart as if she'd borne all six of them herself.

"You're stalling, sis. I signed us in. Let's go."

Rachael snapped out of her memories and took in her surroundings. Even with the subtle scent of sweat, the inside of the building was much nicer than the outside. The steel walls were gray and covered with large, framed black and white prints of boxers and fighters. She recognized Mohammad Ali but the others weren't familiar to her. Not exactly her thing.

MMA announcements were littered across the walls as well. She had no idea what the acronym stood for, but knew it had something to do with fighting. Oh, the irony. She left the abuse a thousand miles away and here she was, standing in the middle of a building that promoted the pounding of fists. Chills ran up her arms, despite the warm air. Rachael clutched her stomach with one hand and her throat again with the other as a bead of sweat formed above her upper lip.

The dark shroud that had lifted over the past few months slowly made its way over her body.

"It's not what you're thinking," Lucy said softly, her arm hooked around Rachael's shoulder.

"And what exactly am I thinking?" She clenched her legs and butt to stop the trembling as her fingernails dug into her neck.

"I can tell by the deer in the headlights look on your face. And you're sweating."

"It's hot in here."

"Not that hot. Listen, the registration fees go to women's shelters and programs for abused women. This place has a good rep. The instructor guy, the hot one I was telling you about, has been teaching these classes for a few years."

Rachael let out a soft sigh and relaxed her hand. "How do you know?"

"I have my own skeletons too, Rach." Lucy stuck a nametag on Rachael's chest. "I know we're not chummy yet, and you don't have to tell me all the deets from what happened."

"Deets?" Rachael only had three years on Lucy but sometimes she felt decades older. With Lucy's pixie do, her dark hair bleached blonde, and overly confident attitude, the adopted sisters would never be confused as blood sisters. Yet she'd always consider her adopted siblings as the real deal. Blood wasn't always thicker. Love was. It's what her parents ingrained into the kids from the moment they signed the adoption papers.

Heck, even before then.

"Details." Lucy gently squeezed her shoulder. "I know the asswipe knocked you around. Physically and mentally. And I get that you don't want to talk to me about it. I'm cool with that. But there's nothing wrong with learning some self-defense moves. No woman should ever let a man have that kind of power over her. If you can knock him on his ass, you can run and get help. Plus, it's a great workout. Let's do this."

It wasn't the pep talk Rachael had hoped for, but she knew her sister meant well, and somehow the veil lifted. Since Maggie had agreed that this would be a good idea as well, Rachael dropped her hand from her throat and concentrated on her yoga breathing techniques.

"I told you I'd try it out. You owe me coffee and a bagel afterward."

"Deal. And if it totally sucks, I'll buy. But if the instructor is as hot as his reputation, the bill is on you."

"Okay." Rachael laughed, the sound surprising to her ears. Lucy quirked her eyebrow, that confident air she had lifting the corner of her mouth.

They followed a narrow hallway to a big open space in the back. Hardwood floors gleamed under the sunlight that filled the room from the floor to ceiling windows. In the front was a large mat, with smaller mats scattered around the perimeter.

There were at least a dozen people in the class already, ranging from their teens to Generation X. All in workout gear. And all women.

"Hey, class. You all ready to get started?" A deep voice filled the room, and everyone stilled, then turned. Except for Rachael. She didn't know if she could go through with this.

"Holy hell," Lucy said a little too loudly.

Rachael had never been one to swoon over a good-looking guy, but when she glanced up and saw the man standing in front, she nearly lost her balance. He towered over the women in the class, his wide, strong shoulders built to carry fifty-pound bags of flour. Or a fire hose. Or a woman.

Hair as dark as ebony, and eyes that matched, should have made him appear menacing, but his enormous grin gave him a boyish charm. The black T-shirt he wore stretched tight over his shoulders and chest, and a tattoo that she couldn't decipher peeked out beyond his shirtsleeves and crawled up his neck. He had trouble written all over him.

Yet she wasn't scared. Not yet.

"Feeling confident in your ability to protect yourself empowers you to live with less fear and more freedom." He paused, and Rachael peered up at him through her bangs. "Welcome to session one. I'm Jake Morgan and I'll be your self-defense instructor for the next few weeks."

"Weeks?" Rachael asked, apparently loud enough for the hot instructor to hear.

"Yes, weeks." He smiled at her and her knees buckled.

"You're welcome," Lucy said, grabbing ahold of her wrist, not taking her eyes off Jake.

Rachael blinked away her trance and forced her head to turn toward her sneaky sister. "You said one class," she whispered harshly.

"Again. You're welcome." Lucy's grin lit up her face, the little devil. "And you're buying."

• • • •

JAKE'S DAY JUST TURNED a little bit brighter. While he loved volunteering his time to teach self-defense classes, the past week had been crazy at work and the gym. He'd logged in almost four hours of sleep last night between designing the new landscaping for the Rocky Harbor Park and taking care of Julia. All he wanted was some shuteye, but when he walked into the sparring room and saw the cute blonde, his body perked.

Usually women her age flocked to the front row, like the rocker-looking girl next to her obviously wanted to do. The blonde's jittery gestures and hunched shoulders revealed a nervousness he was all too familiar with. There were all sorts of reasons why women took his class. To be prepared in case anyone ever tried to attack them, because they had been in an abusive relationship before and wanted to take charge of their life, or because they were looking to hook up.

All too much lately it had been the latter. And while Jake was quite fond of the aggressive woman seeking him out, he'd like to think the women signing up for this class were taking it seriously. The blonde looked like she fit the serious mold, while her sidekick filled the other role.

He'd have to tread lightly with her and tamp down his desire, respecting her skeletons and what brought her here today. Darkness veiled his eyes as he clenched his fists and thought of Julia. If he hadn't screwed up the first twenty years of his life, she wouldn't be in the condition she was in now.

Giggles from the back row brought his attention back where it should be. On his class of new students.

Especially the blonde. Clearing his throat, and his mind, he showed his pearly whites and softened his smile, wanting his new students to feel comfortable and safe with him. "As your self-defense instructor, I'll be teaching you the critical life skill of personal protection. Unlike martial arts, which takes years to master, self-defense is a combination of the correct tactics and strategies with a single scope and purpose. Survival." Jake made eye contact with each person in his class, reading their expressions, identifying who signed up out of fear, and who was taking the class for the sole purpose of kicking ass. They were fun to work with, but often got cocky and forgot about the skills, focusing on the aggression. It was the insecure women he liked working with. Watching them grow and break free of their demons throughout the course and ending up stronger, mentally and physically, than when they started.

"My self-defense training system is the ultimate close combat defensive tactics program. However, before we can begin tactics, we need to understand concepts." Jake paced the front of the room, his arms loose at his sides. His stern voice needed to direct power, but not threaten those who had been or were currently victims of abuse. He gentled his tone even more as he made eye contact with an elderly lady in the back row. "At the very least, it will get you out of trouble, and in the worst case scenarios, it will ensure your survival."

"I'd like to get in a scenario with him," he heard the blonde's friend mumble.

"It's not a sport like wrestling, boxing, or mixed martial arts. I will help you learn combative skills within a short period of time. But I need your honesty, your willingness to work hard, and your best foot forward. If at any time you feel uncomfortable with me or the tasks I ask you to do, please do not hesitate to speak up."

Jake shifted his attention toward the beautiful blonde hiding behind her long hair. "I will never, ever force you to do something you're not comfortable with. Ever."

She didn't make eye contact with him, but her head lifted a little, her gaze remaining on his chest. And he couldn't ignore the odd flutter he felt in his gut. He reluctantly moved his gaze from the blonde and engaged the rest of the room. "You all look like you came ready to work out, but before I teach you the physical techniques..." he paused while some of the younger women snickered "...we must work on the conceptual. Our first task is to talk. I'm going to divide you into four groups. I want you to spend a few minutes sharing with each other what you plan on getting out of this course. What's your purpose? Why are you here?"

As expected, the women's feet didn't move, their heads swiveling around in confusion. The spunky, vocal girl moved first, pulling her blonde friend with her.

"Actually." He stepped in front of them and spoke to the energetic girl first. "I'd prefer if you split up." He looked down at their nametags. "Lucy."

"Sorry, dude. I'm staying with my sister." She draped her arm around her sister, her hand covering the nametag, and gave him the stare down. If his attention hadn't already been captured, he might have enjoyed sparring with Lucy a little more.

"I'm sure your sister appreciates your loyalty, but I've found people tend to be more honest about their purpose for attending this course when they're not with the person they came with."

"Rachael doesn't lie. She's as honest as they come." Lucy pulled *Rachael* in a little tighter, causing her to stumble.

"Lucy, I'm fine. I don't mind separating," the woman's said in a barely audible whisper.

"Yeah, well, I made you come. I got your back."

"I know and I appreciate that. But really, I can handle this," Rachael said a little louder, ducking under her sister's arm. She lifted her chin, revealing the most gorgeous, round blue eyes that didn't quite reach his. "Which group would you like me to work with?"

Her voice was sweet and soft, like his mother's sugar cookies straight from the oven. Hell, with an innocent bat of her eyelashes and a few casual words she had his insides all warm and mushy wishing for his mother's baking instead of focused on the purpose of the class.

An unfamiliar longing lodged in his throat, inhibiting him from speaking. "Mine," he croaked.

Lucy snorted and shook her head, walking to the opposite corner. Jake gestured with his head and watched Rachael move toward the front, where a group of four other women had gathered. Each took their turn introducing themselves and stating whether they were dragged here or joined out of curiosity, while Jake took mental notes.

Angie, solid and rough around the edges, and anywhere from thirty to fifty, started first. "My brother threatens to beat me if I don't give him money. I always give him what I have in my wallet, so I don't know if he'll follow through, but I want to be prepared just in case."

Unfortunately he'd heard stories similar to Angie's. "How about you, Rosa?"

"Wow, Angie. That sucks," said the tall woman who had to be in her late forties. "My mother got mugged when we were in New York last spring. I stood there like a moron not knowing what to do. The bastard got away with Mother's purse, her cell, credit cards and high blood pressure prescription. I want to be ready if anything like that ever happens again."

"I'm glad you two didn't get hurt. You'll learn some simple skills to defend yourself, but if you're ever threatened with a weapon, it's best to back down and not try to ward off the attacker."

"Grizzly bastard didn't show us any weapon, but I'm gonna get a license to carry before I'll go to New York again."

Jake patiently listened to Denise and Cindy's story before looking to the beauty to his right. "And what brings you here today, Rachael?"

"I, uh, my sister Lucy wanted me to come. I'm not sure how I feel about being here," Rachael said quietly, her eyes focused on the floor in the center of their circle.

Not wanting to push, Jake asked, "What do you hope to get out of this course?"

"I'd like to be more...confident. And independent."

"And I'm assuming your sister is here so she can learn how to take a man down."

"Something like that." A smile slipped from Rachael's full lips and he had the incredible urge to drag her to him and devour her mouth, knowing she'd taste like sweetness and innocence. Again, she elicited warm and cozy feelings in him. And Jake was anything but warm and cozy. It must have been her scent. Sugar and vanilla. No wonder he thought about his mother's cookies.

He had to be careful with this one. She fit the profile of a victim of abuse, and he didn't need to get tangled in that mess. Jake preferred to keep his sex life separate from his self-defense class. Jake Morgan was six hundred kinds of messed up and the last thing any of these women needed was to get tangled up in his baggage.

It was too personal. Too close to home. And he knew he'd lose his cool and end up in jail again if he learned about the bastards who drove the women to his class. He didn't ask for their personal stories and he'd never shared his. Save that for the shrinks.

Better to focus on the physical.

And hell if he didn't want to get physical with sweet and shy Rachael.

• • • •

"THAT WAS NOT WHAT I expected." Lucy sipped her coffee while Rachael picked at her blueberry muffin.

"What were you expecting?"

"I thought we'd get to punch something. Maybe learn the best technique to knee a guy in the balls. Poke some eyeballs. Something like that." Rachael laughed at her sister's bluntness. "But for your sake, I'm glad the class had a stoic start. Too much handholding and Kumbaya singing for me. Right up your ally, though. And Jake Morgan. Holy shit. He wants you. Bad."

"I thought the class was nice. I would have been freaked out if we had to actually hit something today."

"Instead you got hit on."

"Do you want a refill?" Rachael stood with her coffee cup.

"You suck at avoidance. I'm the master. Sit. Tell me about Jake."

"There's nothing to tell." But she sat anyway.

"Did he ask you out?"

"No!"

"Will you say yes when he does?"

"He didn't and he won't. I'm taking this class to learn how to protect myself, not to hook up."

"That's not what you told him, and here I thought you were Miss Honesty." Lucy stole a piece of Rachael's muffin and tossed it in her mouth.

"How do you know what I told him?"

"I have ears, girlfriend. *Confidence and independence.* Sure, I believe you want those things too, but you also want to protect yourself from assholes like Dylan. Why couldn't you tell Jake that?"

Rachael shrugged, but she knew why. Only weak idiots would let themselves get into a relationship like she had. After her childhood, after everything Doreen and Keith Riley taught her and brought her up to be, she failed. Miserably.

Sipping her coffee to wash the muffin that got stuck in her dry throat, she berated herself once again for being so powerless. No, Rachael Riley was *not* powerless, but Dylan White had fed her enough lies and abuse over the years that she had believed it and was only now starting to see the truth.

The real Rachael. The strong Rachael.

"Okay. I get the privacy crap. I value it myself. So I won't harp on it. I'm a little pissed at your boyfriend, though, for giving us homework. I didn't know we'd have to read and study for this course."

Ignoring the boyfriend remark, Rachael picked up the folder of information. She actually appreciated Jake's approach. He seemed thorough and studious, not what his appearance screamed.

"Lucy. Rachael. You have to see this. Quick," Mackenzie, the barista and owner of Coast & Roast, called to them. They jumped out of their seats and jogged to the front door. "It's like Christmas, an all-expense-paid vacation to Hawaii and Magic Mike all rolled into one."

Rachael peered down the cobblestone sidewalk toward the town center, where three men in low-slung, worn out jeans and tight T-shirts crowded around a pick-up truck unloading trays of flowers and small plants. They were too far away to see if the heads attached to the strong muscles were actually good looking, but it didn't seem to matter to Mackenzie and Lucy who sighed in appreciation.

"What's going on?" Maggie called from behind them. Since becoming engaged to Rachael and Lucy's brother, Graham, Maggie had become close friends with Rachael. The first friend she'd had since she left California. "Hey, sweetie. How was the class?" she asked, kissing Rachael's cheek and keeping her eyes on the three men down the road.

"It was okay."

"The instructor is jonesing for her," Lucy said, keeping her gaze on the men as well.

"I'm jonesing for *them*." Mackenzie gestured down the road.

"Which one?" Maggie laughed.

"Any."

"All," Lucy chimed in.

"We're making spectacles of ourselves. Let's go back inside." Rachael turned away from the working men and retreated back to her coffee.

Maggie's heels clicked on the hardwood floor behind her. "You're okay? Really?"

"I think so. I'm not going to say Lucy didn't scare me. She did. I expected us to be karate-chopping at each other right away, but Jake was really sweet, and we actually spent most of the class talking to each other. It was kind of therapeutic."

Maggie reached out and laid her hand on top of Rachael's. "I'm happy for you. I see this beautiful, fun-spirited woman hiding inside, and I want her to come out. But I don't want you to rush into anything you're not comfortable with."

"That's exactly what Jake said. When I first saw him I was really scared. He's... he looks like he's done time or is in a motorcycle gang or something. He's all muscle and tattoos, but he has a very kind smile and—"

"And she's jonesing for him too," Lucy interrupted. "He has this sexy tattoo crawling down his neck that wraps around his biceps. You should see the guy's body. Orgasm on a stick."

"Lucy, don't make her feel uncomfortable."

"It's okay, Maggie. I know Lucy is only teasing. You'd be proud. She totally had my back when we had to separate for our group chats."

Maggie hugged Lucy—who hated hugs—and said, "And whether you want to admit it or not, you have a huge heart beneath this façade of—"

"Bitchiness," interrupted Mackenzie.

"Pot. Kettle." Lucy stuck her tongue out and Rachael and Maggie laughed.

This is what Rachael had missed. What had been taken away from her. Girlfriends. Laughter. Freedom. A dark shadow fell over her eyes but was quickly erased when Mackenzie dropped a pad of paper on the table in front of her.

"Memorial Day weekend is coming up. Tourists will be flocking. Think you can double my muffin and scone order?"

"No problem."

While Mackenzie made the best brownies and whoopee pies in the world, she couldn't make anything else and hired Rachael to fill her shop with baked goods. And she kept a pile of catering cards by the front counter. It wasn't a huge moneymaker, but it gave Rachael the sense of independence she needed.

"I hope you don't mind, but Maggie told me about your idea for a Kids in the Kitchen class. Sounds cute." Mackenzie picked up the empty muffin plate and wiped down the table. "When you have a minute, I'd like to toss an idea by you."

"She has a minute," Lucy said.

Rachael appreciated her younger sister's encouragement, even when she tended to stick her nose in everything. Then again, so did Mackenzie.

"Unfortunately, I have plenty of free time on my hands. What's your idea?"

Maggie checked the time on her phone and stood. "I hate to run, but I need to get back to the office. Rachael, I think you'll like what Mackenzie has to say." She leaned down to give Rachael a hug before air kissing her best friend. "See you tonight, Kenz."

Mackenzie sat in the chair Maggie had vacated and rested her chin in her hands. "So, you like to cook. And bake. And you're pretty awesome at it."

"Thank you."

"And Mags told me you want to start this cooking class thing."

Rachael nodded. "I'm thinking of starting off by doing birthday parties for kids. The birthday girl or boy can choose from a simple menu and I'll prepare some of the ingredients ahead of time, but the children will get to prepare and decorate their own food. Pizzas, sandwiches, soups, cupcakes, cookies. And I can offer adult classes as well, maybe for those with special needs but... I figured I'd start with children."

"That's awesome. You just need the space, right?"

She nodded. "It will take a lot of startup money to find a place and buy the equipment. I don't have much money, and while I enjoy being with my mom, I'm also anxious to have my own place."

"Follow me." Mackenzie got up and nodded toward the front counter.

Rachael furrowed her brow and followed obligingly. They rounded the front and wove their way between the two high school students working the counter and headed into the kitchen. A space Rachael hadn't been before.

"It's not huge. I think there's potential. God knows I'm not using it. Coast & Roast was a diner back in the day. Turned into a deli before becoming a coffee shop. I bought it almost two years ago and haven't touched a thing back here. It's not really my forte. I like coffee and chocolate. The rest is foreign to me."

The kitchen needed some updating, but there were two ovens, a gas stove, and a large refrigerator on one wall. A long stainless steel worktable in the middle of the room where eight to ten children could work around, and a wall of shelves and cabinets on the opposite wall. Two windows balanced out the back wall.

"This door leads to the back parking lot." Mackenzie opened the door and the cool sea breeze filled the room. "And there's a small pantry. I have flour, cocoa powder, and sugar in here. This back staircase leads to my apartment. That's pretty much it."

"I didn't know this space existed."

"It doesn't get much use. Which is where you come in. Think it will work for your Kids in the Kitchen business?"

"Are you serious?" Rachael's eyes lit up and she grinned from ear to ear.

"Yeah. I figured you could use the back door as the entrance. Paint it or stick a sign on it or something. That way the little tykes won't have to tramp through the shop. The moms can linger out front and drink my coffee and tea and eat my brownies while you teach kids to cook. That work for you?"

Rachael's heart beat frantically as she opened cabinets and ran her hand across the barren shelves. "Of course it does. But..." She didn't have much in her savings. A few thousand she had hoped to use as her first month's rent if she could find an apartment. And a job.

"Of course I'll need something in return." Mackenzie hopped up on the stainless steel workspace and swung her feet. "You can bake my muffins and scones and pastries back here and use the space for your classes, but I'll want a discount on the baked goods."

Rachael snorted. "Discount?"

"Yeah, you know, kinda bartering for the rent space. I give you this space and you give me a deal."

"Mackenzie. Are you serious?" Rachael's jaw dropped and her heart sped up even more.

"I'm not asking you to give away your baked stuff. We can come up with a reasonable percentage, right?"

"Percentage? This space is worth so much more than a few muffins and eclairs. I'm willing to pay for the space."

"Eclairs? You never mentioned those before. Add those to the Memorial weekend list. What other sugary secrets do you have?" Mackenzie hopped down and closed the back door.

"Wait. You're serious? You're going to let me use this space and still pay me for baking for you?"

Mackenzie shrugged. "It's just sitting here. No one's using it. Seems like a waste. I figure your business will draw in more business for me as well. It's a win-win. I'm not giving anything away and neither are you. Deal?" She stuck out her hand and Rachael looked down at it, mystified.

Tears pooled in her eyes. Her dreams were really coming true. Rachael nodded and grabbed on to Mackenzie's hand.

"Awe, screw the handshake. You're practically family." Mackenzie pulled Rachael in for a hug and patted her back. A few months ago Rachael would have retreated, afraid of the intimacy and close contact, but sessions and friendship with Maggie had helped ease her back to the land of the living. "Mags is like a sister to me, and you're about to be her sister-in-law, which makes us..."

"Sisters-in-law once removed?"

"Works for me. You're cool with this?"

Rachael nodded eagerly and wiped her tears. "Thank you. Thank you so much. I've been thinking about this dream for months, trying to figure out how to make it a reality. You're like...my fairy godmother."

"Only so much younger and way cuter."

"Absolutely."

CHAPTER TWO

Jake didn't normally slap on aftershave when going to the gym, but since Rachael would be there clad in spandex and one of her cute T-shirts, he couldn't resist. Because his Thursday morning class was so large, he asked Erin to help today. It would be the class's first day with contact, and he knew some of them would have a hard time with it. Having another trainer on hand, especially a woman, was pivotal.

His years with Julia had helped soften him, teaching him that every situation was unique. He needed to trust his instincts to act and react in the best way for each student. Pulling on his shirt, he pushed open the locker room door and headed to the back of the gym. It took every ounce of willpower not to seek out Rachael. Instead, he jogged to the front of the mats and greeted his class with one of his favorite motivational quote.

"The goal isn't to beat your opponent; you simply need to refuse to be beaten." He waited a beat for it to sink in then turned on his morning charm. "Good morning. I hope you did your homework."

He skimmed over everyone's head doing a fast count, forcing his eyes to move quickly past the familiar blonde ponytail.

"Last week we focused on awareness and today we're going to work on the psychological preparation. This will help reduce inhibitions in a way that improves the fighting spirit. Hopefully you'll never have to get physical, but if you do, you need to be mentally prepared as well."

"Will we be getting physical with you today?" Lucy asked.

Muffled snickers and giggles echoed through the space. Jake shifted his attention to his left and bit back a laugh. "You read about the fighting strategies. Knowledge is power. Today we'll work on Rear Attack." The usual hecklers, the college girls and Lucy, erupted. He ignored them and moved on. "From my experience working in this field, most attacks happen from behind. Today you'll fight against a padded attacker. The most important thing you can do is be vocal and loud. I want to hear that today. I'll show you some quick, simple moves before you partner up." He showed them how to take their feet and strike the knee area. "Anyone want to come up here and try it on me?"

Of course Lucy volunteered; she made a good student. She wasn't timid and he didn't feel like he had to walk on eggshells around her.

"What do you do if you're being choked?" asked Kelly, a young brunette who had been pretty quiet.

"You want to immediately grab up on the forearm here." He moved Lucy behind him and motioned for her to simulate choking him. "And keep him from choking you and closing off your airway. Then turn your body so it's perpendicular to your assailant." Lucy followed along as he demonstrated the moves on her. He looked in her eyes and saw humor, not fear, so he continued. "From here you will grab onto your assailant's forearms with a firm grip and drop to your knees. By dropping to your knees, he loses his balance and you end up pulling his arm forward. At this point, you can escape."

Lucy dramatically fell to the mat and the class chuckled. "Can we try that again, but this time you're the bad guy?"

"Absolutely." He and Lucy went through the routine a few times before he asked the class to practice with their partners. "And I'd like to introduce Erin. She's a trained black belt and will help you with your form as well."

"As a mother of three college girls, and a survivor of domestic abuse myself, I know what it's like to see your world close in around you. To believe there's no hope, no end in sight. But giving up is not easier than standing up for yourself. Jake believes in you. I believe in you. Now it's time for you to believe in yourself."

For the next hour he and Erin encouraged the women to scream and demonstrated how to kick inside the knee and effectively gouge and poke the eyes, throat, and mouth. And everyone's favorite, the knee to the groin.

Jake hadn't had an opportunity to talk with Rachael during class, so he used her friend to buy him some time after it ended.

"Lucy," he called as the women filtered out. As predicted, she and Rachael turned and waited for him to cross the room. "Thanks for volunteering today. You helped ease a lot of tension in the room."

"Anytime."

Jake shifted his gaze to the blue-eyed beauty he'd spent the previous seven nights dreaming about. "You did really well today too, Rachael."

"Thank you." She didn't make complete eye contact, her gaze fixed on his mouth. He quirked his lips, hoping to put her at ease. "Maybe next week you'll feel comfortable enough to do some demonstrations with me." She flinched and he cursed himself.

"I don't know." She lowered her gaze to his chest and sighed. Her body hadn't tensed but he sensed a lot of self-doubt.

"You're strong. I can see it in your body." He inwardly cringed. Jake hated how that came out, degrading and like a cheap come-on. "I mean," he stammered, "your form is impeccable and your movements fluid. I'm impressed. You're really, really good at this."

A small grin formed and she bit her bottom lip. And then those beautiful baby blues met his and damn if his legs didn't feel like she kicked his feet out from under him.

"Thank you."

Jake was speechless. The woman was stunning when she smiled. Hell, she was gorgeous when she was serious as well. Sunshine and daisies and freshly cut grass. A natural beauty hard to find these days in a world of glamour and fashion. Everything about her made his gut clench—in a good way—and his groin ache, reminding him how long he'd been without a woman.

"I hate to break up this party," Lucy said, "but I have to get to work. Sage is a bear if I'm not on time."

Jake cleared his throat and shoved his hands into his pockets. Or at least tried to. Forgetting he had on gym shorts and not jeans, he slid his hands awkwardly down his thighs, feeling like a clumsy teen talking to the prom queen.

"I'll see you next week." He smiled at Rachael and then forced himself to include Lucy as well. Nothing against the sister, he really liked her, but she wasn't Rachael.

• • • •

"OH. MY. FLIPPING. WORD." Lucy put one hand on the hood of her car to hold herself up and bent over at her waist and laughed.

"What's so funny?"

"He is so hot for you it's pathetic. Or hysterical. I don't know which." Lucy straightened and wiped the tears from her eyes. "And you're playing the innocent virgin role so well."

"I'm not playing any role." Rachael plopped into the passenger's seat and slammed the car door. A moment later Lucy slid behind the wheel and laughed again.

"Maybe not. I don't know you well enough to figure out how you roll, but Jake's dying to ask you out. He must go for the quiet, coy ones."

"I'm not coy."

Lucy snorted as she started the car.

"Or quiet." Well, maybe she was quiet. She never used to be. "Cautious. I'm cautious."

"I'm cool with that. I still say you should go out with the body builder."

"He's not a body builder."

"Defensive much?" Lucy turned left and headed toward Rocky Harbor.

"Whatever. I don't know what he does but it doesn't matter. I'm not interested in pursuing a relationship right now."

"Who said anything about a relationship? I'm talking about sex. Can you imagine him naked? I sure the hell can."

Unfortunately Rachael could as well. She'd been imagining what his tattoo was. She'd never been into them before, always thought of them as a bit dangerous and not her type, but Jake seemed sweet and kind and...maybe a bit into her. Rachael chewed on her lip as Lucy pulled into the lot behind Coast & Roast.

"Thanks for the ride. If I can borrow Mom's car next week I'll drive."

"No biggie. I know what it's like to be stranded. I won't leave you hanging."

Despite Lucy's rough exterior, she had a kind heart. Gone was her pink hair, and face dotted with hardware that she'd donned not long ago. Most of the holes in her ears had closed up, but she still wore three studs in each. The eyebrow and lip piercings were gone, but every now and then she'd put a cute little rhinestone in her nose. Not Rachael's thing, however it suited her sister well.

"Call me if you need a ride home. I should be done by seven tonight."

"Thanks. I have my bike here. I can always ride home."

"'K. See ya."

Rachael invested some money into staples for the kitchen and found some Tupperware, pans, and cooking utensils at yard sales. Her mother was a yard sale fiend and had picked up dishes, mixers, and storage containers for her as well. She loved spending time with her mother, but she needed to break free from the comfort of Doreen's bubble.

She logged on to Mackenzie's laptop that she borrowed and sent out business announcements to the local papers. She printed up flyers to hang at local libraries and coffee shops, hoping busy moms would flock to her birthday party idea.

After six hours of nonstop measuring, stirring, and baking, Rachael had tomorrow's baked goods done and needed to get some fresh air. She finished washing the dishes, wiped down the counter, untied her apron and hung it on the hook by the door. With one hand on the doorknob, she turned around and looked at her workspace and her heart swelled.

Finally. It had taken a year of therapy, self-doubt, and redirection and Rachael's confidence was slowly coming back. She had friends, a loving family, and a new career. With her heart light and free, she walked out into the sunshine and headed toward the center of town. With no agenda, no stress weighing on her shoulders, she tilted her face toward the sun and took in the scent of lilacs and freshly cut grass.

The landscapers had done an amazing job readying the town for the summer tourists. The gazebo had a fresh coat of white paint and thousands of purple and yellow pansies lined the new rock walkways. Rachael was no horticulturist, but she recognized some flowers: lupine, geraniums, and lilies.

Fresh, dark mulch contrasted with the vibrant green grass and the kaleidoscope of colors from the flowers. While rock gardens were artfully displayed across the lawns, gently stacked as if they'd been there for years instead of days.

"So pretty."

"It is, isn't it?" said a deep voice next to her, causing her to jump out of her skin. Fearing the repercussions of being somewhere without asking, she cowered away from the voice.

"Shit. I'm sorry, Rachael. I didn't mean to sneak up on you. I thought you saw me." Jake held his hands up in surrender and stepped back.

"I..." Slowly she steadied her laborious breathing, resting a hand over her heart. "I..." Damn Dylan for turning her into a basket case.

"It's okay. I'm sorry. So, so sorry. I saw you across the road and I thought you smiled back at me. I didn't mean to frighten you. I'd never do anything to hurt you."

It wasn't the first time he said that to her and it made her upset that he thought of her as a fragile, lost soul. Granted, she'd signed up to take a self-defense class and acted like she fit in with the weak, victim crowd.

And didn't that piss her off. No, she wouldn't be a victim for the rest of her life.

Swallowing a gulp of air and taking a deep breath, Rachael met her gaze to his for the first time and pretended to smile. "I'm fine. I was wandering around in my own little world and didn't hear you come up next to me. You did nothing wrong."

Jake stepped closer, concern on his face. "Are you sure?"

So maybe she wasn't good at faking it. Rachael nodded and looked away. "I came out for some fresh air is all." And didn't she feel like an idiot? Jake had said too often in his class to always be aware of your surroundings. But Rocky Harbor made her feel safe and so she let her guard down, just like a fool. She needed to at least be aware of the people around her. And she hated that. Why couldn't she walk freely though the park without fear in her eyes?

Because Dylan. How she hated him. Hated what he did to her. How much control he still had over her life.

"So, you work around here?" Jake shoved his hands in the front of his jeans pockets, filthy with dirt and chunks of mulch.

Rachael appreciated his change of subject. She blinked away her past and put on a strong front. "Yes. You're part of the landscaping crew?" She pointed at his T-shirt that read *Morgan Landscaping & Masonry.*

Jake nodded. "There was a lot of work that needed to be done to these two acres. I'll show you around." He didn't need to, but it was sweet. He pointed out the flower combinations and told her about the plants that deterred mosquitos and deer, those that would bloom later in the summer and bushes that would flower in the fall. Their leisurely walk and his smooth voice calmed her and made her feel almost normal. Like a man and a woman strolling through a park together. All that was missing was a little handholding and a picnic lunch on a checkered blanket next to a fragrant lilac bush.

"The salty air can be hard on some plants, but these are pretty hearty." He reached down and ran the leaves of a bush she forgot the name of between his fingers. "I filled in the old walking path and made a new one that would lead tourists to the shops. They're lined with—" He stopped and swiped his hand across his face. "Sorry. I'm probably boring you. I get caught up in my business."

As if. She could listen to Jake talk all day. Lucy may be attracted to the badass tattoo and biceps he flexed in the gym, but Rachael was drawn to his chocolate eyes and how they twinkled and glowed when he talked about irrigation and masonry and flowers. She never noticed them in class, too afraid to look him in the eye. Or rather, too afraid that he'd see through her eyes and into her soul.

"I think it's great. The only thing I've ever planted was an herb garden last summer. My mom's a decent gardener and I help out when I can, but I don't have a green thumb like her. I do love the fruits of her labor, though. Last fall I spent weeks canning the tomatoes and zucchini and... now I've bored you."

"Not at all." Jake laughed. "What is it you do, Rachael?"

"I bake for Coast & Roast and do a little catering on the side. I've started a business, Kids in the Kitchen, and hope to coordinate cooking parties for kids. Adults too. I was thinking of catering towards those with special needs."

Eyes once smiling now turned soft and tender at her words. An unexpected warmth crept up her spine and circled to her chest, hugging her tight.

Jake cleared his throat. "Now I'm hungry. My crew and I worked through lunch so we'd have this done before the weekend. Care to join me for a bite to eat?"

Rachael twisted her fingers together and chewed on her lip while Jake stood there patiently waiting for her response. She tried not to be affected by the way his dirty navy blue T-shirt fit snugly across his chest, but the hopeful, puppy dog expression on his face made her heart smile.

His scent carried through the light breeze, brushing past her nose. A cross between fresh pine, nutmeg and salt. A unique combination, and one she found captivating nonetheless.

An unplanned meal. Something she hadn't done since...since before her life was stripped away. Determined to get it back, she agreed.

"Sure. I haven't eaten either. Sometimes I forget when I'm baking. When I'm surrounded by food I don't always remember to eat."

"I need to load the empty pallets into my truck and clean up a little. Can I pick you up in about thirty minutes? Or would you feel more comfortable meeting me somewhere?"

A week ago, heck, a few days ago, she would have run away in a panic, but she needed her life back. Plus, she didn't have a car. Rachael pulled out her phone and checked the time.

Channeling the old Rachael back, she decided to jump head first out of her comfort zone. "I'll meet you at Coast & Roast at five. Does that work?"

The boyish smile that made her nearly faint a few weeks ago erupted on his face. "Absolutely."

• • • •

JAKE WATCHED RACHAEL walk down the street to the coffee shop. Thirty minutes ago he was kicking himself for being so stupid by sneaking up on her. The woman had *troubled past* practically tattooed on her forehead; he needed to tread carefully. Hell, he should shuck his steel-toed work boots, lace up his sneakers and run the other way at warp speed.

The gentle sway of her hips kept his feet locked in place and his eyes planted on her curvy backside. When she slipped inside Coast & Roast, he shook his mind free from

Rachael and turned back to his work. It didn't take long to load his truck and send his crew home.

Another job well done. He wished he had known Rachael worked down the street. He would have stopped in the coffee shop instead of bringing his thermos every day. Jake stomped the dirt from his boots and climbed into his truck, coasting the quarter of a mile before parking in front of the brown and white awning.

He looked down at his dirty jeans and chest specked with mulch and cursed. Thankfully he kept a supply of T-shirts in his truck, but not another pair of jeans. Jake climbed out of his truck, stripped his shirt, and fumbled behind his bench seat for something clean. Finding his Batman tee, he unfolded it and shook it out, hoping it wasn't too wrinkled.

A feminine sigh from behind startled him and he turned to find a cute brunette ogling him.

"We don't require shirts for men like you. Just sayin.'"

Rachael appeared behind her, flushed. "Mackenzie," she reprimanded.

"I've been dying to see this guy up close and shirtless for three weeks. Finally. Happy birthday to me."

"Your birthday is in November."

"I know."

Rachael rolled her stunning eyes and brushed past her friend. He slid the shirt over his head and rounded the hood, making his way to the passenger side.

"Oh. My. God. Rachael, you devil."

"Sorry," Rachael mumbled when he reached to open the door for her. "Mackenzie can be a bit... rash."

"Reminds me of your sister."

"Exactly."

"I heard that," Mackenzie called from behind them. "And I'm telling your annoying sister that you've been holding out on us."

Jake worried that Mackenzie would scare off Rachael, but his girl kept her head high and her comments smart. "She doesn't know the half of it." She smiled up at him and he barked out a laugh he didn't know he had in him.

"I like you, Blondie."

"Thanks. I hope I end up liking you as well."

Chuckling, he shut the door, tapped a salute to the brunette, and slid behind the wheel. Maybe Rachael wasn't as fragile as spun glass after all. "Sorry about the grime. I wasn't expecting to have dinner with a beautiful woman tonight." He hoped the superhero shirt didn't make him seem too immature.

"I'm not exactly dressed to go out either." She fumbled with the straps to her purse and crossed her ankles.

Except for the shirt, Rachael still had on the same outfit she wore to class this morning, bright teal sneakers and black tight pants that stopped below the knee. The new, pink fitted shirt had *Roll with Me* printed on a rolling pin. "Nice shirt."

Rachael looked down and pulled her top away from her chest. "My family's been supportive of my new career. Especially my brothers."

"I'm sure they're benefiting from your talent."

"Pretty much. They pay me in silly shirts."

Jake pulled into the nearly empty parking lot to the Lobster Shack which was only a few miles down the road. "In another few weeks we'll never get a parking spot like this. Love what the tourists do for our towns, but it is nice when we can park in the front row again. This okay for dinner? I never asked if you liked seafood."

"I love all food. Well, except for turnips. I've tried a zillion different recipes but can't disguise them enough to taste decent."

"Can't say I've ever tried them." Jake exited the truck and made his way over to Rachael, helping her down. He kept his hands at her waist and made sure she was steady before he slowly pulled away. She needed more meat on her bones, and he was more than willing to feed her and help her gain some muscle.

"Luke puts in the most requests, but I see him more than the others so that makes sense."

"How many brothers do you have?"

"Four."

"Lucy your only sister?" He kept his hand on the small of her back, guiding her to the window to place their order.

"Yes. But I also have a sister-in-law and a soon-to-be sister-in-law."

"Big family."

"Very."

When it was their turn, he let Rachael go first. She ordered a lobster roll and he ordered a fisherman's platter.

"I guess you are hungry."

"I can probably eat it all, but I'll share with you. Just don't eat all the scallops. They're my favorite." He paid the cashier and grabbed a stack of napkins. "Sun or shade?"

A dozen blue picnic tables were scattered behind the small take-out order shack. Some boasted umbrellas while others were open to the ocean view in front of them. During peak season you had to wait for a table like a vulture and swoop in before someone else claimed it. Or you sat on the rocks bordering the ocean.

"Sun. It's beautiful out."

He followed her to a table closest to the ocean and sat across from her. "Tell me more about your family."

"You've met Lucy. She's an artist trying to find her niche. She works for my sister-in-law Sage, who's an event planner. Sage married Luke last year. He's a firefighter in Portland."

"I thought about being a firefighter." When he was ten and before he had a rap sheet. Then again when he was behind bars with too much time on his hands to think about possible career choices.

"It's scary sometimes, but Luke's good at it. Graham is a pilot and recently moved back home. He and Maggie are getting married in September. She's a psychiatrist in town. Blake's a nomad. He builds obstacle courses for those extreme races that are the rave right now. We see him during holidays."

"That must be hard on your parents."

Rachael nodded and rested her elbows on the table. "Dad died a few years ago." Her eyes softened, nostalgia and sadness darkening them before she lifted them to him again with a somber smile. "But Mom's a trooper. She's the glue. We're all...well, she's awesome."

"You've told me about three. Where's the fourth brother?"

Rachael looked out over the ocean, her shoulders slumping. "Afghanistan. At least, he was for the last ten years. We got a call on Christmas Eve that he'd been in an accident and had been flown to a hospital in Germany. Colton has always been the loner. He wouldn't let any of us fly out to see him and he keeps his injuries pretty private. We recently found out he lost his leg and has been in recovery at Walter Reed Hospital. Mom's pretty upset that he didn't let any of us know. I think Blake's going to try to visit him, but Colton doesn't want the rest of us to."

"Wow." Their number was called and Jake got up, welcoming the interruption and needing a minute to process everything Rachael just told him. From the sound of her family, she had a great support system, except for the wounded soldier, and he wondered if they knew all the secrets Rachael held behind those hurting baby blues.

Jake had his share of secrets, his share of pain as well. And like Rachael, he had a support system at home; only he was too stubborn to call on them for much help. Instead, he gave. It was the only way he new how to deal. How to heal.

He returned with the food and they ate in companionable silence. After he cleared their tray and emptied their napkins and plates in the trash, he offered his hand to her. "Feel like going for a walk?"

Rachael looked at his hand, then turned her head to gaze down the sandy coast. At first he thought she'd refuse, but she surprised him by turning her angelic face back to him and brightening it even more with a slight curve of her lips. "Sure." She took his offered hand and flung her long, smooth legs that he'd fantasized wrapping around his body over the bench.

Jake cleared his throat—and his mind of the erotic images of Rachael's blonde hair splayed out on his pillow. She let go of his hand and began the journey over the rocks until they reached the soft sand.

"I guess it's good I'm still wearing my workout gear."

His hand itched to reach out and hold hers as their arms bumped gently against each other. Instead, he wiggled his fingers and kept his hand by his side as they walked in silence.

Once they reached an outcropping of rocks, Rachael broke the silence. "I've told you about my family, what about you? Brothers? Sisters?"

"Sister. And my parents are actually still together. I guess that's pretty rare these days."

"Good for them. Tell me about your sister. Older or younger? You seem like the baby of the family. Spoiled and used to getting your way. Are you two anything alike?"

Instead of answering, Jake said, "The tide's going to be coming in soon. We should probably head back." He didn't know the tide schedule and it wasn't anywhere near the rocks, but he didn't want to ruin the evening by dodging her all her questions.

The last thing he wanted to do was talk about his family. It would lead to his past and the mistakes he wished to leave behind.

"Sure."

Her voice was subdued with an edge of confusion and disappointment. He hated himself for bringing her insecurities to the surface after he'd just made some headway. He couldn't let her think his rush to get back had anything to do with wanting to end their impromptu date.

Jake trotted ahead of her and turned around, now walking backwards. "If I ask you out on an official date, would you say yes?" He wiggled his eyebrows in an attempt to bring back the carefree smile he'd gotten a glimpse of earlier.

As he'd hoped, Rachael giggled. "Maybe."

"Ah, hard to get. I like that." He stopped, letting Rachael catch up with him, before turning around so he faced the rocks. "Let me help you up." Jake jumped up on the big boulder and offered his hand. This time when she took it he didn't let it go, holding on tight as they made their way across the rocks and toward the parking lot. Her hand was thin and delicate, and her skin felt like velvety silk under his giant calloused fingers.

They stopped in front of his truck and he reluctantly dropped her hand from his as he dug out his keys. She licked her lips and lowered her head, averting her gaze and toying with the hem of her T-shirt. His eyes glazed over at the thought of kissing her, imagining how soft and supple her lips would be, how sweet she'd taste. Once again, Jake restrained himself.

After clicking the unlock button on his key fob, he opened the door and held on to Rachael's elbow, gently guiding her into her seat. He walked around the back of the truck, giving himself some more time and privacy to rearrange himself in his jeans. Damn, he wanted her.

· · · ·

WHEN JAKE DROPPED HIS dark gaze to her lips, she thought he'd lean in and kiss her. Thankful and saddened that he didn't, Rachael leaned back in the passenger seat and waited for him to open the driver's side door.

"Are you still hungry? Do you want an ice cream or something?" He fumbled with his keys before finally getting them into the ignition.

She must have said or done something to bring on the sudden changes in Jake. Down at the beach he seemed to enjoy her company, but as soon as she asked about his family he shut her off and ended their night. Now he had a nervous edge to him, fidgeting and fumbling with his words.

"I'm good. Thank you."

"Okay then." He started the truck and backed out of the parking space, their silence no longer companionable.

When he turned down Main Street toward the coffee shop, she slipped her phone out of her purse and started to text Lucy.

Rachael: Can you bring me home?

Jake didn't try to hide his curiosity and leaned over, reading her phone. "Do you need a ride?"

"Do you always read people's texts?" she snapped and tossed her phone in her purse. She'd lived five years with a controlling, hovering boyfriend and had finally freed herself from his possessiveness. If Jake thought he'd—

"Easy. When a girl starts texting during my date I figure something went wrong. Since you weren't talking to me—"

"First, this wasn't a date. Second, you stopped talking to me. Third..." She didn't have a third and didn't want to fight with him.

"I apologize. I didn't mean to pick a fight," he said as if reading her thoughts. "And I didn't mean to pry. But if you need a ride home, I can bring you."

Rachael sighed, berating herself for flying off the handle. "I'm sorry too. I'm a little sensitive to... well, I don't like people breathing down my neck." Although it felt pretty darn good when Jake stood behind her in the gym, helping her hold her stance, and gently breathing on her neck. She shivered at the memory.

"Are you cold? I can roll up the window."

"No, the breeze feels good." Her phone chimed and she pulled it out of her purse again.

Lucy: *Mom will be there in an hour*

She looked up at Jake, his chiseled jaw covered in a five o'clock shadow that only made him appear more dangerous. Then he grinned and an adorable dimple formed in his cheek and her ovaries practically busted

"I swear I didn't mean to peek, but you didn't exactly hide your screen from me."

"If you wouldn't mind giving me a lift to my mom's, I'd very much appreciate it."

"Anytime. Just tell me where to go."

She spouted out directions and he followed them easily. Before she knew it, they were heading down her mom's dirt driveway.

"Nice place."

The rustic farmhouse suited Doreen Riley and the herd of adolescent foster kids she took in over the years. The acres and acres of land gave them all a place to walk, run, ride their bikes, and escape when they needed isolation. But the coziness of the house brought them all together again.

"It's been lived in. Times ten. My brothers were not the neatest, cleanest boys growing up. Still aren't."

"I can only imagine."

And she had no idea what he could and couldn't imagine. He had a sister that he didn't want to talk about and parents who were still married. Rachael had lived through enough to learn that being married wasn't necessarily a good thing either. Granted Keith and Doreen had been model parents and spouses, but her brothers and sister had some crap stories to tell before finding refuge in the Riley abode.

As did Rachael.

"Thanks for the ride. And dinner."

"About that." Jake directed his dark eyes on her and stared, the silence not uncomfortable, but heated. He dropped his gaze to her lips, which she bit in anticipation. Cursing, he turned and hopped out of the truck. Before she could figure out what was going on, her door opened and he pulled her down to the ground.

"A date. A real one. Yes?"

"Um." Her eyes fixated on his twitching lips and she gasped when he lowered his mouth to hers. He turned at the last second, grazing her cheek with his lips.

"Um, yes?"

Rachael nodded.

"Good. Saturday night. I'll pick you up at six. Here or at your kitchen?"

Your kitchen. She liked the sound of that almost as much as Jake's request for a real date. "Here."

"I'll see you then." He winked as he closed the door behind her and rounded the hood.

Rachael stepped away from the truck and slowly made her way up the front walk to the farmer's porch. There she waved, watching Jake drive away.

The front door opened and her mother came out. "I was just heading out to pick you up. Lucy said you needed a ride home."

"I'm so sorry, Mom." Rachael hugged her mother. "I completely forgot to text you back. I went out to dinner with... a friend and he gave me a ride home."

"He?" Doreen beamed. "I won't push for details, but I can't promise the same for your brothers or sister."

"Thanks. We're just friends, though." She stepped through the doorway and waited for her mother to come inside.

"I won't comment on your defensive tone either." Her mother chuckled. Rachael rolled her eyes. "Don't roll your eyes at me."

"You have your back to me, how did you know—"

"I'm your mother. I always know what my children are doing."

She wanted to ask if her mom knew about the abuse she'd lived with for so many years in California, but didn't feel like going down that road tonight. Not wanting to hurt her, Rachael wrapped her arms around her in a tight hug.

"Do you have any wine?"

"Sure do."

"Let's have a glass out on the patio."

"That sounds like a wonderful idea."

Rachael noticed the sentimental tears in her mother's eyes but didn't comment on them. Instead she took two glasses down from the cabinet, waited while Doreen excused herself to the bathroom, and poured two glasses of chardonnay.

The sun had set and the air turned cooler, so she slipped on one of her mother's cardigans hanging in the mudroom off the kitchen before going outside.

"If your brothers were here they'd have a blaze going in the fire pit."

"This is nice, though."

Doreen settled next to her and picked up a glass. They sat in silence, looking out across the field. Back when she and Luke and Graham were kids her dad had a horse, a few goats, and chickens.

"Your father wanted you kids to appreciate the simple things. Like chores and fresh eggs," her mother said, as if reading her thoughts.

"Am I that transparent?" Rachael set her glass down and curled her legs up under her to face her mom. "Jake did the same thing tonight."

"Does he live on a farm too?"

Rachael laughed at the thought. No, Jake had inner city biker boy written all over him. "No, but he spoke as if reading my thoughts. I guess I should never try my hand at poker."

"If you were that transparent I wouldn't worry as much as I do."

"Mom. I'm sorry to have caused you so much worry. I never meant to. That's why I didn't come home and visit often. If you knew what my life was like... you'd be..."

"I would never be disappointed in you, Rachael."

"You sure you're not a telepath?"

"That's why you stayed away? You thought I'd be disappointed in you?" Rachael nodded. "Sweetheart. I love you and respect you and your decisions. We don't always make the best choices in life, but whatever you do, you do with all your heart. Look at what you've started with your new business."

Her mother, always able to see the bright side in everything. "But I wasted five years of my life with an abuser. I should have known. I should have seen the signs."

While Rachael hadn't come from an abusive family, she did experience neglect. She'd only been eight when her neglectful mother tossed her aside for the state to deal with. Thankfully Doreen and Keith Riley swooped in and saved her from a life of misery.

Graham and Luke came from violent homes, and while Doreen and Keith tried to shield her from the abuse her brothers and Lucy experienced before coming to live with them, she heard stories. Ashamed that she missed the warning signs in her own relationship, she chose to cut off her family and suffer the consequences.

Until her brothers caught wind and saved her life. Literally. Rachael shivered and pulled her mother's sweater tighter around her shoulders.

"Tell me about your new friend."

Rachael couldn't help but smile and blush. "I don't know, Mom. He's not what I would have imagined myself being attracted to." While Dylan had appeared to be everything she wanted, clean-cut, from a solid wealthy family, with a college degree and career goals, Jake looked to be trouble with a capital T.

Only Jake's brooding looks and scary tattoo didn't reveal what he had hidden underneath. His sensitive side showed through in his class and his gardening. He listened to her and asked questions about her life instead of filling airtime to build his ego, like Dylan had done.

There was no comparison between the two men.

"Jake is different."

"How did you meet him?"

Rachael told her mother about the self-defense class, their walk around his stunning garden in the town square, and their impromptu date at the Lobster Shack.

"So what's holding you back?"

"I'm waiting for the skeletons. We all have them. I need to know what his are before I move forward. If I want to move forward."

"You've been home for a year now. You're the happiest I've seen you since... well, since you were a teenager coming home with a different boy crush every weekend."

"I remember." Rachael laughed. "I used to write *I love*____ on the paper bags covering my text books. I'd fill in the blank with a name and cross it out within two weeks."

"I don't know if I can even remember any of your crushes. They never lasted long."

"No, they never did." She'd never been serious about a boy until Dylan. Dread filled her again.

"Enough of those morbid thoughts. I like my boy-crazy daughter. Tell me more about your Jake."

"I don't really have much to tell. He has a sister and his parents are married, he teaches self-defense classes and he owns a landscaping and masonry business. Other than that, he's a complete stranger."

"Are you going out with him again?"

Rachael nodded. "Saturday."

"Good. You can introduce him to me when he picks you up."

"Promise not to embarrass me?" Rachael picked up her glass and finished her wine glad she had enjoyed this talk with her mother.

"What kind of mother would I be if I didn't embarrass my daughter in front of her boy crush?" she teased.

CHAPTER THREE

Turning off the ignition, Jake slid his keys into his pocket and wiped his sweaty palms on his khakis before stepping out of his truck. Not since he'd picked up Marcy Stoffer for his junior prom had he been this nervous. He'd already sampled the goods and knew she'd put out that night, but Marcy's father was a cop in town and Jake had a few beers before picking her up. He'd spent enough time in juvie and had no desire to go back, yet the idiot punk he was had still tempted fate.

Tonight, he was stone cold sober, and even though he was not the same punk from ten years ago, Jake couldn't help the inkling of fear that ran through his thoughts. Rachael was special, and he didn't want to do anything that would cause her pain. Or regret.

Running a hand through his freshly cut hair, he climbed the front steps two at a time and before he could knock, it swung open, revealing a perfect angel.

Rachael's long blonde hair hung straight instead of in its usual ponytail. Her face had always turned his insides out and tonight she glowed more than usual. It wasn't the traces of make-up around her eyes or even the gloss on her lips, but her smile that lit the warm spring night on fire.

"You're early." She stepped back, allowing him to enter.

"I didn't want to keep you waiting."

"Just give me a minute to finish getting ready."

"You look...wow." He finally unstuck his gaze from her mesmerizing face and trailed it down her body, taking in her pale blue top and flowing skirt that settled at her knees. Damn, her legs. He'd seen them in workout gear, but the strappy little heels she had on her feet made her legs...wow.

"I wasn't sure how to dress. You didn't give me instructions."

Jake's head snapped up. He'd been out with plenty of women and had never given one *instructions* on what to wear. He may have suggested casual or no clothes at all, but that was about it. "My thing is undressing a woman, not dressing one."

"You must be Jake," an older woman, her mother, said from behind him.

His face heated—a trait he didn't know he had—and he slowly turned. "It's lovely to meet you, Mrs. Riley. I've heard many wonderful things about you."

"Likewise. Would you care for a beverage before you go?"

Rachael cut in saving him from sticking his foot in his mouth again. "Thanks, Mom, but we should get going. I'll call you when I'm on my way home."

"No need to, sweetheart. I'll see you in the morning." She kissed Rachael on the cheek and patted Jake's forearm before heading upstairs. "Have a good time."

Thankful the woman wasn't furious at him for his inappropriate comment, he let out a breath he didn't know he held. "Not exactly the first impression I was trying to make." He studied Rachael's face for a sign of disappointment or embarrassment.

"If she heard one of my brothers talk that way she would have given him the evil eye. You would have peed your pants. It's that scary. No one messes with Mom."

"Seriously? Your mom seemed pretty cool. Almost like she—" He cut himself off before he inserted his other foot in his mouth. *Almost like she wanted us to stay out late. And maybe not come back until morning.*

"Like she?"

"We should get going."

"Are you sure this is okay?" Rachael picked at the hem of her top. "I can change if you want me to."

"You're perfect." He waited while Rachael ran upstairs to get her purse. A minute later she came back down smelling like vanilla ice cream. All he needed was a little whipped cream, maybe a cherry, and... *nope*, he needed to keep a level head. And right now his lower half was anything but level.

They chatted about the weather, about his job, and her recent good news during the ride to the restaurant.

"So, you know my sister-in-law Sage? Well, I know you don't know her, but remember I told you she's married to my brother Luke and she has two sisters?" Jake smiled at her rambling. He liked her this way. Free, unabashed, and happy. "Her sisters have kids. One even started her own day care. I haven't met them yet, but Sage set up a meeting with us next week. Thyme, that's her sister with the twins and a seven-year-old, is going to let the parents at her day care know about my business, and Rayne, Sage's other sister who has two kids, but they're still little, is going to book a party as well."

Rachael came up for air and Jake laughed. "You sound pretty excited about it. I'm happy for you."

"I spent all day making mock menus for the birthday kids to pick from. I have peanut free, gluten free, and dairy free menus as well. And organic options. I know a lot of moms are into natural foods."

"Times sure have changed. For me it was always take it or leave it. I learned to eat what was served."

"Me too."

They continued talking about their favorite foods and before he knew it, he was pulling into a parking garage and they were making their way down the cobblestone walkway to his favorite Italian restaurant in the Old Port. "I hope you like Italian."

"Who doesn't? Of course I'll have garlic breath later. I can—" Rachael stopped in her tracks, nearly tumbling. "I'm sorry. I didn't mean to...I won't have any..."

She looked so distraught and confused he wanted to wrap her in his arms and take the pain away.

"Rachael? You okay?"

She nodded and forced a smile on her lips. "I'm sorry."

"For what? I don't recall you doing anything wrong." Jake reached out and gently tucked her long bangs behind her ear, cupping her cheek before he dropped his hand.

"I'm not used to... I haven't been out on a date in a long time."

"Well then, I'm honored you let me be the one to break the dry spell. Come on. Let's order a bottle of wine and fill up on their garlic knots. They're amazing." He reached for her hand and led her into the restaurant.

Once seated, she relaxed her shoulders and her real smile returned. Jake wanted to know what spooked her. Something about garlic? The man she got away from sure did a number on her. He wanted her to trust him and open up to him, but he knew better than to push.

"I want to apologize again," she said, toying with the stem of her wine glass.

"And again I'll ask why. I don't remember you doing anything that requires an apology."

Rachael opened her mouth, then closed it. Opened, pulled her top lip between her teeth, and looked up at him. "I was in an abusive relationship." She spun her stem of her wine glass between her fingers and looked back down into the rich, red liquid. "He made all the decisions. What I'd wear, what I'd eat, who I could be friends with."

She paused, closing her eyes, seemingly deep in thought. Jake remained quiet, giving her the time and respect she needed to gather her thoughts, to continue talking or to stop, he'd let her set the pace. But he hoped she continued. Listening to Rachael's pain was therapeutic for him as well.

It wasn't like he dated much. Ever, really. He'd pick up a woman and they'd enjoy each other's company for a few hours, but he always left feeling empty. Unsatisfied. Sitting across from Rachael, having a conversation like two mature adults gave him hope for the future. A future that he could be proud of instead of a past he continued to run away from.

"I used to be a pretty independent person and am trying to find her again." She opened her eyes, an apologetic set to her lips." I'm sorry for being awkward. I'm kind of new at this."

"I think you're doing a hell of a job." He reached out and clasped her hand in his. It was a major breakthrough, her sharing her past. He stroked her hand with his thumb and kept his gaze fixed on her downward stare.

Rachael's lips curved into a smile and she finally lifted those baby blues his way. "Thank you."

"Can I ask you a question?" Her eyes turned round as saucers, but she slowly nodded. "Do you like garlic?"

Obviously not the question she had expected. She laughed and nodded again.

"Good. Because I do too." He held out the basket of garlic knots to her, and was pleased when she took one. "I hear if both parties partake in garlic, when they kiss they can't even smell or taste it. Not that I'm suggesting we kiss later, but I wouldn't object if you wanted to test out the theory." Jake shrugged and picked up his wine, keeping his gaze locked on hers over his glass.

They laughed over their salads and talked more about her menu ideas for her Kids in the Kitchen parties. His phone vibrated a few times during dinner, but nothing would distract him from the beauty across from him. After sharing a bowl of tiramisu, he paid the bill and helped her out of the booth.

"That was delicious, thank you."

His phone vibrated again. She must have heard it because she looked down and said, "You look like you want to answer that. It's okay. I need to use the ladies' room anyway. I'll be right back."

He slipped his phone out of his pocket, tensing when he read the screen, and nodded. "I'll wait right here."

Jake watched the tiny sway of her hips until she rounded the corner, then answered his phone. "Is it Julia? Is everything okay?" He closed his eyes and listened patiently. "I'll be right there." He made a quick call to Erin and hung up as Rachael returned.

"I'm so full I don't think I'll eat for a week."

"I'm glad you enjoyed dinner." She looked so happy and he hated himself for breaking the spell. He'd wasted a lot of time by not answering his phone during dinner and had to hurry. Jake offered his hand as he led her through the restaurant and out the front door. "I'm afraid I have to end our night earlier than planned."

"That's okay," she said. "I had a great time."

His chest squeezed under the weight of what he was about to do to her. "I did too, and I hate to end it like this, but I have to go."

"That's okay. I'm ready to call it a night," she said so innocently.

Jake rubbed his hands across his face. "Actually, something came up and I need to leave you. I won't be able to drive you home, but I asked Erin to take you. She lives right around the corner from here. You remember her from class, right?"

Two headlights settled on them as a familiar red Mustang slowed to a stop a few feet away.

"What?" The confusion on her face was quickly erased by hurt.

"Jake? Rachael?" Erin called from her open car door.

"I'll make it up to you. I promise. But I really have to take care of... something." Julia would always come first in his life, and he hoped Rachael would understand. If he ever came to the point of telling her.

"Yeah. Sure. You do that." She turned on her heels and got into Erin's Mustang without a glance back at him.

Damn, he felt like a shit.

• • • •

AN ALL TOO FAMILIAR throbbing burned in her chest. Rachael knew he was too good to be true. After turning off the water and drying her hands, she took one final glance in the mirror.

Julia.

She'd seen the name on his phone screen but wouldn't question Jake about it. When she'd asked Dylan about Lydia's frequent calls and texts, he'd yelled at her, belittled her in front of his friends, and slapped her. He'd apologized the next day and blamed his behavior on stress. A few weeks later, after she caught him with another woman parked outside his apartment building, he asked her—or maybe it was *told* her—to move to California with him where they could escape the clutches of the women who pursued him.

Being a young, trusting, and naive twenty-year-old, she went with him. She hadn't found anything wrong with sharing an account with Dylan when they first moved to California. He had a career and she was a college dropout. It had been in her best interest to have Dylan manage their accounts. But when he didn't come home for four days and left her with no money and barely any food in their apartment, she'd questioned where he was. Asked if he'd been with Lydia.

Three broken ribs and a bruise the size of Texas later, she'd learned to never question him again.

Jake didn't seem like the abusive type, but she hadn't thought Dylan was either, even though he'd slapped her a few times. There was always an excuse. Alcohol. Family stress that he never talked about. Pressure from other women, when he only wanted her, he'd said.

It wasn't until a year into their relationship that she began to realize he'd stripped her from her life. Her friends. Her family. Dylan picked out her clothes, her music, decided on the food she could eat until she became a sickly thin California blonde like the ones he boasted about when she met him in Maine.

Pushing Dylan from her mind, Rachael stripped and turned her shower on scalding hot. She would never fall victim to another man.

Not ever.

After her shower she fell into bed with wet hair and wetter tears streaming down her face.

In the morning her mother graciously stayed out of her way, reading the puffy red eyes and crazy bed head as a clear sign the night did not go as she had hoped.

For the next three days she buried herself in recipes, meetings with Sage's sisters, and cooking. Needing more to do, she made two large pots of soup and pitched the idea to Mackenzie to offer soup and sandwiches to her customers.

Mackenzie sampled the soup and moaned. "This carrot ginger stuff is amazing and the perfect new zen type of recipe for today's organic, all-natural food snobs. I'm a fan of MSG, sugar, and preservatives, but if this healthy stuff sells, I'm all for it."

"I think people like it. What do you think of the gazpacho?"

"It's different. Good. Perfect soups for summer. You're a freaking genius. I'd thought about expanding but I wanted to keep the coffee shop atmosphere. I'm no cook and don't want to start something I can't keep up with. I think soups and your homemade rolls are something I can handle dishing out. You'll sell out quick in the winter. Guaranteed."

Mackenzie left to wait on customers and Rachael used her time alone to knead the dough for her bread. Her arms would be sore by tomorrow, but she needed the distraction or she'd end up crying again.

When Thursday rolled around she pretended she forgot about their self-defense class, only Lucy wouldn't let her off the hook so easily.

"Mom told me to back off, so I did. But I'm not letting you hide behind your cookies and soup and bread anymore. We're going to class this morning. I have no idea what the hell the rat bastard did, but the best way to shove it back in his face is by showing up as if he doesn't matter to you."

Rachael knew Lucy was right. Facing Jake and pretending she didn't care would show him he didn't control her or her moods. Having the strength to do just that was another thing. It was easy to ignore his calls and texts for five days. Coming face to face with him was a whole other level of courage she didn't think she had.

"Sorry, Lucy, but this is a no-go."

Lucy took her sunglasses off and tossed them on the counter. "Did he hurt you?"

Yes. "No."

"Liar."

"Not physically."

"Just screwed with your head like Dickhead Dylan?"

Rachael couldn't even bring herself to smile. "No. Nothing like that. We realized we're total opposites. He's looking for one thing, I'm looking for another." They hadn't talked about future plans other than the love for their jobs, but the lie was easy to tell. "We're not right for each other."

"I thought opposites were attracted each other?"

"Not in real life."

Lucy hopped up on the counter and watched as Rachael cleaned up the mess from the morning baking. She'd gotten into a routine of waking up at four, either biking to work, or taking her mom's car to Coast & Roast, and doing her baking and cooking before returning the car to her mom. At home she hid out in her room, researching recipes online and making shopping lists of everything she needed but couldn't afford.

"Mom says not to pry, so I won't. But if you don't tell me anything then I'm gonna make you go to class."

"I think what Mom meant was to give me some space."

"Nope. She would have said that. Let's go, sweetstuff." Lucy jumped down and pulled Rachael by the arm.

"Hey, you can't make me go." She tugged her arm back but her sister was strong.

"Sure can. What are you gonna do about it?" Lucy swiped her sunglasses off the counter with her free hand slid them over her eyes before pulling open the back door. "Let's show the bastard what you're made of."

And that's what Rachael feared. That she wasn't made of anything. Dylan stripped her of her own personality. All that she had left was an insecure, doubting, lonely woman whose heart kept leading her in the wrong direction.

CHAPTER FOUR

L ucy was right. It felt good to have the upper hand. She walked into the gym, head held high, and plastered on a fake smile, working extra hard to talk to the other women in class. She wasn't so bold as to move to the front row like she'd been in the past two weeks, but still, she showed up, and that was half the battle.

"Strength doesn't come from what you *can* do. It comes from overcoming the things you *once* thought you couldn't." Jake's opening quote wasn't as loud and powerful as it was a few weeks ago. This morning it was soft, almost apologetic. He paced slowly in the front of the room, his hands clasped loosely behind his back. "Welcome back, ladies. Next week is our final class. Today I'd like you to show me what you've learned so far. We're going to start by sparring. I don't want you to hurt each other; don't actually make hard contact. I want you to follow through with the motions. Any volunteers?"

Jake looked straight at her and she avoided his stare, focusing on the wall to his far right. Gina, a woman who'd been shy in the past, raised her hand and moved up front to work with Jake while the rest of them paired off. Rachael kept him in her peripheral vision and avoided making eye contact for the first half of class.

Erin came over once to offer some tips and thankfully didn't say anything about the humiliating drive home last weekend.

Rachael and Lucy were in a good rhythm when she felt his presence behind her, his familiar earthy and spicy scent clouding her brain. He leaned into her, placing one hand on her hip and whispered in her ear.

"Rachael. I'm—"

Without thinking of the consequences, she snapped her head back into his nose, elbowed him in the gut, and spun out of his hold right before kicking him on the inside of his knee.

Taken unexpectedly, Jake grabbed his nose and stomach before falling to the ground. "What the hell?" he groaned.

"Don't ever sneak up on a woman. Especially a pissed off woman." Rachael spun on her heels and ran into the locker room before anyone could question her actions. She grabbed her backpack out of her locker and crashed into Lucy.

"Damn, girl. You kicked his ass."

"Let's get out here, Lucy. Please."

Lucy didn't question her need to flee, and they bolted out of the gym without looking back. They didn't talk in the car and when Lucy dropped her off at home, Rachael ran up to her room, where she let the shakes she'd been holding back take over her body.

Wrapping her arms around her legs, she rocked back and forth until her heart rate slowed to a normal speed. *What was I thinking?* She didn't fear Jake. Didn't think he'd physically hurt her. She knew it was him behind her, but she used the excuse of surprise to take her aggression out on him.

Just like Dylan used to do to her. Rachael broke down in ugly, sobbing tears. She was no better than her ex. How had her life come to this? Anger rushed through her body again. Only this time it wasn't anger at Jake, but at herself. She dropped her arms from her legs and set her feet on the floor.

After years of holding herself together, of looking, speaking, and acting the way Dylan wanted her to, she'd finally let loose. And it felt good. Yes, there was some sense of guilt for taking her physical aggressions out on a man, but she proved she wouldn't be walked all over again.

She lifted her head and stared at her reflection in the mirror over her bureau. She allowed herself to look deeper, beyond the red eyes and puffy mouth, to see the Rachael she once was. A trembling grin escaped her lips. Slowly she lifted her hands and brushed her hair out of her face. There, in the mirror she saw the old Rachael begin to resurrect herself.

Eyes that used to be full of life. A mouth that used to be full of wit and sass towards her brothers. And a body that used to walk with confidence.

In taking Jake to his knees—literally—she proved to herself that she wasn't a fragile weak-minded bimbo she'd been lead to believe. The new, revived Rachael could hold her own. The fire inside roared, and for the first time in years, she felt whole. Confident. Like her old self.

Needing a shower to wash away the tearstains, she stripped and stood under the spray until she felt rejuvenated. A fresh start. Come Monday she'd whip up a new soup recipe, put the final touches on Maddie Montgomery's seventh birthday party for the following weekend, and start all over again.

• • • •

SHE'D HAVE TO START all over. Again. Her sourdough proof didn't look right. Her mind had been distracted all morning and she kept forgetting if she'd added the yeast or sugar. Coast & Roast was normally busy on a Saturday, but today's eighty-degree sunshine-filled day kept people at the beach and at ice cream stands, not in line for hot coffee or soup.

"Rach?" Mackenzie's concerned voice startled Rachael. "Have a minute?"

"Sure." She dumped the batch of starter mix in the sink and washed the bowl.

"I know things didn't go well with shirtless sexy-abs landscaper." Rachael smiled at Mackenzie's lack of proper name usage. "Maggie told me how you punched him out the other day."

"I didn't punch him. And it isn't like Maggie to spread gossip." Maggie was a reputable psychiatrist and would never speak about anyone without their consent. Rachael had confided in her many times and owed much of her emotional growth to Maggie.

"I'll clarify. Lucy told Maggie, who happened to be sitting with me, so I heard the story as well. But only pieces. Mags filled me in on the Mike Tyson move. I'd give you a high-five if I wasn't afraid you'd knock me on my ass." Her smile told Rachael she was kidding. Maybe.

"Let you be warned," she teased.

"Yeah, so about the six-pack... what would you do if you saw him again?"

"I don't know. I still have one more self-defense class to go to." Rachael shrugged. "Maybe I'll apologize. Maybe pretend nothing ever happened."

"Was this over another woman?"

Rachael dropped the dishcloth in the sink and turned. "What do you know?"

"Nothing. Only..."

"What is it, Mackenzie?"

"He may be out there." She flicked her shoulder toward the door. "With another woman."

"*May?*"

"Okay. He's here. With two women. I didn't get a look at them. He ushered them to the back corner table while I was waiting on other customers. Before he came to the counter to place his order, I heard him call one of them Julia. He asked if you were here."

"What did you tell him?" *Julia.* Rachael's throat closed and her eyes misted. She blinked back the tears and struggled to force her belly to stop convulsing.

"That you weren't here. I'm a really good liar."

"He didn't buy it." Rachael toyed with the hem of her shirt. Today's read *I Bake Because I Knead the Dough.* The irony. She couldn't get a batch of dough made for the life of her.

"Maybe. He had this tough-guy-turned-puppy-eyed look as he stared through the back door. I felt bad for him, but then his tattoo sort of slapped me in the face and I remembered he was a badass. I mean, a pain in the ass, and I've totally got your back."

Rachael shook her head at Mackenzie's logic. She and Lucy were two of a kind.

She needed to apologize, and she wanted to see who this Julia girl who meant so much to him he dumped Rachael at the curb was. She wiped her hands on her apron and pulled back her shoulders.

"I'll go out there." The old Rachael would have stood up to any guy who ditched her so disrespectfully. And so will the new Rachael.

"I'll keep an eye out. I have 911 on speed dial if you feel the urge to deck him again. Or should I wait and let him bleed it out?"

It was good to have friends.

Rachael moved ahead of Mackenzie and made her way to the seating area. Jake sat at a table with three paper cups and a pile of cookies in the center. The two chairs across from him were empty. The pocketbook slung on the back of one meant the women were still around. Probably in the ladies' room.

"Jake."

She startled him and he jumped to his feet when he saw her. His nose looked fine, but his left eye had a purple half moon under it. "Rachael." His sad smile left a quavering in her belly. He lifted his hand as if he was going to touch her. When she backed up, he stuffed it in his pocket.

"I came out to apologize for hitting you. And elbowing you." She looked down at his knee. "And kicking you."

"I'm glad my lessons have paid off," he joked. His adorable smile filled his face, making his purple eye look charming and roguish at the same time.

"I hope you're not in too much pain."

"Just my ego," he teased again and dropped his grin when she didn't return his. "Rachael. I'm sorry about the other night. It was rude of me. I shouldn't have left in the middle of our date. I should have driven you home. It was... rude and I'm deeply sorry."

"Yes. Yes, it was. You're a spoiled charmer who thinks he can get his way by flashing his muscles and boyish smile, but you're a... an asswipe." She picked up many appropriate euphemisms from Lucy and figured she might as well share them with Jake.

"What did my son do now?" A dark-haired woman with kind eyes appeared next to her, blowing out a sigh while shaking her head at him. "I taught you better than that. You know how to treat a lady."

"Mother, this is Rachael. Rachael, my mother, Lesley Morgan."

"Rachael. Lovely to finally meet you. I take it this is about Julia?"

Rachael's stomach clenched, her body stiffened and eyes rounded in surprise. She didn't know if she should look straight, to her left, or behind her when she felt another presence at her side.

"Yes." Jake sighed then smiled brightly again when he looked over Rachael's shoulder. "Rachael, this is Julia. My twin sister. Julia? Meet my friend Rachael."

Sister? Hesitantly, Rachael turned, and her body softened when she saw the woman before her. The woman was beautiful, though her expression seemed limited. She met Rachael's eyes slowly, but once she did her face lit up.

"You—re... pre—tty," she said. Or at least that's what Rachael thought she said. Her words were slurred and hard to understand.

"Thank you. You're very beautiful too. You look like your mother."

Julia beamed and rocked back and forth.

"Have a seat, honey. Your hot chocolate is nice and cold now." Lesley helped Julia to her seat. "It doesn't matter if it's a hundred degrees out, when we go out for special treats Julia wants either chocolate ice cream or hot cocoa. They don't serve ice cream here so we settled on the cocoa."

Julia tilted her head, her face skewing as if in pain.

"She'd rather have a glass of wine, I'm sure," Jake added, placing a kiss on his sister's head. A faint smile showed on her lips.

"Please join us," Lesley said, patting the chair in between her and Jake.

Rachael watched the three of them interact; their mother babied Julia while Jake treated her like an adult.

He held out the chair for his mother then sat on the other side of his sister. He brought the cookies closer to her and handed her the biggest one. "You snooze you lose, sis. Better eat up fast or those cookies are mine."

She struggled with the mug and Rachael watched as Jake casually helped Julia lift it to her mouth. The scene was so sweet. So precious. And yet sad.

Lesley continued filling the air with idle chatter while Rachael used that time to process. So the calls were from his sister, who obviously adored him, and he her. After Julia finished her chocolate, Lesley stood. "We're going for a walk to check out your landscape work, Jake. We'll be back in a bit."

Once they were gone Jake seemed to relax. "You left me at the restaurant to go to your sister," Rachael said.

Jake nodded. "She had another seizure and was being rushed to the hospital. Julia responds best to me, must be a twin thing. My mom sent a bunch of texts, and realizing I wasn't answering, sent me one from Julia's phone knowing I'd answer hers right away."

"Why didn't you tell me?"

He looked out the window, staring at nothing. "I'm a private person."

"Are you ashamed of your sister?" That would be a deal breaker.

"No!" He seemed truly offended. "I love my sister more than anything. She wasn't always... she's had a rough life, and the least I can do is be there for her whenever she needs me."

"So why keep her a secret from me? I told you about my brothers and sister."

"No. You told me their names and occupations. Not their dirty laundry."

"Your sister's condition isn't dirty laundry." Appalled at him, she stood abruptly, bumping the table and spilling his coffee in his lap.

"Rachael. That's not what I meant," he called after her but she'd already rounded the front counter and retreated to the safety of her kitchen.

"Ratbastardasswipeprick," she mumbled as she measured and mixed the ingredients for rolls and pounded another pile of worthless dough. With her heart lodged in her throat once again, she slammed around in the kitchen, making more of a mess than usual. She'd worked hard over the past year to get some sense of stability back in her life. The roller coaster ride with Jake only set her back.

She wanted to hate him for his tattooed, biker, badass looks, but they were only a cover to his sweet, sensitive side. He cared deeply for his special needs sister yet seemed ashamed of her at the same time. His incongruous behavior baffled her and toyed with her already sensitive heartstrings.

"Rachael?"

She jumped, knocking a bag of flour on the flour. "What is it with people sneaking up on me? Didn't you learn your lesson the last time?" Cringing at her own snotty attitude, Rachael marched to the corner to grab the broom and dustpan.

"I kept my distance this time," Jake joked. "I don't need another black eye. Seriously though, I didn't mean to startle you. I don't make it a habit to sneak up on women."

"Could have fooled me." Rachael attempted to shush him away with the broom, but he took it from her.

"Let me. I'm the one who caused this mess."

Yeah, in more ways than one. After he dumped the rest of the flour in the trash, he returned the broom to the corner and leaned against the wall, still keeping his distance. The wet spot on the front of his khakis made it look like he peed himself; Rachael bit back a smile and remembered to be annoyed and hurt.

"Will you come to dinner with me tonight?"

"I don't know. Is Erin available to bring me home after?" Her sassy comeback pleased her. No more wimpy, cowering girl.

Jake rubbed his hands across his face and dropped his chin to his chest. The black ink crept its way up his neck but was still indecipherable. Traces of the image showed on his triceps. She'd need him to take his shirt off so she could examine it more closely. *No. Don't go there.*

If he stripped his shirt she knew she'd succumb to whatever Jake was asking.

"I promise never to do that again."

"And if your sister has another seizure?" Great. Now she sounded like a jealous girlfriend. "I'm sorry. That was inappropriate. This isn't your sister's fault. She seems like a sweet woman."

"No, this is all my fault. I could have brought you to the hospital with me. I didn't know how long I would be and didn't want you to have to deal with... this."

"You could have told me." Jake nodded. "Why didn't you tell me about your sister?"

Jake stepped closer keeping the center worktable in between them. "I want to. I will. At dinner tonight. I can meet you somewhere if you'd prefer."

Wanting to know the story and needing to prove to herself she could stand up to any man who got in her way, she agreed. "I'll meet you at the Lobster Shack at six." It would be packed with tourists and they'd likely have to eat on the rocks or beach, but they'd be surrounded by people, and she wouldn't feel so closed in.

Jake's chocolate eyes melted on her and she was tempted to climb over the table and lick him. Why did he have to look so sexy? So sweet? So perfect? He rounded the table and cupped her chin in his palm. "I'm looking forward to it."

• • • •

JAKE ARRIVED TWENTY minutes early and secured a picnic table. When a family with three active children looked at him with hopeful eyes, he gave up his table and paced the parking lot. Maybe Rachael would be more relaxed if they ate down at the rocks or found a spot on the sandy beach.

He checked the time on his cell phone for the fifth time since he'd arrived. Six fifteen. Rachael didn't strike him as the late type. Maybe she wasn't coming. No, she wouldn't leave him hanging.

Yes, she would. He deserved it for being a prick the other night. Although she did get him back pretty good.

Jake smiled when he saw a familiar blonde get out of a maroon sedan. He wanted to jog over and greet her with a long, wet kiss, but didn't think she'd appreciate his gesture.

Instead, he shoved his hands deep in his pockets and waited for Rachael to notice him. In the meantime, he took in her long, tanned legs, the bottom of her denim shorts barely covering the tops of her thighs. She'd changed out of her pink shirt she'd had on earlier. This one read *Does Not Cook Well With Others* with a picture of a cleaver. Message read loud and clear. She was still pissed.

"Nice shirt," he said when she spotted him and was within earshot. Rachael stopped in her tracks. Her sunglasses concealed her eyes and he could imagine her squinting, probably trying to get a read on him. He bit the inside of his cheek to prevent his grin from taking over. "Another gift from your brothers?"

She shook her head. "My mother."

Jake tipped his head back and laughed, startling a smile from her lips. "Not one for sharing her kitchen?"

Rachael shrugged. "I used to like cooking with her. I learned from her and she's the best, but sometimes I like to be alone, especially when I'm trying new recipes. Mom likes to talk a lot and ask what ingredient I'm putting in next and how much. Sometimes I don't know, I wing it, and I get annoyed with her questions."

"Dually warned."

"I don't think you need to worry about that."

"Oh? You're not worried about me bothering you in the kitchen?"

"You won't be in my kitchen, so it won't be a problem." She shook her head in a sassy manner that was probably meant to annoy him but only made him want her even more. Rachael had spunk. He liked that.

A lot.

"Let's get in line. Who knows how long it's going to take to get our food."

They stood in line and talked about trivial things like the weather, the Red Sox's pitiful losing streak, and fishing.

"You like fishing?"

"My brothers used to sneak off to the pond behind our house and I would tag along. They'd only let me hang out with them if I baited their hook. You didn't show your weaknesses in the Riley house or they would be used against you until death. I knew if I showed Luke and Graham how disgusted I was with the worms that I'd find a bucketful in my bed."

"I like the sound of your brothers. I always wished I had one."

"Which brings us to the purpose of this evening."

Not ready to stop the flow of their easy banter, he tried to sidetrack. "Want to share a fisherman's platter with me?"

"You're pathetic."

Jake studied her, unable to read her eyes behind her large glasses, just as she couldn't see his behind his aviators. Thankful for the temporary shield, he played dumb. "You're right. I would probably eat most of it. Want a lobster roll again or something different?"

Rachael crossed her arms over her chest and bit her lip. "Fried haddock and fries and a bottle of water. Please."

He placed their order and they waited off to the side in silence. When his number was called, Rachael grabbed some napkins while he picked up the tray. There weren't any tables free so he followed her to the outcropping of rocks.

"We can sit in the back of my truck if the rocks are too uncomfortable," he suggested.

Shaking her head, she swiped a fry off his plate before sitting down. "This is fine."

Jake hadn't eaten since earlier in the day and his stomach would need to be full to tell her the ugly truth about how he ruined his sister's life.

· · · · ·

THEY'D STALLED LONG enough. Rachael only agreed to this *date* because Jake said he'd come clean about his odd behavior the other night and why he didn't want to talk about his sister. If they were going to have any kind of relationship, she didn't want to learn about the skeletons in his closet later on. She wanted everything up front.

Now. No more secrets.

Or maybe he wasn't interested in a relationship. If not, then she had no business knowing his family's secrets. Torn between her nosey self wanting to know Jake's past, and not wanting to force him to talk about something very personal, Rachael sighed. She'd only touched the surface about her past with Dylan. How could she be so hypocritical, forcing Jake to talk about something that troubled him so deeply?

"I think this was a bad idea." She stood and picked up their tray, dumping the trash in the barrel before stacking the tray in the pile by the takeout window. When she returned, Jake still sat on the rocks, making no effort to get up. "I apologize for hitting you and for prying into your personal matters. It's none of my business."

All six feet of sexiness rose and stood toe-to-toe with her. Rachael had to tip her chin to look at him, his gorgeous eyes shielded behind his glasses. What else did they cover? Her heart pounded at his closeness. He smelled like Christmas and ocean. And trouble.

He took his glasses off and hooked them in the collar of his shirt. Slowly, he reached out and slid her glasses off, tucking them in the deep pockets of his shorts. "What if I want to make it your business?" he whispered into her mouth before making contact, their lips softly touching. His arm came around and pulled her in to his body, one hand resting on her hip while the other cupped her cheek.

Dear God. Jake sucked her bottom lip between his then released it, tracing it with his tongue. Her hands could no longer stay numb at her sides. Afraid to wrap her arms around him like she really wanted to, Rachael placed her palms on his chest, feeling the powerful curves of his pectoral muscles and the rapid beating of his heart.

Her mouth responded to his. There was no keeping it still. She darted out her tongue and played with his, enjoying the loud moans vibrating from his body. Her toes curled into her flip-flops and she pressed harder into him.

"Damn." Jake pulled his lips away and rested his forehead against hers. "You make me forget we're in a public place."

"Sorry."

"Don't apologize. And keep doing that."

"Doing what?"

"Making me forget." They stood like that, forehead to forehead, until their breathing steadied. "Let's go for a walk." He took her hand and led her down the tiny path in between the rocks and the sea grass until they reached the flat sand.

They walked hand in hand for nearly a mile before he broke the spell, his fingers falling limp in hers. "Julia has Diffuse Axonal Injury."

"What is that?"

"Brain damage."

"Oh. Wow." Rachael and her siblings had lived through an array of emotional and physical abuse, but they were all healthy. She couldn't imagine the strain on Jake's family.

"Was she always...how did she...?" Wanting to know the details but knowing how personal and heartbreaking they must be, Rachael conceded. "Jake."

They stopped and she turned to face him. "If it's too much, you don't have to tell me. I'm sorry for prying."

He tightened his grip again. "You're not. It might actually feel good to talk to someone about it. But I need to keep moving." He squeezed her hand and pulled her along. "To answer your first question, no. Julia was not born this way. She lived twenty-three happy and healthy years before the accident. An accident I caused."

"Oh, Jake." Rachael couldn't go on any further. She slipped her hand from his and wrapped her arms around his taut body, resting her head on his shoulder. "How horrible for all of you." She didn't let go, not even when he kept his arms at his side, ignoring her hug. "You can't blame yourself for an accident. It's obvious how much you love your sister, and I could tell by the look in her eyes that she loves you too."

"You're just going to take it at face value? That the accident wasn't my fault?" He reached back and removed her arms from his waist.

"Did you intentionally try to hurt your sister?" Knowing he wasn't anywhere near the same kind of man as her ex, she could safely ask that question.

"Maybe I need to sit." Jake headed toward an outcropping of rocks. "Or you need to sit. I don't know." He paced in front of the rocks, keeping his back to Rachael. She finally sat and waited patiently for him to continue.

"Julia and I were close as kids, but when I hit my teens I got into some trouble. Ran with the wrong crowd. My sister didn't like me not hanging out with her anymore and became a constant thorn in my side. We fought a lot. I'd tell her I was going to the movies with my friends but really, I'd be in town. Shoplifting or finding free alcohol. She'd make plans with her girlfriends to go the movies and would get pissed when I wasn't there with my gang. We didn't have cell phones yet, so avoidance was easier."

"My brothers used to do that to me as well."

"They let you fish with them."

"Yeah, but they ditched me as well. I think that's normal sibling behavior."

Jake shook his head and shoved his hands into his pockets. "We stopped talking by the time we were seniors in high school. Julia was part of the National Honor Society kids and I hung out with the losers. The kids who skipped school to smoke pot. The ones who took five years to graduate or decided to drop out."

Rachael wanted to ask what he found so appealing in that crowd, but kept quiet and let him talk. "She graduated top of her class. Made a speech and everything."

"You must have been very proud."

He shrugged and turned away. "Never heard the speech. I was in town getting wrecked on Jim Beam and a line of coke. Never marched across that stage either."

Her hands itched to touch him, so she sat on them. The Jake Morgan she knew wouldn't behave that way now, and that was all that mattered. Her brothers had troubled pasts and they worked through it, cleaning up their act and aton-ing their wrongs.

"I was the model bad boy. The one mothers warned their children about." He dug his toe in the sand and kicked a pile into the wind.

She could sense him shutting down and he still hadn't told her about the accident. "What happened to Julia?"

"She got a full ride to UMass Amherst. Studied business. Got her master's. Mom and Dad threw a college graduation party for her. I hadn't seen her in five years. I'd been...busy. Julia insisted on going out with me after her graduation par-ty. We were out in Portland, bar hopping. She wanted to fit in with my friends and they...wanted her."

Jake let out a sigh and pulled at his hair with both his hands. "We had an argument and, to spite me, she took off with one of my *friends*. I didn't find out about it until later. When I did, I made my posse come with me and track her down."

Rachael's heart sped up, wanting to know what hap-pened to Julia, but not wanting Jake to go through the pain. She got up and made her way toward him, not touching, still giving him his space. He wouldn't look at her as he kept talk-ing.

"Long story short, I got a call the next morning that she'd been in an accident. She was in the hospital, hooked up to life support. If I wasn't such an ass that night. If I'd paid attention and didn't let her leave with Snake. If I'd looked harder for her..." His jaw ticked as he glared out across the ocean.

"You can't blame yourself."

"If I wasn't so messed up she'd be making millions in some corporate office doing her marketing thing."

"You've been playing the *If I only* game for a long time."

"Six years."

The five years he didn't see his sister probably didn't feel quite as long as the years since. Clutching at her chest, Rachael inched closer but Jake shook his head. "Don't give me the pity look. It'll piss me off. Don't tell me it wasn't my fault. That it wasn't my hands that...just don't. Okay?"

Clearly he didn't want to give her the specific details. The guilt from the past six years had done its damage. Knowing her brothers liked their space when they were dealing with the demons from their past, she attempted to lighten the mood.

"Your mom and sister are beautiful. Doesn't seem fair that you got stuck with the ugly genes."

Jake cocked his head at her. The tension slipped away, replaced with heat radiating from his eyes. "I told myself I'd be slow and gentle with you."

"What if I don't want you to be gentle?"

He cursed before he kicked Rachael's legs out from under her and cradled her to his chest as they fell to the sand. She landed on top of him right before he devoured her mouth. His hands clamped hard on her butt, pulling her harder into his body.

Oh, he felt delightful. Hard and rigid. Everywhere. From his six pack abs rubbing against her belly, to the man of steel arms casing around her hips, to the obvious arousal making an impression against her crotch. They fit each other well.

Her five foot seven frame nestled in all the right places of his hard body.

Jake's tongue didn't have the same gentle caresses as earlier. He licked and tasted the inside of her mouth, leaving no spot untouched.

Rachael gave as much as she received, grinding her body into his, forgetting they were on a public beach. She felt like a wanted woman who was about to be ravished.

Jake abruptly switched positions, pinning her into the sand and hovering over her body. "Damn. You did it again."

"Sorry?"

"You make me forget."

"Oh. Sorry."

"No. Never be sorry. You're good for me, Rachael Riley. I like forgetting things when I'm with you."

Truth be told, Rachael forgot about her skeletons when she was with Jake as well. Or rather, she forgot she was insecure and afraid of a man's touch. Forgot to fear saying the wrong words, wearing the wrong thing, being the wrong person.

With Jake, Rachael could be herself.

"I like forgetting things too."

"Yeah?" That gorgeous rakish grin erupted. "Like what?"

"Like we're on a public beach and I was dry humping your body."

His chocolate eyes turned darker and his gaze landed on her mouth. He licked his lips like a predator getting ready to go in for the kill. Or at least the bite.

Jake kissed her neck and murmured in her ear. "We can be at my place in fifteen minutes."

Cold water splashed on her—literally. The tide had come in and soaked her lower half. Jake swore before hauling her to her feet. "I didn't know the tide would be coming in so quickly."

The cool water brought her back to reality. Rachael wasn't the type to do pelvic grinds in public. Her girly parts tingled at the memory, so wanting to relive it. Soon. But logic took over and cooled her down once again.

"That's okay. I should get going anyway. I have to get up early."

Jake nodded in defeat and took her hand in his. Their walk back to the parking lot was too short. He'd occasionally bump shoulders with her and she'd knock him back, trying to throw him off balance. Once Jake knocked her too hard and she nearly toppled, but he caught her before she could fall. Not that she would have minded him falling on top of her again.

"You're stronger than you look, Blondie."

"Don't you forget it."

"Doubtful I will. My purple eye is a constant reminder."

He walked her to her car and engulfed her in his strong embrace. They held on to each other for a long time before breaking free. "I'm not going to kiss you again."

"Oh." Her heart frowned, as did her face.

"Come on, Blondie. Don't make that lost puppy face or I will kiss you again."

"You say it like a bad thing."

"It is. I'm trying. Really trying. I pride myself on my self-control, only I seem to lose it when I'm around you. I'm tempted to toss you in my truck and haul your beautiful ass back to my place and show you six ways to Sunday how amazing I think you are."

"Oh."

"You're not the type of girl who goes for my kind, so I need to work a little harder to gain your trust. Prove to you I'm not the same kind of guy who hurt you."

Rachael's gut dropped to her feet and she gasped. She wanted to lock away the last five years of her life, to pretend they never happened.

"I won't ever hurt you. And when you truly believe that, I'll show you how un-freaking-believable we can be together." He took her sunglasses out of his pocket and slid the frames over her ears.

No poet could sweep her off her feet like rough-around-the-edges Jake Morgan. He dropped a quick kiss to the top of her head and opened her car door for her.

"See you on the flip side, Blondie." He winked before jogging over to his own truck.

Six ways to Sunday needed to happen.

Fast.

etween prepping for her first Kids in the Kitchen party and crafting recipes for Rocky Harbor's Strawberry Festival, Rachael barely had any time to come up for air. Jake had stopped in twice while she'd been in the middle of making strawberry-port jam and couldn't leave the stove. He'd distracted her with kisses on the back of the neck until she nearly lost her balance and fell into the pot of strawberries. She poured herself the leftover port after he left.

Delighted with the reviews of her strawberry-pistachio tart, she made an extra batch for Mackenzie to sell during the festival. The strawberry and cream éclairs she'd save as a surprise for Saturday morning. With the strawberry pops for the kids tucked away in the freezer, all she needed now was an unbiased taste tester for her new drink recipe.

"Hey, Blondie."

"Perfect timing. I need you."

Jake growled and took two giant steps across the kitchen, locking his lips on hers. Rachael couldn't help but swoon a little before she started giggling.

"Not the impression I try to make," he grumbled.

"Sorry. This wasn't what I had in mind."

"Oh." Disappointment was etched across his face.

"Not that I had any problems with your greeting, but I'm on borrowed time. I still have a ton of prep work to do for tomorrow's party. I wasn't thinking when I booked it. The town is going to be packed for the Strawberry Festival."

"That's good, isn't it? Good PR?"

"Yes, but I was already swamped with baking for Mackenzie, and now the birthday party."

"What can I do to help?"

"Try this." She handed Jake the glass and studied him as he sniffed it.

"It smells like a girl drink."

"Do they make boy drinks?"

"Yeah. Beer. Whiskey. Scotch."

"Sexist, are we?"

"Not at all. But this smells like a drink I'd rather taste off of you." He nibbled on her ear, tracing his tongue across her lobe and down her chin. Her knees buckled and she held on to the table for support. Jake smirked and peered at her over the rim. "What is it?"

"Strawberry-ginger caipirosca."

"Yeah, no guy is going to drink something he can't spell, much less pronounce. What the heck is in it?"

"Vodka, muddled strawberries, mint leaves, lime, fresh ginger, and sugar."

"Have you had any yet?" Rachael shook her head. "You try it first." He handed her the glass and she rolled her eyes as she sipped.

"Oh, that's good. Maybe a little more ginger."

"Let me try a taste." Jake took the glass from her and set in the counter before leaning in and kissing her. Deeply. His tongue swirled and danced with hers before he sucked her bottom lip. "I'd say it's perfect just the way it is."

He must have sensed her lack of coordination and picked her up, sitting her on the counter, pushing her legs apart with his thighs. Jake slid her forward, her butt nearly hanging off the counter as he scraped his calloused palms up and down her arms, her neck, and into her hair.

"Well, I guess you found her. Looks like I'm not keeping her busy enough."

They broke apart and Rachael blushed. She pushed at Jake's chest until he backed away so she could hop off the counter.

"I'm sorry, Mackenzie. It won't happen again. I—"

"Easy girl. Kidding. Ha ha. Lover boy, you can drop the death stare. It's not like you were going to get lucky on the counter. Unless..."

"No!" Rachael lowered her head in mortification. She respected Mackenzie and her place of business. She'd been so kind, letting Rachael use the space and selling her food. The last thing she wanted to do was break any type of rule.

"Hey, can't blame you if you have. Can't deny the temptation's been there, just haven't had the opportunity. I say go, girl. And you, sexy abs." Mackenzie waltzed closer, jabbing her finger into Jake's chest. "You don't hurt my girl. I need her. When she's pissed she can't cook worth crap." Rachael gasped. "Sorry, hun. You know it's true. You throw random ingredients in a bowl and can't remember what you put in there." She placed her hands on her hips and returned her glare to Jake. "And when she's sad she bakes like a fiend. Right now, she's making all sorts of recipes. It better be because of business and not a broken heart." Mackenzie looked to Rachael and lifted an eyebrow. "By the look of the lip-lock I broke up and the steam on the windows, I'd say all is well."

Rachael resisted the temptation to check out the windows. "Wow. Am I that transparent?"

"No. I'm just that good." Mackenzie clicked her tongue before exiting.

"I'm not gonna lie. She scares me a little." Rachael picked up the drink and took another sip. It was good, but a touch more ginger and it would be amazing.

"Me too, Blondie." Rachael's face heated again when Jake turned his back to discreetly adjust himself. "Listen," he said, facing her. "I have a meeting with a new client but I really want to see you again."

"You're seeing me right now," she teased.

Jake shook his head. "Not good enough. I've competed with your kitchen this week. I don't want to share you anymore. I want you to myself."

Had he been angry or possessive when he said those words, Rachael would have backed away in fear. But instead he was only passionate. His eyes darkened to pitch black and he licked his lips as his gaze locked on hers. Shivering with anticipation, she nodded and he closed his eyes with a groan.

"I need a cold shower." Jake placed a chaste kiss on her lips and walked out the back door, leaving Rachael hungry for more.

• • • •

EXHAUSTED AFTER A LATE night baking and a long morning teaching nine six-year-olds how to make homemade pizza and strawberry shortcake, Rachael dropped onto the old wooden chair by the back door, sitting down for the first time in what felt like days. She'd cleaned up the mess, booked two events with some of the moms from the party, and kept Mackenzie's front counter stocked full of strawberry desserts.

"Your keeper said you were all done back here." Jake filled the doorway, one massive shoulder leaning against the frame, his arms crossed over his sculpted chest. Rachael was no virgin, but the thought of being naked with Jake terrified and delighted her. He looked like the kind of man who knew his way around a woman's body and would enjoy pleasing her.

She squirmed in her seat and licked her lips.

"Don't look at me like that, Blondie. I only have so much self-control."

Her cheeks warmed and she ducked her head, hiding behind her bangs. "I'm sorry."

"What is it with all of your apologizing?" She heard him sigh in frustration as he approached her.

If he only knew. Jake thought *he* was damaged goods, but Rachael had him beat. At least the path he chose was his own, his decisions. While she let someone else mold her into his little puppet, stripping her of all self-worth, independence, and pride. There were times when she forgot about her baggage, when she felt free and young again. Jake made her feel that way, but stupid ghosts from her past kept creeping in, making her doubt herself and her abilities.

"You look like you could use a break. Let's check out the festival. My mom said your strawberry things sold out within minutes."

"Which ones?" She perked up in excitement. The festival was the perfect marketing tool for her children's cooking parties and the catering business.

"The ones with the nuts." He pulled Rachael to her feet and wrapped his arms around her, untying the apron and slipping it over her head.

"My strawberry-pistachio tart?"

Jake nodded, touching his lips to hers. "You taste like whipped cream," he murmured into her mouth.

Rachael looped her arms around his neck and drew him deeper into the kiss, blocking out all coherent thoughts except for his clean, forest scent. They stood in the middle of her kitchen, touching head to toe, and had a good old-fashioned make out session. There was no groping, no words, no music. Just the sound of their sighs and gentle caresses.

If she wasn't careful, she'd find herself head-over-heels in love with her badass boyfriend. *Boyfriend?* Did he think of her as his girlfriend? Was Jake the type to have a few girls on the side?

No, he spent too much time working, volunteering at the gym, and caring for his sister to have another girlfriend. They'd barely had any time together with his busy schedule and her new career.

Unless...

No, the jealous Rachael got her nowhere in life. Actually, it got her into the hospital. Which lead her back to Maine.

"Should I be offended?" Jake tipped her chin up so he could see into her eyes.

"What?"

"I lost you. One minute you're totally vested into this." He tipped his head back and forth between them. "And the next you're off somewhere else."

"How could you tell?"

"So I'm right? Damn. I'm losing my touch." Jake stepped back, putting a little space between their bodies, keeping her hands in his. "Want to talk about it?"

Badass but observant. Yeah. Totally in love. She loved that he cared enough to read her signals and not be put off by her distractions. Rachael stood on her tiptoes and planted a hard kiss on his lips. "Let's go check out the festival. Mackenzie got a special liquor license so she can serve my strawberry-ginger caipirosca."

"That's that drink that tastes so good on you?"

Rachael laughed and pulled him through the kitchen, grabbing her purse before yanking the back door open.

They held hands as they strolled through the center of town, checking out the storefronts all decked out for the festival. They peeked in the windows of the various gift shops, ice cream stores, and boutiques giggling at the silly knickknacks that drew tourists in.

Jake's landscaping was beautiful, the masonry giving an elegant yet cozy feel. Tents were set up along the cobblestone walkway with vendors selling jewelry, artwork, crafts, foods, and services. He stopped in front of a local crafter and picked out a teal sea glass bracelet.

"Think Julia will like it?"

"Is it her birthday? Your birthday?"

"No. She doesn't go out much so I like to pick her up things I think she'll like when I see them. She used to love searching for sea glass when we were little. And teal is her favorite color."

Touched at his sentiment, Rachael leaned her head against his shoulder. "She'll love it. That's very sweet of you."

After he paid, Jake picked up her hand, lifting it up to his lips and kissed her knuckles. They were admiring some artwork when Rachael spotted her brother on the far end of the square, with a small one-seater plane parked in the blocked-off road. He talked to the kids who played around the plane, picking one little boy up and setting him in the seat.

"Let's go say hi to my brother." She didn't realize the significance until Graham noticed her and his gaze quickly moved to her right. The protective brother stare was in full effect. She should have known.

"He doesn't look happy to see me."

"He's harmless. It's my other brothers you should be worried about."

"I'm looking forward to it."

Rachael peered up at Jake and smiled. Yes, she'd be bringing him by to meet her family. And they would love him.

• • • •

BIG BROTHER DIDN'T look too happy to see a man holding Rachael's hand. He'd met her mother, but Jake had a feeling Rachael hadn't told her family much about him. He'd been a cocky son of a bitch in his teens and early twenties, not caring what a girl's family thought of him. It wasn't until after Julia's accident that he cleaned up his act. Still, the damage had been done. He knew he wasn't boyfriend material before and hoped he'd rectified his image to deserve someone like Rachael now.

Hell, not someone *like* Rachael. Just Rachael. She was the only one he wanted.

Graham, the pilot brother, said something to another guy before making his way to them. His eyes had been locked on Jake's since he spotted his sister and he didn't look too happy to see her. Or rather, him. Jake would follow Rachael's lead on this one coming across as defensive probably wasn't a good first impression.

"Rach. How was the party?"

"Yeah, Graham. I'm over here."

Jake held back his chuckle at Rachael's sass until Graham moved his gaze from him and looked at his sister.

"Sorry. How was the party?"

"Awesome. I booked two more already."

"I'm proud of you." Graham kissed her cheek and stepped back before nodding in Jake's direction. "This the guy?"

The guy. So she'd talked about him. He wondered what she'd said, if she painted him in a good light. Or if she told her family about how he'd screwed up their first date.

"Lucy's approval doesn't mean much in my book. You're going to have to prove yourself."

Jake opened his mouth to reply, but a beautiful redhead stepped into their circle, pulling Rachael into a big hug. "I heard about your party this morning. I'm so happy for you." The woman—who Jake assumed was Graham's redheaded fiancée—glared at Graham before shaking her head. "Be nice."

Rachael stuck her tongue out at her brother and Jake laughed.

"You must be Jake. I'm Maggie. It's a pleasure to meet you. You won't find a sweeter woman than Rachael."

"No need to sell me on her, Maggie. But I'd appreciate you convincing Rachael that I'm not such a bad catch either."

Maggie laughed.

"Oh, God," Graham moaned.

"You look and sound just as charming as someone else I know." Maggie elbowed Graham in the ribs, keeping her sparkling eyes on Jake.

"You're all embarrassing me. Be nice or Jake and I are out of here." Rachael tugged at his hand but he kept his feet firmly planted in the grass. He enjoyed watching her spunk and sass come out when she was with her friends and family.

"Have you had eaten yet? I was coming over to pick up Graham for a late lunch. We'd love it if you'd join us."

"I've been too busy to eat. Are you hungry, Jake?"

"I can always eat." He winked at Rachael and looked over at the brooding brother. "Mind if we join you?"

"Might as well."

"Gee, thanks, G. The brotherly love is simply oozing out of you today."

The four of them stopped by the food trucks, made their selections, and found a patch of grass in the shade. "So tell us about yourself, Jake. Are you from around here?" Maggie rested her back against Graham's chest and unwrapped her sandwich.

Graham looked to be a few years older than him. Jake hoped his old rap sheet hadn't made its way to the nice families in Rocky Harbor. He figured if it had, Rachael's brothers would have been beating at his door, warning him away from her. "I grew up in Westbrook. My mom, dad and sister are still there." It was only thirty minutes away, but Maine was small and people with reputations like his had a hard time hiding.

"Do you do anything besides play at the gym all day?" Graham asked and *oomphed* as Maggie elbowed him in the gut. "What? I'm Rach's big brother. I have to ask these questions."

Jake would act the same way toward any man who showed interest in his sister, if only she'd have the chance to date again. Not wanting to go there, he gladly answered Graham's question. "I'm a landscaper."

"So you cut grass?"

"Graham." Maggie gasped and he liked her instantly. He also appreciated Graham's sarcasm.

"Yeah, I cut grass. And plant flowers." He could have fun with the big brother.

"Jake is the one responsible for the town center. He did all the landscaping. He designed the new layout of the gardens and built the rock walls."

And his heart did an unfamiliar flutter thing. Never had a woman stuck up for him or sounded so... proud of him.

Graham looked around and nodded. "Nice work."

"Thank you."

"So what are you doing over at the gym?"

This is where he got uncomfortable. He wasn't a saint and didn't want to come off like one, but he didn't want to lie either. "I volunteer during the week."

"Checking people in? Cleaning the locker room?" Again, the tough guy sarcasm.

Jake laughed. "Not exactly. I teach self-defense classes."

"Must be great for picking up women."

"Good God, Graham. Will you shut up?" Rachael tossed her fork at her brother, but Jake didn't mind replying.

"Actually, I've never dated any of my students."

"And we're supposed to believe that?"

"Graham!" both Maggie and Rachael yelled.

"It's okay, ladies. I don't mind the third degree. I'm glad you have an overprotective brother. I'd be concerned if you didn't."

Yeah, if he'd been the overprotective brother his sister would be living a happy, healthy, normal life. He hoped all of Rachael's brothers hovered over her. Forever.

Picking up on his mood change, she came to his rescue, resting a hand on his thigh and giving him a gentle squeeze. "How we met is none of your business. You have a right to ask questions, but don't be rude."

"Sorry. One last thing." Graham wadded up his trash and clenched it tight in his fist. "It's gotta be said. You hurt my sister, you'll have me and my brothers to deal with. Understand?"

"Completely. I appreciate that you're looking out for her. Whether it's me or some other guy, I hope you and your brothers keep her safe."

Graham nodded in appreciation.

"Enough of this interrogation, I want to try that strawberry drink of yours." Maggie wiped her hands on her legs and stood.

"I can honestly tell you, I've never tasted anything so good in my life," Jake said, winking at Rachael as he helped her to her feet.

CHAPTER SIX

Another week flew by with little contact with Jake. It wasn't until she entered the gym for their last self-defense class and spotted him sparring in the boxing ring with the owner, Tony, that she realized how much she cared for him. His tight gray T-shirt was drenched in sweat, with only a small patch on the bottom still light in color, while black gym shorts hung low on his hips and showed his glorious backside. Triceps, biceps, and shoulder blades ripped with muscle threatened to tear through his shirt like the Incredible Hulk.

Rachael couldn't help but stare.

Jake noticed Rachael and he stilled, standing a little straighter. His classic grin changed the serious lines etched in his face to something more relaxed, more Jake. Tony took advantage of his distraction and sucker punched him across the chin. Jake's head whipped to the left and Rachael let out a loud gasp.

Finding his balance, Jake grinned and saluted Tony with his glove.

"Seriously?" Lucy huffed.

"What?" Rachael rolled her shoulders in an attempt to appear casual.

"Why don't you two head back to the locker rooms and get it over with?"

"I don't know what you're talking about." Rachael turned and tried to focus on her sister when all she wanted was to make sure Jake was okay. The laughing and taunting from behind her told her he was and that Tony thoroughly enjoyed throwing him off balance.

"Please. You practically tore his clothes off with your eyes, not that I can blame you. I can't believe you've been seeing each other for this long and haven't stripped him naked yet. You're not a prude, are you?"

Rachael knew Lucy wanted to rile her up, so she shrugged off her offensive taunt. "We're taking it slow. I'm not ready to rush into anything."

"Understood. Didn't mean to pressure you. I don't exactly know what happened with dickwad in California, but I get that you need some time. Seriously, though, Jake seems like a good guy. You should at least get a peek at the goods. Watch him mow the lawn in his underwear or something."

Laughing, Rachael rolled her eyes and shook her head. "Such a one-track mind."

"What do you know about his friend? Tony, is it?"

Of course Lucy would know the man's name. "Not much. He owns The Warehouse and seems like a big brother to Jake."

"He can't be that much older?"

"Down, girl. Tony has a girlfriend."

"Your point?"

"You're pathetic." Rachael turned back to the boxing ring and was rewarded with a strip show. Jake reached the back of his collar with one hand and pulled the sweat-drenched shirt over his head in one slow, erotic move.

"Holy crap." Lucy let out a low whistle.

For the first time, Rachael saw his entire tattoo. Black ink covered his left shoulder and part of his chest. She couldn't decipher what it was exactly, more an intricate marking of symbols and lines. Using his shirt to wipe the sweat from his forehead, he said something to Tony that made him laugh before catching Rachael's eye again.

Tossing his shirt over his shoulder, he kept his gaze fixed on hers as he carried his solid frame toward her. "You're early."

Finding her voice buried deep under the pile of lust in her chest, Rachael cleared her throat. "Yeah. We, uh, we... we are."

Lucy snorted. "Nice tat. What is it?"

Jake broke eye contact to acknowledge Lucy. "It's a warrior tattoo."

"It's hot."

"Um, thanks?" Clearly embarrassed by Lucy's blatant ogling, he shifted on his feet. "I need to take a quick shower before class. I'll see you ladies in a few minutes. Feel free to warm up on the mats." He started to lean in to kiss Rachael, but eyed Lucy and retreated.

"Someone's getting lucky tonight."

"I'm not seeing him tonight."

"Why not?"

Rachael headed toward the back room where the class was held. "He has a new project for a housing development and a late meeting with the association." They stretched out on the mat, loosening their hamstrings as Jake had instructed.

"So meet up afterwards and get naked with him."

Laughing, Rachael lightly smacked her sister. "What's this obsession with me getting naked with Jake?"

"I want you to be happy."

"I am. I truly am."

"So make it work tonight."

"I need to be at Coast & Roast at three in the morning to start baking and cooking. He won't be home until late. Tonight isn't good."

"So you'll get naked this weekend."

"I don't know. Maybe."

"Ladies." Jake came up behind them, startling Rachael. By the predator look on his face she'd bet her strawberry trifle he heard her confession.

· · · ·

WITH NO WAY IN HELL to hide his obvious arousal, he lowered the stack of towels in front of his crotch and bounced on the balls of his feet. "All warmed up?"

"Oh, we're plenty warmed. You took care of that earlier when you took your shirt off and did your Magic Mike thing."

"Lucy!"

The sisters were nothing alike that was for sure. Jake wanted to learn more about Rachael's family. Hell, he wanted to hear her story. There was so much he wanted to learn about her past. When was she adopted? Why she was adopted? What the hell happened with the guy who messed her up?

Before he got her naked, as Lucy so delicately stated, he needed to get to know her better. To understand her and to make sure he never crossed any of those delicate lines he knew she had laid out all around her.

The past few weeks had been fun. Going to festivals and walking on the beach weren't in his normal repertoire of dates. Not that he had normal dates. Hook ups at bars were as complicated as he got.

And whatever the hell was going on between him and Rachael was definitely complicated. She was relationship material.

He was not.

Thinking about their obvious differences helped lower the rush of blood in his shorts. There were skeletons in his closet he didn't want to share with her, but he knew he needed to. If she found out through the wrong people, well, her trust in him would never return.

He'd screwed up once by keeping his sister a secret. Maybe this weekend he'd come clean about his past. And his present.

"'K, loverboy. Take your sexy eyes off my sister and let's get going with this last class." Lucy shoved him aside and he stumbled backward, grateful for a distraction.

After an hour of lessons, skills, and drills, he dismissed the class, suggesting those who were interested in more self-defense techniques sign up for his taekwondo lessons on Tuesday nights.

"It's been real. Maybe I'll see you around." Lucy patted his chest, lingering a little too long with her hand before she gave him a devilish grin. "Meet you in the car, Rach. Don't be too long. I have to get to work."

"I can drive you home or work or wherever you need to go," he offered when Lucy left.

"Thank you, but I have a lot of prep work I need to do today." Rachael bit her lower lip, a sign he'd learned to read. She was nervous. Probably about their weekend plans. He could be a gentleman and pretend he didn't hear her say there was a possibility of sex this weekend, or he could address it and tell her there was no need to rush.

Since a gentleman he was not, he opted for option B. "About this weekend." A crimson blush took over her face and she lowered her head, her hair falling out of its ponytail and disguising her face. "I'm not going to lie and say I don't want to... get naked with you."

He tipped her warm face up and waited until her blue eyes made contact with his. "However, I'm not rushing or pushing you into anything. I never thought I'd say this to a beautiful woman, but being with you is enough. We don't have to take it any further than we've already gone."

Yeah, he was totally whipped. God's honest truth, he'd never spoken those words to a woman before.

"I'm sorry—"

"Eh, eh, eh," he tsked. "I told you to stop apologizing when you've done nothing wrong."

Rachael nodded and blinked fast. "Okay. I, uh, I really need to go. Lucy has to get to work."

"Yeah, I'm going to be late too. I'll walk you out." Once outside, he spotted Lucy's beater and followed Rachael to the car. He kissed her lightly on the lips. "Saturday. I'll pick you up around six?"

"That sounds good. What should I wear?"

A devilish grin he couldn't control took over his face and worked its way down to his shorts.

"Babe, you can wear anything you want. As much or as little as you'd like."

When the taillights couldn't be seen anymore, he jogged back into the gym, tossed on his work jeans, boots, and shirt, and sped to his latest job site.

Digging holes was backbreaking, hard, sweaty work, and it helped him get out his sexual frustration. He wasn't frustrated in the sense that he was annoyed. Yet every minute he spent with Rachael it became harder and harder to keep his hands in gentlemanly places. Come Saturday night he'd ask her about her scars.

And then, come hell or high water, he'd at least make it to second base.

· · · ·

IN TWO MONTHS HE'D be done with his Friday afternoon meetings with Ross Noles. Eight more visits with his probation officer and then he'd be a free man. For real.

In all honesty, Noles was a decent officer, but every time Jake left their thirty-minute check-in he was reminded at what a failure he'd been in life. It didn't matter that he'd spent the last five years of his life making up for his crimes; he had twenty-four years of loser behavior to rectify.

Well, he'd been a decent kid. It was the past sixteen years of his life he'd like to redo. Still, trust was easily broken and took years to build back up. He'd ditched his thug buddies from the past and worked his ass off to prove to his sister and his parents that he was a changed man and, because they were better people than him, they'd forgiven him.

He was a lucky son of a bitch blessed with an amazing, supportive family, and now the sweetest, kindest woman.

Now he needed to forgive himself.

"You look like hell." Ross stuck out his foot and hooked it around the leg of the chair across from Jake, pulling it out before taking a seat. "That coffee for me?"

Ross didn't have to ask. They'd been meeting here for nearly two years, Jake showing up early at the diner on Marginal Way in Portland and ordering two black coffees.

They both didn't care for the retro places or fancy coffee shops, although Coast & Roast was growing on him. Or maybe it was the woman who worked in the back. He'd prefer her tasty concoctions over coffee any day. Or a taste of that strawberry drink on her lips.

"Looking better now. What's going on in that thick skull of yours?"

Jake had lucked out with Noles. He had a decade or so on him but came from a similar tough-guy adolescence. He didn't judge Jake or make him feel like an ass. Their friendship grew over the months, with Noles taking on a big brother role. Not that at twenty-nine he needed a big brother.

Hell, he'd always wanted a big brother. At five, at ten, at sixteen. And if he was honest with himself, he'd still want one when he turned forty as well.

"Just thinking." Jake sipped his coffee and stared out the window, watching cars rush by on their way home to see their perfect families.

"Whatever you were thinking about when I first got here didn't look so great, but now your cheeks are all rosy and you have that stupid dumbass grin on your face. Is it the girl?"

He'd told Noles about Rachael last week. It was the first time he ever talked about a woman with him. Because no one else had ever mattered.

"Maybe." He grinned.

"Good for you, man. You deserve a little bit of happiness in your life."

If Jake hadn't been so badass his eyes would have teared up. Outside of his parents, no one ever admitted to believing in him. His landscaping business started taking off last summer after Noles recommended him to a rich guy with a house on the coast that probably set him back quite a few million. Pocket change.

Jeff Sherman hired him on the spot, no questions asked, and loved Jake's ideas for a natural rock garden and gazebo overlooking the ocean. From then on, he'd had no shortage of jobs. Without Noles's recommendation, Jake would still be pushing the lawnmower Graham teased him about.

"How's your sister?"

"The same."

"No sign of improvement?"

"Not yet. The doctors are still hopeful. You never know in cases like hers. The damage could be permanent or she could make a mild recovery. It took her three years to talk again, maybe in a few more she'll be able to really communicate."

"And the seizure? How is she recovering from that?"

"A typical setback. She went fifteen months without having one. They're more sporadic now. So that's good."

They continued their idle chatter, Noles asking about Jake's family who he'd never met but talked like he knew them. The Morgans didn't need the constant reminder that their son was a criminal and had to meet with a parole officer every week. So he kept his meetings fairly private and never talked about Noles with his family.

"How about you? Kids done with sports for the summer?"

"Christopher is in Little League. Doesn't seem to ever end. Melissa has her gymnastics once a week and Kate keeps active with her reading group."

"What about you? What do you do when you're not meeting up with hardened criminals in coffee shops? My offer still stands. I think you'd like taekwondo."

Noles laughed. "You just want an excuse to kick my ass."

"Something like that." Truth be told, Ross Noles and Tony Carver were the only friends he had. If you could count a parole officer and a gym owner as your friends. He liked the men on his crew, but he didn't socialize with his workers, needing to keep the boss and employee relationship strong. Besides, the kids were young. High school dropouts who lacked academic skills but were hard workers.

Jake saw potential in them when no one else would. To hang out with them would make them lose their respect for him.

"And work? Business is good?"

"Hell yeah. I barely have time for Rachael." He couldn't help the tug at his lips and Noles laughed.

"You're whipped, man. I can see it all over you."

"No, not whipped."

"You love her?"

Love? How the hell would he know? Jake shrugged. "We're just having fun."

"I've seen you the morning after you *just had some fun.* You never looked like this."

"We're taking it nice and slow. One step at a time." Painfully slow, but worth every damn second.

"I'm happy for you, Jake. I'm not gonna lie, though. I'll be happy when we can stop meeting like this. Filling out reports and checking in. It'll be nice to meet up somewhere else. Grab a beer. Shoot some hoops."

"I'm looking forward to that too." More than he could possibly imagine.

CHAPTER SEVEN

Rachael opened a new razor and spent an extra ten minutes in the shower until her legs were smooth, her skin lathered twice, and her hair deep conditioned. Wrapping herself in her towel, she wiped away the fog from the mirror and checked out her reflection. What the heck did a man like Jake Morgan see in the skinny blonde in the mirror?

He belonged with someone strong and athletic, not a scrawny washed-up twenty-six-year-old who still lived with her mother, who had no car and barely a career.

Damn Dylan and his emotional abuse! It was harder to get past than the physical beatings she took. Squeezing her self-doubting eyes closed, Rachael shook off her negativity and then re-evaluated herself in the mirror.

Jake liked Rachael just the way she was. In the past few months, she'd put on some of the weight Dylan had made her lose and there were the beginning signs of muscle definition in her legs. Probably from all the biking to and from work. She had excellent skin, shiny natural blonde hair, and when she wasn't pouting and hiding behind her bangs, she had pretty eyes.

She did it! She looked in the mirror and saw her true self, not the façade of what Dylan made her see.

In high school she used to play up her eyes, coating on too many layers of mascara. Her long black lashes made her bright eyes pop and she used them to get her way and out of more than a handful of jams growing up. Not in a mean way. She worked her charm on her brothers and often got the last brownie, or the front seat, or got to tag along with them when they'd go to the movies. Even her mother couldn't say no when Rachael smiled, kissed her cheek, hugged her tight, and batted her eyelashes.

Her bright, bubbly self had been stripped away and she'd turned into the skinny robot Dylan wanted her to be. Not tonight. Rachael pranced across the hall to her room, shucked her towel, and slid into a silky pair of pale pink underwear Lucy got her for her birthday in April. At the time Rachael didn't think she'd ever have a reason to wear them.

Lathering herself in her favorite orange cream lotion, she made sure to smooth it across parts of her body often neglected. Giddy with excitement, Rachael slipped into her teal striped skirt and found a white sleeveless blouse hanging in her closet. It was old, from her high school days, and it still fit—a little loose, but it would do.

Not knowing—or caring—what they were doing tonight, she left her hair down and spent a little more time than usual on her make-up. Jake hadn't seen her with make-up on before, nothing more than a little lip gloss and a quick swipe of mascara, so tonight she added a light layer of pale pink eye shadow, outlined her eyes with a thin line of black, and put on four coats of mascara.

"So, her inner vixen comes out," Lucy said from Rachael's open doorway. They may have become closer over the past few months, but they still weren't comfortable revealing their darkest secrets. She and Lucy were starting to talk about normal things, though. Boys and the future and food. Rachael enjoyed Lucy's abrupt nature and admired her ability to speak her mind and without caring what other people may think. "Hot date with Jake?"

"I don't know about *hot,* but yes."

"Anything you do with Jake is hot." Rachael bit back a smile. "See, you can't deny it."

"No, I can't deny Jake is hot, but it doesn't mean we're getting naked this weekend either."

Lucy snorted. "I'll tell Doreen not to wait up."

Rachael shook her head and marched past her sister, refusing to give in to the taunts. She found her mother in the kitchen stirring sauce on the stove.

"You look beautiful, sweetheart."

"Thanks, Mom." She leaned in and kissed her on the cheek. "Jake should be here any minute."

"You two have a good time. Lucy and I will save some lasagna for you to take to work tomorrow. Rosie is picking me up in the morning to go yard sale hopping, so you can have my car if you need it."

The doorbell rang and Rachael's heart flipped in her chest. "I, uh, I'm not sure what time I'll be home tonight."

"Or if she'll be home at all," Lucy said behind her. "I'll get the door."

Thankful for a minute to catch her breath before she saw Jake, she bit her lip and hugged her mom one more time.

"Have fun and be safe. It's okay if you don't come home tonight, but you call me if you need me. Anytime. Okay?" Doreen placed her hands on Rachael's cheeks and kissed her nose. "I love you."

"Magic Mike is in the living room." Leave it to Lucy to break the mood. "Should I send him in here or ask him to put on a show for me until you're ready?"

"Who's Magic Mike?"

Rachael laughed. "Never mind. It's just Lucy being Lucy. Love you, Mom. Have fun shopping with Rosie tomorrow."

She rounded the corner and spotted six feet of muscle in her mother's old-fashioned living room looking totally incongruous to the setting. Yet he still fit in, like her brothers at Christmas time or during family gatherings. The lace doilies and heavy drapery softened his hardened exterior, making him appear like he belonged. He'd gotten a haircut and had shaved. Normally by the late afternoon he had a light layer of scruff.

He'd shaved. For her. Just as she had. For him.

Rachael's neglected girly parts tingled in anticipation.

"You're...wow. I've never been a man of many words but never been speechless either. Until you. You're gorgeous." His long legs ate up the living room in two strides. When their bodies nearly touched, he lowered his mouth to hers and pressed a gentle kiss against her lips. "You taste like strawberries."

"I had a drink earlier. To settle my nerves."

"There's nothing to be nervous about. I promise."

Noises from the kitchen and Lucy's loud laugh hurried them along. "Let's get going."

"Is your mother here?"

"Yes. Why?" She cocked her head to her side and studied his face, wondering about his intentions.

"My mother would have my hide if I left without saying hello. She taught me to use my manners, it's only recently that I'm listening to her."

And her girly parts exploded. No way in heck was she coming home tonight. "You want to say hi to my mom?"

"Of course."

Rachael stood on her tippy-toes and kissed him. "She'll talk your ear off if you encourage too much discussion."

"Will she tell me embarrassing stories from your childhood?"

"Probably."

"Let's say hi." He pulled her into the kitchen, keeping his hand in hers. "Hello again, Mrs. Riley."

"Oh, Jake. So nice to see you again. Please call me Doreen."

"Doreen." He let go of Rachael's hand to step closer to her mother, lowering his tall frame to kiss her on the cheek.

"How come I didn't get a kiss?" Lucy whined from the barstool at the counter where she chopped tomatoes and cucumbers for a salad.

"I figured you'd smack me or take my shirt off. Neither one looked too favorable to me."

"I like you." She pointed her knife at him before picking up her wine and studying him over the rim while sipping.

"You're crazy, but I like you too."

"Where are you taking my big sis to dinner?"

"I don't know. I figured I'd ask her." Jake turned to Rachael. "What do you feel like?"

"Or you can have dinner with Mom and me. She made two trays of lasagna, figuring our brothers would be by tomorrow."

Rachael growled inwardly at her annoying sister. She wanted alone time with Jake so she could finally touch him the way she'd been dreaming yet doubts still lingered about her not being good enough for him.

"We can eat here if you prefer." Jake rubbed his thumb across her knuckles and those neglected parts of hers begged to be touched by him.

Maybe a little family distraction would help her contain her lust and give her time to make sure she was...sure.

"I thought we'd go to the Drive-in later."

"To watch a movie or to make out in the back seat?"

"Lucy!" Doreen reprimanded.

"Whatever Rachael wants." He winked before returning a more serious look to her. "What would you prefer?"

"We can eat here before we go out, if that's okay with you."

"As long as I'm with you, I'm good," he said softly so only she could hear.

"Oh, get a room already."

"Lucy!" Doreen scolded again.

Or maybe it wasn't quite so softly.

"Are you sure you and Mackenzie aren't twins separated at birth?" Jake asked. Rachael snorted and Lucy flipped him the bird when Doreen wasn't watching.

The four of them ate out on the patio, laughing over stories of Rachael's desperate attempts to tag along with Graham and Luke when she was in middle school. It wasn't until

Blake and Colton had come along that she'd backed off a tad, being a little intimidated and very outnumbered.

Sensing Lucy's unusual quietness, she changed the subject to include her, knowing Lucy didn't have any fun stories to tell. By the time Doreen and Keith had adopted her, everyone had moved out. She didn't get to fight with younger or older sisters. And only had Keith as a father figure for less than a year before he died.

Her backstory was still vague to Rachael. The Riley siblings had taken an unspoken oath not to ask others for details of their life before being adopted, but remained available to listen when a sibling wanted to share.

Lucy hadn't shared her story, and Rachael hadn't divulged her secrets either. This summer she'd change that and include Lucy more in her life. And welcome her into her secrets. Just as she'd open up to Jake. He deserved to know about her screwed-up past as well.

• • • •

JAKE PARKED HIS TRUCK toward the back of the Drive-in. Not so secluded she'd be nervous, but not right in front of the crowd either. "This good?"

Rachael nodded. He kept it light while they waited for the sun to set and the previews to start by playing the I Spy game.

"You're making it up. I can't find anything else that's purple."

"Keep guessing, Blondie."

"Is it something in the back of your truck?" He shook his head. "And I can see it from where I'm sitting?"

"Maybe."

Rachael looked around the close quarters of the cab of his truck. He'd cleaned it since the last time she was in it. Vacuumed and stored his tools somewhere else. "I give up."

"You know what that means?"

"I don't recall making any rules before we started this game."

"Oh, we definitely did." Rachael raised an eyebrow at him. "Well, I did."

"Uh-huh." She crossed her arms over her chest and did her best to cast an evil eye his way. "And what exactly are the rules?"

"The rules clearly state"—she interrupted him with a snort—"that if someone is unable to find said I Spy object, the loser must kiss the winner."

"I don't know." She played along. "Seems a little Catch 22 to me. Maybe I should keep guessing."

"Too late. You already gave up."

"Did not."

"Did so. It's your toes. They're purple."

Rachael unhooked her leg from under her and rotated her foot. She forgot about the purple polish she put on last night while talking to Jake on the phone. "You couldn't even see them from where you're sitting." She straightened in her seat, slipping her feet out of her flip flops and rotated her ankles.

"I noticed them when I picked you up."

"You didn't even look down at my feet."

"Babe, I looked at every inch of you." The heat smoldering in his voice sent shivers of lust through her body.

"Oh."

"And when you look at me like that..." He let out a breath and turned away from her, staring ahead at the blank movie screen.

"When I look at you like what?" she whispered, moving her aching body across the bench, closer to him. She studied his profile, noticing his Adam's apple bob as he swallowed. A look of concentration became etched into his brows as a bead of sweat formed on his forehead. Feeling brave and bold for the first time, she slid her hand across the seat and onto his knee. It twitched and he growled.

"Rachael," he warned.

"I'm paying up." She skimmed her hand up his thigh, keeping it safely on the outside and away from the bulge between his legs. She moved it up his chest until she reached his neck. Caressing his chin, she turned his face toward hers and looked deep into his magnetic eyes. "I'm going to kiss you now, is that okay?"

"Babe."

Rachael leaned in towards him and brought his face closer to hers, taking the time to smell his clean, rustic sent before lowering her lips on his. Her tongue found entrance to his mouth and slowly sipped the sweetness from it, feasting upon his kindness and generosity. Jake's hands made a leisurely trip up her back until they settled in her hair.

Needing to be closer, Rachael shifted to her knees and leaned even further into his strength. She tried to fling her right leg over his body to straddle him, but her thigh rammed into the steering wheel and her foot got caught on the gearshift. In all the movies she'd seen and romance novels she'd read this never happened.

"Sorry."

"No. Don't." He made his point the other day about her apologizing, but she couldn't help it. Old habits were hard to bury. Jake slid his body across the bench so they were in the passenger seat, with her still straddling him. "Better?"

"Much." She studied his caring eyes as he positioned his hands on her waist.

"Now, where were we?"

Rachael wiggled her eyebrows and her butt. "I don't remember. Something about purple toes and—" He cut her off with a searing kiss that ended too quickly as the movie flickered on the big screen and music came out of the speakers.

"This is probably a good thing." Jake held her face in his hands and gently pushed her hair back. "There's only so much I can take right now. I may need to go for a walk. Cool down for a bit."

"Want me to come with you?"

"Babe. That would defeat the purpose. I can't promise I wouldn't pin you against a tree and... never mind. I'm good. I'll grab the cooler out of the back." Jake picked her up and moved her to the side before jumping out of the truck. She watched him scrape his hand across his face before wiggling around in his jeans.

Smiling at the effect she had on him, Rachael calmed her breathing, applied another layer of lip gloss, and studied her disheveled hair in the mirror.

From the back, he said, "I have water, soda, and one of those fruity girly drinks my sister used to love before... it's basically spiked lemonade."

"The girly drink sounds good."

He climbed back into the cab, a bottle of water and her bottle of Mike's Hard Lemonade in one hand and a bowl of popcorn in the other. "Can't watch a movie without popcorn."

"You made it ahead of time?"

"I'm picky about my popcorn. The movie theater stuff is good, but sometimes I like to make my own."

Rachael grabbed a handful and nearly melted. "Oh, wow. What's in it? This is amazing."

"Parmesan, garlic, and rosemary."

"You're kidding me. You can cook?"

"I didn't say anything about cooking. My mom spoiled us on good food growing up. She loves to make fancy healthy stuff and I learned how to make the things I really liked."

"Tell me more. What other foods did she make for you?" Rachael continued to shovel popcorn in her mouth, ignoring the movie, while he fed her stories and recipes.

"My dad's Irish and, in case you couldn't tell, my mom's pure Italian. She'd be proud of your mom's lasagna. It was pretty good."

"Mom is an awesome cook, although she doesn't do much of it anymore. I've sort of taken over in the kitchen since I've been home. Although I've been slacking lately since I've been so busy." Not only with her cooking, but with Jake as well.

"I'd hardly call it slacking." He took a swig of water and screwed the cap back on the bottle, setting it in the cup holder. "I'm looking forward to having you cook for me. And I don't mean that in a sexist way. I've sampled some of your recipes and I'm hooked. Consider me a food snob, so really, that's the highest compliment anyone could give you."

Rachael laughed. "Thank you. How about next weekend I cook dinner for you?"

"I'd like that." Jake picked up the bowl of popcorn that separated them and placed it to his left, moving into her space. "I'd like that very." He kissed her lightly. "Very." He settled on her lips a little longer. "Much."

When the movie ended they looked up in surprise, not having watched a single minute of it. "Are you tired? I know you have an early morning tomorrow. I can bring you home if you don't want to stay for the next movie."

"Actually, I'd like to stay, if that's okay." Rachael loosened her arms from his neck and dropped her legs from his lap."

"I suppose I can sacrifice a night of debauchery for you, Blondie." He picked her legs back up and set them across his lap, pulling her into his side with his strong arm.

They cuddled together and actually watched the second film. His hands were in constant movement, skimming up and down her arm, in her hair, or intertwined with her fingers. Jake pressed gentle kisses to her head, which rested on his shoulder, and held her tight when she jumped at the scary parts in the high-action thriller.

It was nearly one in the morning when the double feature was over, and Jake drove her home. She had a hard time keeping her eyes open, but wanted to make sure Jake stayed awake. He walked her to the door and gave her a slow, passionate kiss that played with her girly parts again.

The pale pink satin underwear stayed on but would be coming off next weekend.

For sure.

• • • •

"YOU CAN'T KEEP WORKING seven days a week." Mackenzie swung her legs back and forth, sitting contently on Rachael's workspace.

"I'm not exactly working."

"You're here every morning, and covering shifts for me when someone calls in sick."

"I'd be baking at home anyway. This gets me out of the house."

"That's working seven days."

"Pot calling the kettle black. Have you taken a day off since I've met you?"

"I live upstairs, so it only seems like I work every day."

"Ha. You check in with your staff, serve the patrons, and clean up whether you're *working* or not."

"Yeah, so speaking of that." Mackenzie hopped down and wiped her hands on the thighs of her jeans. "Any chance you can cover Deanna's shift this afternoon? She came down with the flu and I have a hot date later." She wiggled her eyebrows. "I don't plan on getting much sleep tonight."

Rachael still had a zillion things to do like grocery shop, shower, change her clothes, and bake five dozen muffins. She figured she'd have a late night too and had planned on doing Sunday's baking this afternoon and not coming in tomorrow.

But she couldn't leave Mackenzie hanging, not after the support she'd given Rachael. She'd have to call Jake to cancel.

"Sure. I can close up." Coast & Roast opened at five in the morning and closed at six in the evening during the summer months. Normally Rachael was gone before closing, but she'd put in a few long days and watched Mackenzie close down the place, so she knew what to do.

"I'll come in early tomorrow, so don't stress about anything. As long as the food is put away and the counters clean, I'm good. And really, thank you. I hope I didn't crash any plans you had tonight."

"Nothing I can't reschedule."

"You're a peach. I'll see you tomorrow."

After Mackenzie left, Rachael pulled out her phone and sent Jake a quick text. Thirty minutes later, as she was wrestling with the espresso maker, he walked in, clearly annoyed.

He waited until her two customers had their drinks and had walked off before leaning over the counter and studying her. "What gives? Last thing I knew you baked for this place, you didn't work the front."

"I know." She sighed, rounding the counter and walking into his arms. "I'm sorry. Deanna's sick and Mackenzie was in a bind. I told her I'd help out. I should be out of here by six-thirty, I just won't have time to change or shop for food. I promise I'll make you dinner another time." Rachael rested her head on his chest, snuggling into his steady heartbeat.

"First, don't apologize unless you poisoned Deanna so she'd be sick and you'd have to cover for her, or unless you were looking for an excuse to bail. Second, I'm not mad that you're not making me dinner. Was I looking forward to it? Hell yes." He kissed the top of her head. "Mostly I was looking forward to being with you. I can hang around here until you close up and then we can grab a bite to eat. Or I can whip up something at home."

"I have my mom's car so I can meet you at your place. There's no need to wait around here for another hour."

Jake squeezed her one more time before stepping away. "Watching you for an hour would be no trouble at all, but if you have a car then I might as well meet you back at my place. I'll stop at the store and start on dinner."

"Are you sure?"

"Hell yes." He nuzzled her lips with his until the ringing of the front door separated them. "I'll text you my address."

"I'll call you when I'm on my way."

Jake kissed her lightly one more time before slipping away. The late afternoon crowd was thin and Rachael used the time in between customers to sweep the floor, fill the napkin dispensers, and rearrange the glass cabinet that housed the baked goods. Sunday mornings were busy and she'd have to come in pretty early to get a jump on the muffins.

At least dinner wasn't a total washout. Once the shop was cleaned and locked up for the night, Rachael hurried into the employee bathroom and washed her face, brushed out her ponytail, and inspected her make-up. Not one for carrying cosmetics in her purse, there wasn't much she could do to glam up for her date.

At least she wasn't wearing one of her tacky shirts her brothers got her. The plain white shirt would have to do. It wasn't like Jake was the dressy type anyway, not like...nope. Not going to go there.

Checking her phone for the address, she typed in the information to her GPS, locked up the back door, and got into her mother's car. Next week she'd go car shopping. The second step to independence.

Then would come her own apartment where she could have sleepovers with Jake and not feel self-conscious about it. Because come hell or high water, she was sleeping over his house tonight.

• • • •

JAKE HAD NEVER BEEN self-conscious of his little house, but he'd never had a woman over either. It complicated things too much. Besides, his humble home was nostalgic, and bringing a one-night stand into his home seemed inappropriate.

When his grandparents passed away two years ago—first his grandfather after complications from a stroke, then his grandmother, who died of a lonely heart—he'd inherited their tiny two-bedroom. Their faith in him, that he'd treat it like a home and not a headquarters for drugs and crime, was heartening.

While the home needed a lot of upgrades, the last being done back in the eighties, it was paid for and in his name. Eventually he'd build on. For now the small living room fit his second-hand couch and modest television. The orange and yellow linoleum kitchen floor had seen better days, but would be one of the last modifications. He tracked in a lot with his work boots and didn't want to worry about ruining his floors. The eat-in kitchen area still had his grandparents' chipped and yellowing Formica table and four metal chairs, and the spare bedroom housed the large oak desk his grandfather used to sit at and make model airplanes with Jake when he was younger.

He ran the vacuum over the brown, frayed carpet and did a quick clean of the bathroom before Rachael came over, not wanting her to be disgusted with his bachelor ways. Jake wasn't a slob, but with his workload, and trying to squeeze in as much time with Rachael as he could, he hadn't devoted as much time to chores as he should have.

When he opened the door to her a little while later and she stepped into his arms, all insecurities fell by the wayside. He poured her a glass of wine and he laughed as she pushed him aside so she could make the salad.

"I see what your mother means about you being a grouch in the kitchen," he teased.

"I am not. I just gets complicated with too many hands, and I like things done... the right way."

"Meaning *your* way."

"Maybe." Rachael grinned.

Twenty minutes later, Jake looked down at the sleeping beauty on his couch. He'd gone outside to take the chicken off the grill and had come in to find Rachael snoring like a lumberjack. Her face was smushed into the back cushion and her gorgeous ass stuck out, begging him to stare. She'd been up since four this morning and worked nearly fourteen hours. Poor woman was wiped.

The house was warm, but he pulled a light sheet over her body before lying next to her, spooning her backside into him. Before he knew it, he'd fallen asleep as well.

"Christ!" Jake yelled when he hit the floor sometime later.

"Jake?" Rachael sat up, her hair disheveled and pillow lines creased into her cheek. "What... did I fall asleep?" He hadn't pulled the shades, but it was dark out and he had no idea what time it was. "I'm s—... uh, I didn't mean to."

Proud of her for stopping her apology, he got to his knees and faced her. Their eyes were level and he filled his face with a smile. "You sleep like a log."

"I do not."

"And you snore."

"Shut up."

"Like a chainsaw on steroids. Damn woman, you crashed hard. I copped a cheap feel and you didn't even stir." Her cheeks turned red and her blue eyes rounded like saucers.

"I'm kidding. Although you'd never know. In all seriousness, you didn't move an inch when I tucked us in."

"What time is it?" She stretched and God love her white T-shirt for showing him she was a bit chilly.

Jake shifted his gaze and slipped out his phone. "Almost eleven."

"I'm so—so hungry. Have you eaten?"

"Nice save, Blondie. No, I didn't eat. Let's go see what we can salvage."

He hopped to his feet and held out his hands to Rachael. She took them and he pulled her up. "I didn't realize I was so tired."

"Part of it's my fault. You get to that bakery early every morning and I keep you up late at night."

When they couldn't make their schedules match to have dinner during the week, he'd call her after work, or class and they'd talk for hours. Mostly about nothing. He'd make her laugh, she'd make him laugh then he'd get horny.

He held her close, massaging warmth back into her arms. Thinking her neck could use some attention as well, he nuzzled his lips into her softness then made a pathway to her mouth. Sweet. Always so sweet. The loud grumbling of his stomach turned her lips up and she pulled away.

"Let's get some food in you, big guy."

Thankfully he'd had enough common sense to put the chicken in the fridge before taking a three-hour nap with Rachael. The salad still sat on the counter and he figured it was fine.

"Do you want cold chicken, or should I warm it up?"

"Cold chicken sounds perfect. I'm—" His eyebrows shot up in warning, sensing she was about to apologize again. "Thankful for your cooking."

"Another good save, Blondie. Let's eat."

He enjoyed watching her nibble around the chicken bone, then delicately wipe her mouth with her napkin, wishing he were either one. The bone or the wet napkin.

Jake stirred in his seat, adjusting himself. Again. He hoped when they finally had sex—and he prayed it would be sooner rather than later—he wouldn't get hard at the sight and sound of everything Rachael.

He hoped.

After they cleaned and put the dishes away, he swatted her butt with the dishtowel and she laughed, getting him back with her own towel. They danced around the kitchen, play fighting with their towels until she caught his and he pulled her his way, wrapping his body around hers like a blanket.

"Cold?"

"Not anymore," she said before she yawned.

Shit. He really wanted to show her his bedroom tonight, but the woman still looked dead on her feet. "You should probably go soon. I don't like the idea of you on the road when you're so tired."

"Oh." She frowned and stepped back. "I didn't know if you wanted me to... to maybe stay over tonight."

Hell yeah. "What time do you need to be at Coast & Roast?"

She plopped herself down on a kitchen chair and lowered her head. "Early. I had planned on doing all my Sunday baking this afternoon so I could... so I wouldn't have to go in tomorrow, but I didn't get a chance to do so."

And there went his jeans again, growing snug in the crotch. Smiling to himself, he went to fridge and pulled out a cold bottle of water. She had hoped to get naked tonight. Maybe the gods were looking out for him. He unscrewed the cap and chugged the entire bottle, hoping it would cool him down and buy him some time to come up with the right answer.

She wanted to stay the night. Who was he to say she couldn't?

She needed her sleep and had to get up early in the morning and so should probably go home. If she left now, she'd get in three hours of shut eye.

But if she stayed at his house and they went right to bed, she could get three and a half hours.

Choices.

"Want to sleep over?" his mouth asked before his brain could decide what to do.

"Are you sure?"

"Babe." He slowly screwed the cap back on the empty bottle and placed it on the counter before taking one long stride across the kitchen. He stared down at her, willing her to look him in the eyes and question if he was sure. Like he knew she would, her head tilted and she swiped the long bangs from her eyes, batting thick, black lashes, and twisting her plump bottom lip between her teeth.

There wasn't much room left in his jeans. They needed to come off or she needed to leave.

"Okay."

They were coming off.

Jake gripped her shoulders and, pulling her to her feet, crushed his mouth into hers, feeding off her sweetness until he could no longer stand. Rachael's hands massaged his back and lowered to his ass.

God help him, this woman drove him mad.

"Where's your bedroom?"

The one room he put a little investment into was the master bedroom. He'd slapped a few coats of navy blue on the walls last winter and ripped up the old rugs. But at the moment, he couldn't remember what they looked like. The room was just large enough to fit a queen-sized bed and a tall bureau. All he really needed.

Besides Rachael. Scooping her up in his arms, he kept his lips locked with hers as he carried her down the hallway to his bedroom. Slowly he set her down, her thin, soft body sliding against his until her feet touched the floor.

"Jake," she gasped as he cupped her ass in his hands and squeezed.

"Are you sure?" She nodded. Closing his eyes, he leaned his forehead against her shoulder, struggling between right and wrong. No, not wrong. Loving Rachael tonight wouldn't be wrong, but it wouldn't necessarily be right, either. "You have to get up in a few hours. I don't want to be responsible for an unproductive day at work tomorrow."

"You don't want to be responsible for an incredibly sexually frustrated woman who's only had three hours' sleep. A satisfied woman can run on virtually no sleep at all." She slid her hands under his shirt, and in one quick move that totally turned him on, she had it flying in the opposite corner of the room. "Now, are you going to unbutton those jeans or do you want me to do it for you?"

• • • •

AFTER THREE ORGASMS and an hour of sleep, Rachael couldn't help smiling as she stood under the warm water in Jake's shower. Despite being six feet of solid muscle and the sexy yet dangerous-looking tattoo covering his left shoulder and chest, he proved himself to be gentle and selfless in their lovemaking.

Not once, not twice, but three times he'd pleasured her, sliding his large, strong hands up and down her body, exploring every inch of her, touching her in places she had no idea could be so erogenous. Shivering at the memory, she picked up his shampoo and lathered it into her hair.

"You're not getting away that easily." Jake opened the shower curtain and stepped into the tub with her. "I woke up and you weren't there."

"I need to get to work." Proud of herself for not apologizing first, she tossed him the bar of soap and a grin before turning around. "Wash my back?"

"Babe."

"Why am I sometimes *Babe* and other times *Blondie*?" she asked, enjoying the feel of his hands on her behind. "And I said my back, not my butt."

Jake growled in her ear. "I'm going to wash every inch of you, *Babe*."

Rachael giggled and tried to squirm out of his reach when he pinched her cheeks. "I have to go to work. We can't do this again."

"Oh, we can. I'll leave you alone, but I'm not going to stop myself from looking. And touching. Just a little." He reached his arms around her and lathered her front, taking extra care to make sure her breasts were clean.

Shaking her head with a smile, she spun around to face him and leaned back under the spray to rinse her hair. "You didn't answer my question."

"Mmm." He continued the journey with his hands, the bar of soap leading the way toward her thighs. She slapped his hand away and he chuckled. "You tell me."

Sighing in frustration, she turned quickly to rinse off the soap before shutting off the water. Jake opened the curtain and yanked a towel off a hook and began slowly, methodically, drying her body, starting with her legs.

"If you're going to dry me, you should start at the top. My hair is dripping water down my legs faster than you can dry them."

He looked up at her from his squat, the tattoo incongruous to the white walls but synonymous with his devilish smirk, his face dangerously close to the apex of her thighs. "Then I'll just have to spend more time down here." He blew gently on her and she quivered.

"Jake," she begged. For what, she didn't know. To stop? To continue? She'd let him make the call.

He stood, bringing the towel to her head and gently patted her wet hair. "You're beautiful."

Suddenly self-conscious, she crossed her arms across her chest. She kept her gaze locked with his as he worked his way down her body, taking special care around particular parts—the ones he spent so much time studying last night—before handing her the towel.

"Don't I get to dry you off?"

"I don't think so." He stepped out of the tub and wrapped a towel around his waist, but it did nothing to hide the impressive erection. "If you touch me I'll likely explode."

"Isn't that the idea?"

"Babe."

"See, there you go again. Why not *Blondie*?"

"You really want to know?" She nodded and he held out his hand to help her out of the tub. "*Blondie* is when you're being cute. Fun. *Babe* is..." He moaned before leaning in and sucking on her bottom lip.

"Oh." Her body went limp and fell against him when he worked his tongue into her mouth. The kiss ended too quickly, with a devilish grin on Jake's face revealing he knew exactly how much it had stimulated her.

Somehow she managed to get dressed, finagling her clothes out of their twisted heap on the floor. There was a chocolate stain on her shirt and traces of strawberry on the hem of her shorts from yesterday, but she didn't care.

Jake tugged on a pair of running shorts and a Patriots T-shirt before sitting on the edge of the bed to tie his sneakers. "You're not going back to bed?" she asked.

"No. I'm coming with you." He stood and placed a quick, chaste kiss on her lips. "I'll make us coffee, unless you want the fancy stuff from the shop."

"What?"

"Coffee. How do you take it?"

"You don't need to make me coffee. Go back to bed. There's no reason for both of us to be dead on our feet today."

"I know my way around the kitchen. I can help."

"Jake." She followed him down the hall. "You're very thoughtful. Really though, I'll be fine."

"Kindness has nothing to do with it." He measured coffee, filled the machine with water, and pressed a button. "I have purely selfish and lustful intentions. This way I get to spend more time with you, maybe cop a feel or two in between muffins, and then you'll get out earlier so you can rest. Or we can do something. Or go back to bed. Your call."

"I still call it kindness."

He shrugged off the compliment. "Milk? Sugar? You look like the cream and sugar kind of girl." He grinned before turning and taking down two travel mugs from his cabinet.

She wanted a soy latte from Coast & Roast but couldn't refuse his sweet gesture. "You're sure?"

"Stop second guessing me, Blondie. Let's go before you blame me for making you late." He handed her a mug, swiped a kiss across her lips and patted her butt toward the door while he grabbed his keys off the counter.

Blondie. She'd bet her first batch of scones he'd be calling her *Babe* before the sun rose.

CHAPTER EIGHT

They were both so tired by the time they wrapped up her baking that they parted ways in the parking lot, not before a hot and heavy make out session, and agreed to play hooky from work on Tuesday.

Jake planned to pick Rachael up on his motorcycle, a refurbished Harley he spent a great deal of time telling her about on Sunday while they baked side by side. She'd snipped at him occasionally for getting in her way or opening the oven door before the timer went off. Jake took her scolding with ease, laughing and making fun of her for being so territorial.

"How would you feel if I hovered over you while you were working on your motorcycle?"

"I'd pull you down into my lap and make love to you right then and there."

"Seriously?"

"Seriously."

"Well, I can't do that here, but maybe I'll try that tactic while I'm cooking in your kitchen."

"Babe," he'd warned and she'd smiled smugly when he squirmed and covered his crotch with his hands.

With all his big talk about helping her out, his presence in her kitchen actually slowed her down. Rachael spent too much time gazing at his butt when he wasn't looking and he spent too much time giving her gentle caresses and kisses on the neck while she was mixing her ingredients.

Tuesdays weren't especially rushed, so she worked extra long on Monday to make sure the shop wouldn't run out of treats. Jake had given his workers the day off as well, telling them to take advantage of the beautiful weather. She knew this would set his current project back a bit, and that he'd have to put in extra hours later in the week, which made her fall for him even more.

The loud engine coming down the drive revved up her heartbeat with anticipation of the day. Nothing on the agenda but a long ride and time together. Perfect. Dressed in jeans, black work boots and a white T-shirt, he reminded Rachael of an old-fashioned movie star.

Jake removed his helmet, kicked out his stand, and slung one long leg over the bike. Her ovaries tap-danced, reminding her how much she enjoyed being nestled between those thighs.

"You look hot," she admitted.

"You like?"

Rachael nodded and skipped down the steps. He welcomed her with a searing kiss before strapping a helmet on her head. "I've never been on a motorcycle before."

"I'll go slow. We're in no rush today anyway. Figured we'd take the scenic way up Route One and stop when we see a good place to stretch our legs. That okay?"

"Perfect." Rachael swung her leg over the seat of the bike and licked her lips in anticipation.

"Babe," he growled. "*You* look hot." Jake put his helmet on, his gaze staying locked on hers the entire time, before turning around and straddling the bike. "Hold on tight but let me know if you want me to slow down or if you need a rest. Okay?"

"Okay."

He revved his engine, kicked up his stand, and made a slow descent down the driveway. She hugged him tight, keeping her hands clutched on his sides. Jake tensed under her touch and slowly relaxed as they made their way down Route One. The warm sun and the ocean breeze tickled her bare arms as the vibration of the bike between her thighs made her think of Jake and how his hands had warmed and tickled her body a few nights ago.

When they slowed at a stoplight Jake turned around. "You doing okay?"

"This is awesome. I can't believe I've never driven up the coast on a bike before. Everyone should experience the view from here."

"The view is pretty kick-ass." Jake's chocolate eyes darkened before he turned around and accelerated through the intersection.

They stopped at a deli and ordered sandwiches, deciding to eat them at Pemaquid Lighthouse. The view never got old. Maine's coast was dotted with hundreds of islands and lighthouses, all unique and beautiful in their own right. Every beach was a completely different experience, from York to Rocky Harbor to Casco and Bar Harbor.

And none were like California, where the beaches looked similar: sandy and littered with lifeguard stations and surfers. There were beautiful beaches in California but the only areas she was allowed to go were touristy. She supposed it wasn't fair to give California beaches a bad rap, but they weren't for her. Rachael had wanted to visit Santa Barbara but Dylan wouldn't let her go by herself, and he never wanted to go.

This. The rocks, the lighthouses, the islands, and the sound of the waves crashing against the jutted shore, this was what Rachael appreciated. The beauty of nature, not an open space to lay out and get a tan.

Jake parked the bike in a shady area and turned backwards in his seat, facing Rachael before taking his helmet off. "How are your legs?" He rubbed his hands up and down her thighs, a mischievous smirk taking over his face.

"They feel like rubber." She unhooked her helmet and handed it to Jake. "Can we walk a little before we eat?"

"As you wish." He took their lunch out of the bag strapped to the back of his bike and held out his hand for her. "Lead the way, Blondie."

They followed a path that led to the Fishermen's Museum. "Can we look around first?"

"Of course."

She warmed at Jake's casual response. It had been years since she'd been able to make decisions, call the shots, or even make suggestions. To be heard and appreciated made her heart swell with happiness. They took their time reading the history of the lighthouse and maritime heritage, and examining old artifacts from over the years.

She looked up the steep, circular stairs leading to the top of the lighthouse and then turned to Jake. "Can we go up?"

"You don't have to ask, Blondie. I'm following you. You lead the way."

Rachael gave him a quick hug before rushing to the stairs. "I haven't been up here since I was in middle school. And I didn't make it to the top. I got scared and turned around. Graham and Colton teased me but Luke stayed behind while my brothers raced to the top."

"We don't have to go to the top if you're not comfortable."

"Nuh, uh. I'm overcoming all sorts of obstacles. This is just another on my bucket list."

"Oh yeah, what's another?"

"Maybe I'll show you later."

"Show?" Jake stepped closer, pinning Rachael to the wall. She licked her lips and nodded. "Babe."

Grinning until her cheeks hurt, she pushed him back and slipped under his arms. "Let's go." The stairs were narrow and they climbed slowly until they reached the top. "Wow." You couldn't buy a better view than from the top of a lighthouse. They could see for miles and miles across the Atlantic. The quarters were cramped, and they had to make their way back down soon so the next group could come up.

"Where to now?" Jake picked up her hand and kissed her knuckles.

"Let's eat before our subs get warm." Once again Jake let Rachael take the lead. It was all so new to her. They followed a path toward a shady area and found an empty picnic table. They sat next to each other facing the ocean and ate, occasionally bumping shoulders or thighs. Sometimes on accident, sometimes on purpose.

Jake liked to touch her, and she liked it when he touched her. A lot. He wasn't possessive or domineering; his gentle caresses were more natural. Like he simply wanted to touch her, not control her. "Feel like exploring?" he asked.

"Absolutely." She gathered their trash and placed it in a bin before leading the way out on to the cropping of rocks. "I've always wanted to find a sand dollar. In all my years at the beach, I've never found one."

"We're not going to find one in these rocks, but we'll put it on our list of things to do this summer."

She liked that. *List of things to do.* It meant they'd be spending more time together. Like a couple. They climbed far out on to a large rock and sat, dangling their feet above the waves.

"I was never a beach kid growing up. Julia liked going to the ocean with her friends, while I was more of a city boy. I used to give my parents such crap when they'd make us go to the beach for a family day or camping in the White Mountains."

"Why didn't you like it?"

"I was too cool."

"I think you're pretty cool now and you're at the beach."

"Yeah, well, if I knew you'd be at the beach when I was a kid I wouldn't have given my parents such hell."

"As if." She bumped his shoulder with hers and he looped his arm around her waist.

"I'm glad I didn't run into you when I was a puke teen."

"Oh yeah? Why is that?"

"I was a messed up kid. Drugs. Alcohol. If I was in another state I'm sure I would have joined a street gang."

"You're doing pretty well now."

"Only because..."

Not wanting to ruin their perfect afternoon with too much serious talk, Rachael changed the subject. "Do you bring Julia to the beach?"

"My mom does for walks."

"We should bring her with us next time. Not on the bike, obviously, but we can pack a picnic and you can be our hero and find us sand dollars and sea glass."

Jake shifted sideways and lifted his hands to her face. "You'd do that?"

"Of course. She's your sister."

"But you don't have to give up a day to take care of her. It's not easy."

"You and your mother handle her differently."

"You picked up on that, huh?" Jake played with her hair and pulled gently on her ponytail. "Mom can hover. She forgets Julia's brain still functions. It's just slow at sending messages to the rest of her body. You can see it in her eyes, though. Or maybe it's the twin vibe thing we have going. She wants to be treated like an adult. It's tough. For her. For my mom."

"I'm sure your mom could use the break. And with us both there with her it won't be too bad. I'd like to get to know her. Help make her feel... normal."

Jake studied her face, an unfamiliar look in his eyes. Something between lust, surprise, and compassion. He lowered his mouth to hers and her body melted into him. The kiss was tender, sweet like his iced tea, and so gentle she nearly collapsed in his arms.

"You're a really good kisser," she said when he finally broke away.

"No. It's you. There's something about those lips. And those eyes. And that body."

"Excuse me." A voice from behind them prevented them from another make out session. "Would you mind taking a picture of our family for us?"

"Sure." Jake stood and helped Rachael to her feet. The gentleman gave Jake his phone and gathered his three kids and wife to pose. After he took a few pictures, Jake gave the man his phone back.

"I can take one for you if you'd like," the woman offered.

Rachael hadn't even thought of having their picture taken, but she'd love to have this day captured forever. She handed the woman her phone and stood next to Jake. He drew her near with his arm, his hand placed lovingly on her hip, and she wrapped her arm around him as well, resting her head on his shoulder.

"You're a lovely couple," the woman said when returning the phone.

"Thank you. Your family is beautiful as well. I hope you're enjoying your vacation."

"When the kids aren't fighting we are." She laughed. "We always enjoy our trips to Maine. Take care."

Jake asked, "Ready to hit the road, or do you want to walk around a little more?"

"It's pretty warm out here in jeans. We should probably head back anyway." They mounted the bike and took their time traveling back to Jake's house.

"Are you hungry?" he asked after opening a water bottle from his fridge. "I can make us dinner."

"Not yet." Rachael took the water and drank, watching Jake's throat bob with each sip she took. Feeling brazen, she set her bottle down, toed off her sneakers, and unbuttoned her jeans. "I'm feeling a little sweaty from all that sun. Mind if I take a shower?"

"That depends," Jake said as he whipped his shirt off over his head. "As long as I get to join you."

· · · ·

JAKE COLLAPSED ON THE bed, trying to catch his breath. He rolled onto his back and pulled Rachael to his side. Still breathing heavily as well, she draped a leg over his thigh and rested her head on his shoulder.

"Damn." He didn't have the strength to say much of anything else. Rachael's fingers traced the tattoo on his left shoulder. Her caresses were not helping his breathing rate any.

"Tell me about your tattoo."

"Give me a second. You damn near killed me, Blondie."

"Me?" she laughed. "You're the one who made our foreplay last so long."

He had to stop thinking about the laughing and teasing and moaning that had happened in the shower, against his wall, and on his bed over the past hour or he'd never catch his breath. "Yeah. Well." He slid his fingers along her side. "Like I said before. You're hot."

"I'm average."

"This is one argument you're not going to win." He swept her hair out of her eyes and nipped at her shoulder. "I bet you were an adorable kid."

"I don't have any pictures from before I was adopted so I suppose we can pretend."

Jake hadn't meant to bring up the past, determined to move on with the future but since it was out there, he wanted to know more.

"You were eight when Doreen and Keith adopted you?"

"Yeah. They already had Luke and Graham. I thought they were so cool. They hated me." She chuckled. "I don't remember trying to be a pest, but I couldn't help wanting to be with them. I'd been alone and bored my entire life."

"Do you mind me asking about your birth parents?" When her body didn't tense he figured he hadn't crossed the line.

"Not much to tell. I really don't remember much about them. I don't remember my dad. He took off when I was young. My mom was poor and often didn't feed me. I remember having an accident in kindergarten and having to go home. The next day I showed up at school with the same underwear and pants on. My mom hadn't washed them. I can't imagine what I smelled or looked like."

"Sweetheart." He hugged her close, unable to imagine sending a child to school that way.

"I hated school vacations and long weekends. I wasn't sure when I'd eat next. A least at school I got free breakfast and lunch. I don't remember my mom yelling at me or hitting me. I don't really remember her at all. My bus dropped me off not far from our apartment in a rough section of Lewiston. I thought I was so mature having my own house key and staying home alone. I'd have tea parties with my dolls all afternoon and played with my imaginary friends until my mom got home. We didn't talk much. I'd put myself to bed. Wake myself up. I guess I was a pretty responsible kid."

Jake stroked her back and listened to her tell more stories of her loneliness. No wonder she latched on to Graham and Luke when she joined the Riley family. And succumbed to Dylan's abuse. All she wanted was someone to pay attention to her. His heart squeezed tight in his chest, wanting and needing to give her all the love he had inside of him.

But how much did he have? Hell, other than the love he had for his sister and parents, he didn't know if he had any in him to give. And didn't that make him feel like a shit? He'd come from a solid family with two loving parents and a sister who worshiped him, yet he threw it all away for a life of drugs and crime.

While sweet little Rachael was sitting at home in her soiled pants, hungry, playing make believe with her dolls. He hated himself, hated her birth mother. Hated the neglect and stupidity of others. Including himself.

"Have you heard from your mom since your adoption?"

"No. She opted to have no contact with me."

It had to hurt. Complete and utter rejection, yet there was no trace of agony in her voice.

"I'm sorry your life started out the way it did." He slid his hand through her silky hair and kissed her temple. "I'm grateful for Doreen and Keith and the love they gave to you. You've thrived and are a model to others. Not just in this body." He squeezed her hips. "But in your attitude. I'm proud of you. All that you've faced in your childhood and adulthood, and look at you now."

She was completely awe-inspiring.

"Yeah." Rachael lifted her head and grinned. "In bed with my sexy biker boy."

"Enough with the biker boy already."

"It's true," she teased, tracing the outline of his tattoo with her finger. "Why did you choose a dragon?"

He took his time answering, knowing he needed to tell her about more than just the tattoo. She shared her past, even though none of her sad story was her fault. His messed up tales, unfortunately, were one hundred percent brought on by his own stupidity. Not wanting to see the disappointment in her eyes, he pulled her back down to his chest.

"In Japanese tattoo art, dragons are generous, benevolent forces that use their strength to do good for mankind. The Celtic dragon is related with a warrior or a fighter that had strong power and character to fight or battle. I combined the two. It's a Japanese Celtic dragon. And it covers up a stupid tat I had done when I was in juvie."

"Wait." Rachael pulled herself up onto her elbow. "You were in juvenile hall?"

"Yeah. I told you. I was a puke."

"What happened?"

"I had some inexperienced idiot tat me with a pot leaf on my chest. The dragon's scales cover it up pretty well."

A curtain of blonde hair fell across his face as Rachael leaned over and inspected his chest. If this was the kind of inspection she was going to give to his ink, he wished he had tats in other places as well.

"Oh, I think I see it." Her soft fingers traced the outline of one of his many mistakes. "It's barely noticeable."

Thankfully his tattoo artist covered it up pretty well, but Jake could easily spot the leaf. A constant reminder that it didn't matter what you did to try to fix or cover up your stupid mistakes, they'd always be there.

Rachael rested her head against his shoulder again and circled his nipple with her fingers. He thought he'd need at least an hour to recover, but if she kept touching him like that she'd be on her back in minutes.

"Why were you in juvenile hall?"

"Stupid stuff. Drugs. Drinking. Stealing. Fighting. Like I said. I was a puke."

"I can't imagine you like that. You're so caring. Not just to me but to your sister. To the women in your class. You were even kind to my brother when he was taunting you." Rachael's hand slipped lower, stroking his stomach. His abs contracted and his eyes rolled back into his head. The woman had no idea the effect she had on him. "And you've been nothing but thoughtful and considerate to me. You're a good man, Jake."

She hadn't flinched or made him feel ashamed of his past. Instead, she accepted him without judgment and made him feel like a man worth...worth something. She'd restored in him a new sense of pride. Not in the egotistical way. God knew with his track record he didn't have an ego to stand on.

Heat flowed between them, elevating his pulse, heightening his senses. She smelled delicious, a mixture of vanilla, orange, and their mingled sweat.

He couldn't take any more. "Babe," he growled, tucking her beneath him and attacking her mouth with his. He was anything but gentle and considerate with his mouth as he sucked her tongue and bit her lip, then trailed kisses down her neck, leaving tiny love marks all the way down to her core.

• • • •

"YOU SURE YOU CAN'T stay the night?" Jake trapped her naked legs between his and pulled her on top of him.

Rachael smiled at his boyish pout, her chest pounding against his. "You have an early start as well. We need our sleep and you and I both know we won't get any if I stay the night." They'd made a simple dinner of spaghetti and meatballs to regain energy and then fell into bed again.

"I didn't ask you to *sleep* over, I asked you to stay the night. At least I'm being honest with my expectations."

She nuzzled his naked chest and shook with laughter before rolling off him and dragging the sheet with her as she slid out of bed. "Things will slow down when the tourists leave."

"That's not for another six or seven weeks." Jake stood, unabashed in his nakedness, and picked up his jeans off the floor. Forgoing the underwear, he stepped into the jeans and yanked them up his strong legs, covering his sexy, firm butt. Rachael smirked, remembering how he moaned when she dug her fingernails into his backside earlier. "What?" he asked, looking over his shoulder. "You keep looking at me like that and I'm going to think you have second thoughts about going home."

Rachael crossed the room to grab her bra off the windowsill and picked up her panties from the end of bed. "Of course I have second thoughts, but I'm sticking to my guns.

I need some sleep. You've completely worn me out and I'm going to be useless tomorrow."

"I'll come help."

She crouched to reach her jeans under the bed—how they got under there she had no idea. "You make it twice as hard to get anything done."

"I'll take that as a compliment." Jake came up behind her and kissed her neck while he undid her bra clasp.

"You're a pleasant distraction, I'll give you that, but I'm starting my business and need to be professional." She slapped his hand away and refastened her bra.

"I hardly think Mackenzie's going to give you a bad reference because you're so smitten with me." He slid his fingers under her bra straps, kissing her bare shoulders.

"Smitten?" She fixed her straps and scooted out of reach of his busy fingers.

"Isn't that a word?"

"Yes." Rachael lifted up the comforter at the end of the bed and untangled her shirt. "But not one I picture coming out of your mouth." She ducked under his outstretched arms and slid into her shirt.

"What exactly do you expect coming out of my mouth?"

Refusing to go there, she cocked her eyebrow and crossed her arms. "Get dressed, biker boy. It's time for me to go home."

"Biker boy, huh?" Jake opened his dresser and reached in blindly, pulling out a T-shirt and slipping it over his head without even looking at it. The Jameson Whiskey shirt had seen better days but looked good on him.

She held on tighter than necessary during the ride home, not out of fear, but because she didn't want to let him go. The roar of the engine was the only sound in her ears while the cool evening air kissed her thoroughly loved skin.

"We'll do this again," Jake said instead of asking after he kissed her on her doorstep.

"Which part? The bike ride?"

"That." He kissed her again. "And the other stuff."

"Oh, yes, the lighthouse was fun." She smiled coyly and toyed with the frayed collar of his T-shirt.

"Babe."

"Good night." She kissed him lightly before turning and letting herself in the house, her body humming and tingling from her toes to her ears.

CHAPTER NINE

"Dinner with your parents?" Rachael slid deeper in the tub, keeping her cell phone barely above water. "And my sister."

"A family meal? Really?" She blew at the bubbles covering her chest and wished Jake was in the bath with her.

"I'm assuming you've had them before, with your herd of brothers and sisters."

"I have, but I've never had a family meal at someone else's house. I know how loud and obnoxious my siblings can be at the table."

"You don't have to worry about that at the Morgan household."

"Oh, Jake. I'm sorry." She sat up, sloshing the water in the tub. Rachael only meant to say the craziness was normal to her only she'd put her foot in her mouth and offended his family.

"Are you in the bathtub?"

"Uh, yeah."

"Babe." Apparently he wasn't as offended as she thought

"Seriously, Jake. You have a one-track mind. We're talking about a family meal and you're thinking about me naked."

"Babe. You are naked."

"People tend to be when they take a bath."

He growled on the other end and a flutter of goose-bumps trailed down her arms. She sank as low as she could under the blanket of bubbles, wishing she was in bed so she wouldn't have to keep her phone dry.

"You're killing me here."

Good. She enjoyed being wanted. Having the power to weaken a man's senses so he could barely think straight. No, not any man's, just Jake Morgan's.

"I'll see you tomorrow night then."

"I may need to drop in for a muffin or one of those cream-filled things again."

"Eclairs?"

"Yeah. Those. Do you know what I want to do with that filling?"

"Jake," she warned. He ignored her and told her exactly what he had planned.

• • • •

THE NEXT DAY HE SURPRISED her at the back door of the kitchen with a kiss and a box of her eclairs he'd purchased up front tucked under his arm.

"You didn't have to buy them. I would have given you as many as you'd like."

"Oh, sweetheart, they're going to be worth every penny." He gave her another quick kiss and a mischievous smile before backing out the door.

She enjoyed his surprise drop-in visits. They were usually short; he'd drive out of his way for a cup of coffee or a brownie and then head back to his work site. Jake wasn't the type to have a coffee preference beyond black and strong without the frills, so his frequent trips to Coast & Roast were all an obvious ploy to see her.

And she didn't mind one bit. He wasn't stopping by to check on her, he stopped by because he liked seeing her. And she liked seeing him too.

Once home, she showered, shaved, lathered on lotion and packed a bag, knowing she'd cave and spend the night at his place after dinner. The overnight bag was like a big billboard with flashing neon lights saying, *I'm sleeping over my boyfriend's house and going to have sex.* Not something she wanted to advertise to her mom. After saying goodbye to her mother, she grabbed the trifle from the fridge and rushed out the door before Jake could get out of the truck. She felt like a teenager going out with her boyfriend—sometimes the excitement of it was fun—however, she really wanted a place of her own.

Not just so she could have noisy sleepovers with Jake, but it was the last piece of pride she needed to restore.

"Hey beautiful. In a hurry? I would have come to the door. Said hi to your mom."

"She's fine." She didn't want Doreen to look from Jake to Rachael, knowing they'd be sleeping together tonight. It was too mortifying.

Jake's playful smile turned serious. "Is something wrong?"

"No. Everything's good. You can go now." Her silver sandals tapped nervously on the floorboard as she held on tightly to the trifle resting between her legs.

"Hey. What's wrong?" Jake cupped her chin, turning her face toward him. "Rachael?"

Puffing out her cheeks, she blew out a mouthful of air she didn't realize she was holding in. "It's embarrassing, okay?"

"What is?"

"You. Me." She gestured between them and Jake dropped his hand, pulling back as if she'd slapped him.

"I'm sorry you feel that way. I never meant to embarrass you. I know my past is shady, but I've—"

"Oh, no. Not *you*." It crushed her to see the hurt flash across his face. Rachael turned in her seat, being careful not to tip the dessert. "I'd never be embarrassed of you." She picked up his hand and held it over her heart.

No matter how tough and badass Jake appeared, there was a hurting, sensitive chunk inside of him he liked to hide.

"Then what?"

"I told my mom I wouldn't be home tonight. I packed a bag." She nodded to the floor where her backpack sat on its side. "She knows we're...sleeping together. It's embarrassing."

"Blondie." Jake's lip lifted in a sly twist. He moved their joined hands to her neck and drew her towards him. "You're so freaking adorable."

"You can't kiss me now. We've been sitting out here too long and my mom is probably watching from the window." Jake peeked over her shoulder and grinned. "Oh my God. She is, isn't she?" Rachael shifted her body around so she faced front again. "Drive. Please. Let's get out of here."

Jake barked out a laugh before starting the engine and pulling out of her driveway.

• • • •

DAMN IF SHE WASN'T the cutest thing he'd ever seen. Her blue sundress—as Caribbean blue as her eyes—made her look sweet and innocent, which she was. He noticed the extra time she put into smoothing her hair and putting on make-up. He understood her nerves and the thought she put into her first impression with his parents, not that she had anything to worry about.

She'd met his mother briefly a while back at the coffee shop, but they hadn't really had a chance to talk. Jake knew his mother would love her. Probably start talking babies and wedding dresses. For some odd reason that didn't worry him either.

Jake reached over and laced his fingers with Rachael's. "Nervous?"

She shook her head, but her body language said otherwise. In the short time he'd known her, he'd watched Rachael grow from a meek girl in his self-defense class to a woman who started her own business and had no problem telling Jake exactly what she wanted.

He especially liked it when she bossed him around in bed. Not wanting to show up at his parents' house with a hard on, he back-burnered that visual for the ride home. She had packed an overnight bag. He smiled and stroked her palm with his thumb.

"Julia is very excited to see you again."

"Really? She remembers me?"

"You're the pretty lady at the coffee shop who makes the best chocolate brownies. They're her favorite. I usually pick her up a few when I stop in."

"Jake, you should have told me. I would have brought her a batch." Instead she'd made a strawberry trifle.

"They'll love what you made. And if not, we'll bring the leftovers back to my place and I'll serve it off of you. Like I did with those eclairs." She'd been surprisingly responsive to his suggestions and even offered a few of her own.

Damn. He needed to stop thinking that way. He flicked on his blinker and turned left onto his parents' road. He grew up in a modest cape in the outskirts of Westbrook. Close enough where he could walk in any direction and find trouble, but far enough out of the way to avoid the daily grind of the city.

His childhood home didn't have much of a yard, but his parents kept it well landscaped, and his father bitched every few years about the repairs he secretly enjoyed doing. His mother left her teaching job when Julia was in her accident, while his father worked as many overtime shifts as he could at the paper mill to try to make ends meet. They'd never been well off, middle, probably lower-middle class, but he didn't care about social status as a kid. None of his friends, if he could call them that, had much either. Not that it ever stopped any of them from getting what they wanted. If they saw something they'd like, they'd use the five-finger discount and take what they could get away with.

Jake was the slickest of the group. He'd worked his way up from pocketing candy bars in the checkout aisle when he was twelve to shoving pocket-knives from Walmart down his pants before he could drive. Not a part of his past he was proud of. Hell, he wasn't proud of anything from his past.

Jake slowed his truck and parked at the curb in front of his house. Rachael's palm was sweaty in his, her tapping foot ready to bust through his floorboard at any minute.

"Don't be nervous."

"Easy for you to say. Remind me to tell you the same when you come to one of my family dinners."

His chest filled with hope and excitement. "I look forward to it."

"Ha. You say that now. What you experienced with Graham was nothing. I'm waiting until Colton comes home, then I'll invite you over."

Rachael didn't talk too much about him. All Jake knew was that Colton had been injured in Afghanistan and was holed up in some VA Hospital in the Midwest. Graham seemed decent, although he had alluded to Luke's massive size, which would crush Jake into smithereens if he ever hurt Rachael.

Which he never planned on doing.

Jake hopped out of the truck and rounded the hood, opening the door for Rachael and taking first the strawberry dessert, then her hand.

"I'll carry it in. I need something to do with my hands." She took the dish back and they walked the short distance to the front door.

"I can come up with a few ideas for those hands—Mom. Hi." He smiled innocently at his mother when she opened the door, and he kissed her on her cheek. "You remember Rachael."

"Of course I do. And I'm so glad you could come tonight. Come in." She opened the door wider and Jake gestured for Rachael to go in first. Partly because his mother had taught him to be a gentleman—he just chose not to be one—but mostly because he wanted to check out Rachael's butt.

Unfortunately the dress billowed around her backside and her legs, but he'd get another good look later tonight. Jake closed the door behind him and looked around the living room for his sister.

"Where's Julia?" She didn't often leave her seat in front of the television.

"She wanted to help make supper."

Pride filled his chest at knowing his sister wanted to make a good impression on Rachael. Julia may not be able to communicate with words, but he knew her mind still functioned normally. Not being able to control her speech or her fine motor skills frustrated the hell out of her.

When people treated her like a mentally challenged person, he could see the aggravation in her eyes and feel the attitude inside her wanting to come out. Julia used to have a wicked temper and Jake prayed every day that someday soon he'd witness it again.

The doctors had no prognosis. She could be in this state for the rest of her life or she could regain nearly one hundred percent of what she lost. Only time would tell. His parents took a second mortgage out on the house to pay for therapy and Jake contributed a good chunk of his paycheck to her medical bills as well. One of the many reasons he still lived in an eighties throwback. He'd do anything for his sister, to pay for his wrongs.

His father came out of the kitchen, wiping his hands on a towel. "Dad, this is Rachael. Rachael, my dad, Stan Morgan."

"Nice to meet you Mr. Morgan." She held out a hand and his father ignored it, drawing her in for a hug.

"Pretty girl like you should be calling me Stan. None of this mister business. I hope you like barbeque chicken. I made my special sauce. Been simmering on the stove all day."

"It smells amazing. Oh, I made dessert. I hope that's okay." She handed the glass dish to Jake's mom, who had been eyeing it since they walked through the door.

"This looks delicious. Maybe we should start with dessert." His mother headed toward the kitchen and they followed.

"That's what I'm always telling her."

Rachael stopped, causing him to bump into her back, then turned around and scrunched her nose in a pissed off sort of way. Only it made her look ridiculously cute. Jake lightly tapped her butt, ushering her ahead of him.

The kitchen wasn't huge but it had an eat-in area that could comfortably fit six. Julia sat at the table with a head of lettuce, carefully tearing pieces into a bowl, the bracelet he bought with Rachael last month dangling from her wrist.

"Julia is making the salad. It's one of her specialties." He knew his mother meant well but Jake's twin-sense could tell his sister was offended. She didn't have enough motor skills to handle a knife, and on a good day could carry an empty plate to the table. She'd dropped so many over the past few years that his mother stopped having her do any chores that could hurt herself or any more dishes.

"Hey, gorgeous." Jake kissed the top of his sister's head and whispered in her ear. "I'm still waiting for my lasagna. Mom's been ruining it for years. Someday soon you'll be cooking her under the table again." She went still and looked up at him. He swore he saw a twinkle in her eyes but it could have been the reflection from the kitchen light.

"You remember Rachael, right? She's the girl who was yelling at me and tossed her coffee in my lap at Coast & Roast a few weeks ago."

"Nice way to reintroduce me, Jake." Rachael gently pushed him out of the way and pulled out a chair next to his sister. "Your brother didn't tell me how much you liked brownies until we were almost here. I'll bring you a whole batch the next time I see you."

"I like... to... cook."

"Really?" Rachael grinned and tapped her finger to her lips. "You know, I've been twirling this idea around in my head for some time now. I'd like to offer a cooking class for adults who... who need a little extra help in the kitchen. Think you'd mind being a guinea pig one day? I could do a test run with you and you can give me your honest feedback. So far I've only done a class for kids. I'd like to do one with grown up food. Maybe some wine and appetizers."

Jake's heart swelled. He hadn't seen a smile on his sister's face this big since before the accident.

"An-d brow... nies."

Rachael cocked her eye. "Only if you promise not to share my brownie recipe with anyone else."

Julia nodded and handed Rachael some lettuce and said, "You... help... me."

"I'd love to. Let me wash my hands first." Rachael scooted her chair back to get up. Jake kissed her nose and showed her to the bathroom. "I could have used the kitchen sink," she said when they were out of earshot.

"I know. But I really needed to do this." He drew her in and crushed his lips against hers, breathing in her sweetness. He let her go before he got too carried away. They had all night to finish what he'd started.

"Oh. Well then."

"Stop being so perfect or I'm going to lose the tiny bit of self-control I have."

"For a man who is trained in martial arts, you sure lack a lot of self-control."

"Babe." Jake backed away and went into the kitchen before his parents came looking for them.

"I like her, Jake."

"Me too, Mom."

When Rachael returned to the kitchen, Jake and his father were outside on the deck manning the grill, but he could see and hear the women inside through the screen door.

"I love your hair. I always wished I had thick, dark hair like yours," he heard Rachael say before she stood behind his sister and started playing with the long ponytail. "I didn't have a sister until I was in my late teens. I always wanted one so I could play with her hair and she could play with mine. Do you like to do hair?"

Julia used to put her hair in fancy braids while playing field hockey, but she didn't have the motor skills to do much more than brush her hair, and even then she needed their mother to help.

"Maybe after we eat, you'll let me do your hair?"

"Yes."

"Julia and I used to fight all the time when she was little. She hated having me brush her hair. All I wanted was to put it in a ponytail so it would stay out of her food, but she insisted on wearing it down. It wasn't until she hit middle school that she wanted to learn how to French braid. I never learned how, so she had to ask her friends to do it," his mother said as she busied herself at the stove.

Jake almost felt like an interloper listening in on the conversation between his three favorite women.

"My mom taught me how to do it but I only learned on myself. I can try to French braid your hair if you'd like, Julia."

"Yes...please. French...braid."

Warmed by the scene inside, Jake turned his back on the women before he did something stupid like confess his undying love to Rachael.

CHAPTER TEN

Baking for Coast & Roast had been a perfect jumping off point, but Rachael wasn't going to make ends meet by making muffins every morning and hosting the occasional birthday party. She had a few bookings, but even then, she was nickel and diming it.

The weather was warm for so early in the morning. With the sun starting to rise in the horizon and a forecast in the low seventies for later, she opted to ride her bike to work, cruising through downtown and past the Rocky Harbor Inn. The newly hung Help Wanted sign in the front window caught her attention. Rachael kept peddling to the coffee shop and let herself in the back door, all the while thinking about the beautiful inn. After her morning baking was done, she checked her face in the mirror for any traces of flour and took down her messy bun, opting for a sleek ponytail instead.

She'd worn gym shorts, tennis shoes, and a tank top to work today, hoping to get a little sun on her shoulders during her ride home. Not exactly job interview clothes. Still, she was curious as to what the job was. Rachael looked up the inn's number on her phone and dialed. A woman answered on the third ring, sounding winded.

"Rocky Harbor Inn."

"Hi, my name is Rachael Riley. I saw your Help Wanted sign and was wondering what the position was."

"I'm looking for a breakfast cook. The kitchen hasn't been used in a while and needs some serious updating. I'm currently serving a simple continental breakfast to my guests but I'd like to offer more home-cooked food. I'm useless in the kitchen. Eventually I'd like to open for dinner on the weekends. Probably just during tourist season."

"That sounds perfect. Can I come by and fill out an application?"

"Sure. If you're available, this afternoon is a perfect time. I'm slow today and my son is at a friend's house. Are you local?"

"Actually, I'm just down the road. I do the baking for Coast & Roast."

"Oh, well then, if you're the one responsible for adding ten pounds to my hips this summer, you're hired. And fired. I've been buying your muffins and serving them at breakfast to my guests."

"You should put in a special order and avoid the middle-man cost. I can deliver to you daily if you'd like." She'd hate to take the business away from Mackenzie, but if the owner was buying so much, it was the right thing to do. She'd talk to Mackenzie about it.

"That would have been the smart thing to do. I'm still new at this." The woman laughed. "Anyway, can you come by today?"

"Sure. But just to warn you, I'm not exactly dressed for an interview. I rode my bike to work and have been baking all day."

"Bring me one of your white chocolate macadamia nut cookies and I'll forgive you."

"Deal. Can I bring you a coffee as well?"

"You really want this job, don't you?"

"I do." Rachael danced around the kitchen with excitement. "Oh, I didn't even ask you your name."

"I was so excited to hear you're the mastermind behind my secret vices that I forgot to introduce myself. I'm Ellie Fairfield. Oh, and I'd love an iced coffee with skim milk and sugar. The real stuff. I'll see you in a bit." Practically skipping down the cobblestone sidewalk twenty minutes later, Rachael smiled at tourists as they window shopped, at the little kids licking their cones as ice cream melted down their hands, at couples walking hand in hand down the street. While she hadn't grown up in the heart of the town, just outside of it, Rocky Harbor would always be home to her.

It was where she wanted to raise her family. She could picture mini-Jakes tugging at the bottom of her shorts as she baked in the kitchen. Little girls with their Daddy's chocolate eyes and dark hair, boys who would be the charmers in their preschool.

They'd never talked about too far into the future. What if he didn't want to marry or didn't like children? No, Jake's gentle nature with his sister and even the students in his class proved he'd be an excellent father.

As she neared the Inn, Rachael forced her thoughts back to her job interview. Ellie sounded fun. Hopefully they'd have a good working relationship like she had with Mackenzie. If the job only required breakfast, she could do the baking for Coast & Roast at night, or maybe get up a little earlier and multi-task.

The Rocky Harbor Inn was at the end of the square and had served as a centerpiece of the town for many years. There was great history to the place, but Rachael didn't know the story. She couldn't wait to hear about it from the new owner.

The house was exquisite, old and well cared for. A classic white three-story colonial that faced the main road, while the back yard sloped toward the ocean, giving guests a million dollar view from their room. Rachael tried to calm her excitement at the prospect of another job. It meant everything to her.

That constant struggle for complete independence.

Not that she didn't love living with her mother. Doreen was amazing, but she really didn't want to be living at home anymore. Bounding the steps, she reached out to knock when she heard a loud scream from inside. Yanking the door open, Rachael rushed into the foyer and followed the noise toward the back of the house.

"I hate you!" she heard from the kitchen.

Fear and tension filled her body. The moves Jake had taught her during class kicked in. Looking around for the nearest weapon, she picked up a pewter bell from an end table and slowed her pace, inching around the corner, scared of what she'd find.

"Stupid, stupid, stupid," yelled a petite brunette as she kicked an ancient looking refrigerator.

The pressure in her chest let out and her grip around the bell loosened. "Hello?" The brunette, presumably Ellie Fairfield, screeched and turned. "I'm sorry. I never meant to scare you." How cruel of her to sneak up on Ellie. Rachael knew how it felt to be spied on.

"Oh, hi. Sorry. I'm having a brawl with this fridge from the forties and I think it won. Or lost. Not sure how to look at it. She's totally useless. It's cooler in the kitchen than it is inside this honking thing. All my food has gone bad. Looks like takeout until I can get a new one." Ellie rubbed her hands on her jean-clad thighs and then stuck one out. "You must be Rachael. Sorry to look so sordid, but I was hoping to have the kitchen cleaned up for you before you arrived."

"Oh, don't go to any trouble. You were clear on the phone that it hadn't been used in a while. Here's your coffee and cookies." Rachael handed her the bag and cup and looked around the space. It would be perfect for her Kids in the Kitchen classes. Roomier than Mackenzie's.

"So, what do you think? Minus the I Love Lucy refrigerator. I'll get you a new one. Well, C.J. and I will need to use it as well."

Rachael took a few minutes to walk around. The room was amazing. Open and airy, with a view overlooking the lawn and ocean and a large eat-in area that could probably seat twelve kids. The kitchen space was gigantic, built and designed to serve the patrons in the restaurant area of the Inn. The butcher block island had to be at least eight feet long and four feet wide.

Pale yellow walls kept the kitchen bright and airy, as did the white farmhouse-style cabinets. She trailed her hand over the beautiful woodwork as she checked out the two Viking wall ovens and eight-burner stove. "They paid top dollar for these, I wonder why they didn't upgrade the refrigerator."

"The appliances were replaced as they broke down, which makes sense. I guess this girl is the last to go." Ellie kicked it with her bare foot and bit her lip at the pain.

"I'd love to hear the history of the Inn." Rachael opened an oven door, impressed with the size.

"Let's go out back in the Adirondack chairs. It's beautiful out today and I haven't had a chance to sit yet."

Once they settled in their chairs, Ellie began. "The previous owners stopped serving lunch and dinner about a decade ago, but they kept the dining room open for breakfast for guests. The terms of my owner's contract state that I have to have the restaurant up and running in the next year. At least for breakfast, and ideally dinner as well. I can only fit fifty in the dining room so it would be more intimate setting. Long, leisurely meals with a slow turnover. Think you're up for the challenge?"

"Don't you want to interview me? Sample my cooking?"

"If you're as great as everyone says you are, then why not? I like you, we seem to get along pretty well, and I need a chef."

"Who is everyone? We barely met and you haven't even tasted any of my recipes yet other than my muffins."

"I'm assuming the soup at Coast & Roast is yours as well?" Rachael nodded. "I've sampled every baked good there and it's all amazing. I don't know her well, but the few times I've talked to Mackenzie she's raved about you. I don't know why I didn't think about stealing you from her before. Oh, is that going to be a problem?"

"I don't think so. I have a pretty good routine going, and now that I know the bulk of my order is coming to the Inn anyway, I can kill two birds with one stone."

"I met Maggie O'Fallon briefly. I don't know her well either, I don't know anyone, really, but she lit right up when she heard Mackenzie and me talking about you. I remember her talking about your cooking."

"You have quite the memory. Maggie is engaged to my brother, so she has to say nice things about me."

"Maggie attested to your cooking skills. And we won't be serving dinner until next year anyway, and then probably just for guests. They'll have to order ahead of time so there'll be plenty of time to prepare. We can see how that goes and then build from there."

Rachael laughed. "It sounds like you've thought this through." She liked Ellie. "Can you tell me what kind of breakfast you'd like to serve?"

"Don't ask me. My meals consist of Frosted Flakes in the morning, macaroni and cheese for lunch, and spaghetti for dinner. I'm sure whatever you come up with will be wonderful."

"First, I'd like to hear about the Inn. Maybe it will give me some recipe inspiration. Or maybe there are some tucked away in the cabinets."

"Could be. I haven't had much time to snoop through the kitchen. C.J. has, but I doubt he's been looking for recipe cards."

"Your husband?"

Ellie's smile faded and she shook her head. "No. No husband." She sighed and slowly the smile returned to her face. "C.J. is my son. He's my world. He doesn't eat much, mostly snacks. I've been trying to put more meat on his bones, although I can't blame him for not wanting to eat my cooking."

"I can't wait to meet him. Sounds like he may be a willing guinea pig if I want to try out new recipes."

"Absolutely."

"So, tell me about this place. I heard you won it through an essay?"

Ellie pulled her knees toward her chest and wrapped her arms around her shins. "Over a hundred years ago, James and Charlotte Peabody built the mansion expecting to have dozens of children, only to find out Charlotte was infertile. For years they opened their doors to the less fortunate, giving them a place to stay in exchange for honest work. Cooking, cleaning, landscaping, and the sort. Then one day Charlotte had the grand idea to turn the rest of the rooms into affordable rooms to rent. When she and James passed away they left the house, completely paid for, to their head housekeeper, Eleanor Smith. She continued operating the house in the same manner as the Peabodys, but as she got older, she knew she needed to figure out a way to keep the integrity of the Inn."

Rachael, totally enchanted by the story, shifted her body so she was facing Ellie. "And Eleanor started the essay contest."

Ellie nodded. "She didn't have children and wanted to give back to the community. She met with a lawyer and had a contract written that made sure whoever took over the inn would not renovate, only upkeep, would not change the name or the colors on the outside, would keep the integrity of the inside, keep rates affordable, and wouldn't sell it off."

"Smart lady."

"Yup. I'm the fourth person to earn the Inn. It's mine until I want to pass it on to another. I'm required to keep the building up-to-par, the grounds groomed and the guests fed. Well, at breakfast. Unfortunately, the last of the help left with the owner. She'd been getting up there in age and couldn't handle the responsibility."

"Doesn't the contract say everything had to be status quo? I thought you said the restaurant hadn't been used in ten years."

"There's a clause in there somewhere. Actually, there wasn't a restaurant back when Eleanor Smith ran the place. She provided three meals for the guests, but that wasn't even required in the contract, just breakfast. Susan Kennedy added that piece right before she left."

"She could do that?"

"I guess. Again, clauses. I haven't read them too carefully. I was thrilled to win and to have a place to start over with my son. I've always loved Maine."

Respecting her privacy, Rachael didn't pry even though she wanted to know more about the intriguing woman.

"Well, Ms. Fairfield, it looks like you found yourself a new head cook. When do I start?"

"How about tonight?" She joked. "I have no clue what to cook C.J. and myself for dinner. You can move in whenever you'd like."

"Move in?"

Ellie nodded. "Per the contract, anyone who works for the Inn gets free room and board."

Independence. Exactly what Rachael needed to feel whole again. Tears filled her eyes and she blinked fast in an attempt to bat them away, not wanting to appear weak.

"Hey, are you okay?"

"Allergies. I'm wonderful. You've made my day, Ellie. No, you've made my world complete. Thank you. Wow. Thank you."

They stood and shook hands. "Heck, is it inappropriate for me to admit I'm a bit lonely and in need of a friend? And a hug?" Ellie hugged Rachael. "Welcome to the Rocky Harbor Inn. I think we're going to work fabulously together."

Rachael raced back to Coast & Roast. She wouldn't leave Mackenzie high and dry, which meant she needed to figure out a plan to keep both jobs.

"Have a minute?"

Mackenzie looked up from her laptop and beamed. "You got the job. Congratulations."

"How did you...?"

"Small town."

"I left the Inn less than five minutes ago."

"Ellie called before you went over. She wanted to make sure she wasn't stealing you from me. I told her we'd work it out."

"We will. I promise. I'll keep up with your orders here. I promise."

"I know. You're honest and reliable. I have no doubts. Besides, I'm capable of baking a few things. My brownies are kick-ass and were doing just fine before you brought more variety to the counter. I need to make some business decisions anyway. Do I keep status quo or expand and offer lunch? Maybe expand and open a bookstore? I'm still not sure what I want to do with my life. You gave me options. Things to think about."

"I'll keep up with your orders. I promise, Mackenzie. If it weren't for you I wouldn't have gotten the job at the Inn."

"Sure you would. You're awesome. I just happened to be the first person to take advantage of your culinary skills. Besides, with you out of the way I'll have more opportunities to christen the counter out back. Unless you and Sexy Abs have already done that."

Close, but no. "It's yours to christen."

Rachael wanted to race home and pack and tell Jake her news. Maybe she wouldn't tell him about her room yet, but surprise him tomorrow night after she moved in. She hadn't even asked to see what the room looked like. She didn't care. Her own personal space. Rent free and private.

It took forever to get home—granted, it was more uphill going inland. Finally, speeding down the driveway, she parked her bike in the garage and hobble-jogged to the house. Her mother had texted her earlier saying Maria had picked her up to volunteer at the shelter in Portsmouth, New Hampshire, and that Rachael could use the car.

She jumped in the shower and got ready in record time. She found a cute pink skirt and black sleeveless top in her closet, slid her feet into black sandals, and checked her reflection one more time. The glow in her cheeks was either from the sun or from her news. She didn't care.

Rachael drove out to Jake's worksite, a new development in Saco, and got out of the car looking for him. She recognized some of his crew who Jake had introduced her to a few weeks ago and waved. Joey nodded, dropped his shovel and sauntered over.

"Hey, Rachael. You looking for the boss?"

"Hi, Joey. Is he here?"

"He had a meeting at the diner on Marginal Way. Goes there every Friday at three."

"Thanks. I'll see you around."

She could wait for him here, stalk him at the diner, or go home. Too anxious and excited to wait, she drove to the diner. It wasn't far and she got there in less than twenty minutes, hoping he'd still be finishing up.

She found Jake's truck in the parking lot and pulled up next to it. Not wanting to crash his meeting, she rolled down her windows and waited. Rachael wondered what type of meeting he could have every Friday afternoon. A business meeting? But that didn't make sense, since his clients were always changing and his projects lasted different lengths of time.

At four o'clock he came around the building with another man dressed in slacks and suit coat. They talked for a minute and shook hands before the other man walked toward a Cumberland County police car.

Rachael's head swam with questions.

Jake pulled out his phone and read the screen as he headed toward his truck. A smile appeared while he tapped the screen and Rachael's phone beeped, signaling a text.

He slid the phone in his pocket and looked up, stopping suddenly when he spotted Rachael. Jake turned his head, looking toward the man in the police car, who just pulled out of the parking lot, before he made his way over to her.

"Rachael?"

She got out of her car and leaned against it, the heat radiating through her thin clothing.

"What are you doing here?"

"I came to see you."

"I just got your text. You've some good news?" The smile that reached his eyes a minute ago while texting wasn't the same one he donned now. This one was forced, as if was covering something. Jake wasn't one to squirm, but his shoulders and feet twitched and his eyes looked everywhere but at her.

Rachael spent too many years with a man who spent more of his time covering up his lies than telling the truth, and she didn't want to live that life anymore.

"It's probably none of my business, but are you in some sort of trouble?"

"No. I promise. I'm not."

"So why the secret meeting?"

"It's not a secret meeting."

"Joey said you meet here every Friday. Do you meet with the police every week? Why didn't you ever tell me?"

"I don't run my schedule by you, nor do you give me yours," he snapped.

Rachael shot back as if slapped. "I apologize. Carry on with your schedule. I have my own to keep." Wanting to get away before she completely broke down, she yanked open her car door and slammed it shut before he stepped closer.

Jake didn't chase after her. He stood in his spot as she drove off, the dagger in her heart twisting as she sped home.

CHAPTER ELEVEN

There were no texts. No calls. No Jake at her doorstep ringing her doorbell, begging to talk. Saturday morning Rachael rolled out of bed before the sun came up, left her mom a quick note, and rode her bike to work again. By the time she neared the center of town, the sun was making its way over the horizon, casting rays of a beautiful sunrise across her path.

A new day. A beautiful, picture perfect day for the people of Rocky Harbor. Except for Rachael. She had no idea why Jake seemed so shocked and upset at her yesterday, but he wasn't the Jake she'd fallen in love with.

Yes, she loved him. And that's why the dagger he'd twisted in her heart hurt so freaking much. She'd packed up her bedroom last night and asked Lucy to help her move into the Inn this afternoon.

Not one to wake before she had to, Lucy agreed to load her car with the boxes and meet Rachael at the Inn at two. For hours Rachael mixed and stirred and baked. She had promised Julia a batch of brownies and nothing Jake could do would make her back down from her promise. Rachael layered the brownies in a box and set them aside.

The kitchen was clean, the dishes put away. Now she could move in to her new space and start over. Again.

Surprisingly on time, Lucy stood outside her beater of a car, packed full of boxes, in the Inn's parking lot. "Nice place. Where is your room?" Lucy asked as they carried the first load up the front steps.

"I have no idea. I haven't seen it yet."

"What if it's a crap hole?"

"I'm sure it isn't."

Rachael shifted the box under her arm and reached out for the front door as Ellie appeared.

"I got it."

"Thanks." Rachael stepped through the doorway. "Ellie, this is my sister Lucy. Lucy, Ellie owns the Inn."

"Nice to meet you. Thanks for taking my sister off our hands. She's a real pain in the ass."

Ellie laughed. "We can swap and you can take my son. He's driving me up a wall this summer. I hope it's only a phase he's going through."

"Uh, which way to my room?"

"Wow. I'm not usually so scatterbrained. I didn't even show it to you yesterday. I'm so sorry. If you don't like the space you can pick another room. Or I can add to your salary."

"I'm sure I'll love it. I haven't had much privacy since I've been home." That wasn't totally true. Her mother respected her space and let her be alone when she chose to hole up in her room, but Rachael looked forward to not checking in with her mother every time she wanted to go somewhere. It wasn't like Doreen made her, but her mother appreciated the courtesy.

Rachael and Lucy followed Ellie into the kitchen and down a private hallway. "Back in the day this was the maid's quarters. I think it's absolutely adorable, and if I didn't need two bedrooms I would have taken this space for myself." Ellie unlocked the door and handed Rachael the key. She stepped into the room and hurried over to the window opening the blinds.

The windows overlooked the patio off the kitchen. Beyond it a large grassy area stretched at a slight slope before reaching dune grass and the ocean. "It's gorgeous."

"You get a million-dollar ocean view, but you don't have much privacy if we have guests on the patio, or events on the lawn."

"I'll survive." Rachael hadn't even looked around the room yet, too enamored with the view. She turned and took in the space. The walls were painted a bright blue, the wide white casings around the doors and windows making a stunning contrast. The long dresser and four poster bed were white, as were the two wicker chairs by the window.

The blue and white striped cushions matched the pillow shams, while the bedding and comforter were a country chic yellow flowered print. Dark hardwood floors contrasted beautifully with the décor.

"You have a private bath that was recently remodeled. The clawfoot tub is my favorite." Ellie led Rachael to the bathroom. It wasn't huge but she didn't need much space.

The sink sat in a beautiful piece of dark cabinetry that was too elegant to be in a bathroom; the large white marble tiles having the opposite effect as the bedroom, making the floor bright and vibrant instead of dark and homey. She couldn't wait to soak in the tub while looking out across the ocean. With a romance novel to keep her company, since Jake wasn't talking to her.

"The original space didn't have a closet, but the last owner insisted on making the maid's quarters more modern.

You've got a pretty nice walk in space here." Rachael left the bathroom and peeked in the door on the opposite side of the room.

"Sweet closet." Lucy whistled.

"It's more than I could have ever expected. I love it."

"Good. And you have free use of the kitchen. CJ and I have a small kitchen in our living quarters at the end of the hall, but he likes the convenience of the big kitchen. That's what we call it. The big kitchen. Oh, and I ordered a new fridge. It should be here by Wednesday."

"I'll respect your privacy."

"Don't be silly. If we wanted privacy, I wouldn't be running an inn. Besides, we can eat in our private quarters if we need the escape. Since you don't have a kitchen, I consider the big kitchen yours. We'll try not to intrude if you have guests."

"I don't plan on hosting any dinner parties, but thank you."

"She'll be making me dinner at least once a week." Rachael scowled at her sister, but Lucy continued, "As payment for driving you around the past few months." Yes, she did owe her. Now that Rachael had an apartment and a few thousand in her bank account, she could afford a car as well.

"I want you to feel at home here, Rachael."

"I already do."

It didn't take long to unload the car. Lucy had places to go, people to see, so she didn't stick around to help unpack. Not that Rachael expected her to. She emptied her suitcases and hung up her clothes first, not wanting them to wrinkle. When her clothes were stored, she tackled the few boxes of odds and ends she brought from home. A few pictures of her family, some costume jewelry, scented lotions, and recipe books. There were still hours left in the day and she had no plans. No one to spend time with. No one to call. No one to talk to.

Maybe she should have stayed at Coast & Roast. Mackenzie was always good for a laugh. And Maggie stopped by often.

Yes, Maggie. She'd be marrying Graham on Labor Day. Maybe she'd like some sister time. Rachael dug through her purse, searching for her cell phone. She found it and turned it on. Four texts popped up. She read the first one from Luke.

I would have helped you move. Congrats on the new place. Can't wait to see it.

Rachael smiled. Luke had always been the thoughtful, caring brother.

There was one text from Graham.

No sleepovers until you're 30.

She laughed at his bluntness and protectiveness. And there were two from Jake. She didn't want to read what he had to say. Nothing could erase the cruelty of his words to her. But she still yearned for him, wishing it was all a terrible misunderstanding and he'd come begging for her forgiveness.

Dylan had never asked for forgiveness. He'd toss out an apology that lacked any type of sincerity and would move on as if he hadn't destroyed another piece of Rachael's soul.

Except Jake wasn't Dylan and she needed to stop comparing the two. Nothing Jake could do or say would ever be as cruel and deliberate as Dylan. Except his words had hurt more than Dylan's fist to the rib. Her body would heal, the bruises would lighten, and her hatred for Dylan would never go away.

Jake's words, however, made a more permanent scar on. Her heart had never been in her relationship with Dylan. It hadn't been stomped on, just her pride. That could be repaired with time.

Her heart, not so much. Still, the pull to Jake was like a magnet to steel. No matter how hard she tried to fight it, she couldn't stop the attraction. She slid her finger across the text and read the first one.

We need to talk.

And the second text read

Please.

No excuses. No begging for forgiveness. No answers. Should she respond? Yes, she wanted answers. Needed answers.

Needed Jake.

. . . .

HE WOULDN'T BEG, BUT he needed to see her, to apologize for being such a shit. She'd surprised him, to put it mildly. He didn't want her anywhere near that part of his life. Didn't want anyone he cared about mixed up in his past shit.

Jake's meetings with Noles were the constant reminder of the baggage he carried around with him everyday. No matter how hard he worked to right his wrongs, it was always there, tattooed on his forehead, on his soul. And no matter how hard he worked to push it away or cover it up, there

would always be traces of his mistakes marking him as a failure. A deadbeat. Unworthy.

Rachael didn't need to be exposed to the evil in his life.
Not that Noles was evil; he was a good guy. But their Friday
coffee chats were a symbol of what Jake once was. A symbol
he couldn't erase but tried like hell to burn from his life.

Needing to see her, to apologize, to right yet another
wrong, he'd sent two texts, one last night and one this morning. Knowing Rachael, she needed time to be pissed at him,
but she'd also want answers. And he needed time as well.
Time to work up the courage to come clean about his past.
His present.

About everything. Once she heard it all, if it was too
much to be with him, he'd walk away.

Hell. Who was he kidding? Jake wouldn't let her slip
away that easily. He didn't want to have this serious talk
while she was working, so he waited until he thought she'd
be home. Only Rachael still hadn't responded to his texts.
Not knowing what else to do, he hopped on his bike and
sped to her house.

Doreen Riley's car was in the driveway, which meant
Rachael would be home. And probably her mom. Having
this discussion at Coast & Roast didn't appeal to him, but
neither did having it in front of her mom. But if Rachael
didn't agree to leave with him, he'd stay on her front porch
and beg until she agreed to listen.

Jake shut off the engine and removed his helmet. After
stalling, hoping she'd come outside to greet him—or yell at
him, hell, he didn't care—he finally made his way up the
front steps when she didn't show.

Doreen opened the door with a welcoming hug. She obviously hadn't heard what a bastard he'd been to her daughter.

"Hi, Mrs. Riley. Is Rachael home?"

"Home? Here? I figured you would be at her place."

"Her place?"

"She didn't tell you? Oh, I hope I didn't ruin a surprise she had planned for you."

Jake had two options. Be honest with Mrs. Riley, telling her how Rachael wasn't talking to him, or play off her innocence and get the inside scoop.

Damn Rachael for making his honesty card come out. "The truth is, Mrs. Riley…"

"Uh oh. Why don't you come in and I'll pour you a glass of lemonade."

"You probably don't want to be fraternizing with the enemy. I've uh, I said some hurtful things to Rachael and I came over to talk to her. To try to explain a… situation."

Doreen studied him intently for a few awkward moments before coming out on to the porch. "Let's sit out here then, and you'll explain to me how and why you hurt my daughter."

Jake had never talked to a girlfriend's mother before. Hell. He'd never had a girlfriend. He didn't know what to do. Come clean with Rachael's mom or keep their issues private?

"I'm not one to pry, but I'm very protective of my children. Tell me how you hurt her." Direct and stern she was, just as Rachael had warned.

"She found me in a situation I didn't want to be in and I snapped at her. Told her it was none of her business."

"You cheated on Rachael?" She placed a hand over her heart and reared her head back in shock.

"Oh God, no. I'd never do that to her. I swear."

"Phew. I didn't peg you for the philanderer." Doreen relaxed in her chair and pushed off with her foot setting the glider in a slow sway. "This situation. She misread it?"

"I've been fairly honest with her about my past." He was upfront about being a shit, yet hid the specific details. "I wasn't a kid you'd bring home to meet your mother. I'm sure my high school teachers and everyone at juvie hall would be having a good laugh if they could see me now. Sitting on the front porch of my girlfriend's house talking with her mom."

"So you were in some trouble as a teen."

"And in my early twenties. I've been on the straight and narrow for quite a few years. I'll never go back to the person I once was. Life has, well, stuff happened that changed my outlook on life. There are some things I need to talk to Rachael about. She saw me talking with my parole officer... I had yet to tell her I had one." The words slipped freely from his lips. Something about Doreen made her easy to talk to. There was no shame in her voice, in her eyes, or body language.

"I see."

They sat in more awkward silence. Jake fidgeted in his seat while Doreen rocked, staring out into the open fields, deep in thought. "You would have fit in quite well in my house as a teenager."

"I don't think you'd have wanted me around."

"Don't think I could've handled it?" She chuckled and turned to him. "I could tell you stories that would blow you over. And then some. My children have experienced horrific things in their childhood. In their adolescence. My Rachael is the only one who seemed to come out of it unscathed. Always the perfect angel, just wanting to fit in with her rowdy brothers."

"Yeah, she told me about that."

"I won't lie, my boys gave me a run for my money. My husband and I knew every police officer and detective by first name. Knew their families. Their birthdays. Their favorite foods. I'd hate for anyone to hold my children's mistakes over their heads for the rest of their lives. They've grown up to be fine individuals. They have their demons they struggle with, but they're each fighting a good fight. They're good people. I'd like to think that you are too, Jake."

Touched by her honesty and understanding, he picked up her hand and squeezed. "You remind me a lot of my mom. I think you two would get along great."

"I'd love to meet her sometime."

"I'd like that too."

Doreen patted his hand. "Rachael is living at the Rocky Harbor Inn. She called me about a half hour ago. She'd planned on going for a walk and then back to her apartment to take a bath."

"Apartment?"

"She's the new breakfast cook at the Inn. The job comes with a small apartment. Lucy helped her move in today."

"Thank you, Mrs. Riley. I appreciate this more than you know. And whatever happens with me and Rachael, know that I never meant to hurt her. I care about her. A lot."

"I never doubted that for a minute." She squeezed his hand while he leaned down to kiss her cheek.

Racing to his bike, he strapped on his helmet and took off for the center of town. Cursing Saturday night tourists, he steered out of traffic and took a longer but less traveled route to the Inn, knowing he could get away with going ten over the speed limit, taking the curves like a pro. Jake scanned the park and the sidewalks, looking for Rachael, but didn't see her. He parked in the guest lot, tucked his helmet under his arm, and marched up the front steps, not taking the time to read the signs or appreciate the landscaping.

A bell rang above the door as he opened it, stepping into the entryway. It was as open and welcoming as he presumed an inn would be and smelled like the lemon oil his mother used when polishing the wood furniture. He'd never been in an inn before. Hadn't been in too many hotels either. A cement ten-by-ten cell with a cot and a toilet had been all he'd seen besides his small room at his childhood home. And once he hit his teens, he stopped spending many nights there.

A tall desk nestled in the corner with an open laptop greeted him, but no innkeeper.

"Hello?" he called, looking into the room to his left.

The scraping of a chair from down the hall alerted his attention toward the back of the house.

"I'm sorry. I was on the phone in the kitchen and wasn't expecting any arrivals tonight. How many nights were you hoping to stay?"

Hopefully quite a few. "I'm looking for Rachael Riley. Is she here by any chance?"

The innkeeper's gaze dropped to his helmet, then down his jean-clad legs, stopping at his steel-toed work boots before making its way back to his face. On the way, she scrutinized the tattoo peeking out of his shirt. Not exactly inn material. Or Rachael Riley material. "Is she expecting you?"

"I sent her a text." Partial truth. Not that he'd be by, but that he wanted to talk.

"I don't like to disturb my employees during their off hours, but I'll check to see if she's available. And your name?" The young woman eyed him as would a lioness guarding her cubs, and he had to appreciate her protectiveness of Rachael. Only it hurt that she viewed him as the enemy.

"Jake. Thank you, Miss..."

"Fairchild." She gave him another once-over before turning on her heels and heading back toward what he presumed to be the kitchen.

Jake paced uncomfortably around the front room, feeling incongruous to the bright decor. All around him were seashells and picture frames and knickknacks. He was afraid to sit in the chairs; the thin spindle legs didn't look like they could hold anyone much larger than Rachael.

He smelled her before he heard her. Vanilla. Jake turned around, hesitant to face her. "Hey."

Rachael stood with her arms crossed, leaning against the doorframe, looking pissed at the world. Or more likely, at him.

"Can we talk?"

"About?" She didn't budge. Not her body. Not a muscle in her face.

"Me being an ass?"

She cocked an eyebrow and sucked in her cheeks. When she got angry at him for ditching her during their first date, he had been kinda turned on by her temper. Tonight, though, she didn't look angry. Her usually bright blue eyes were shielded, not trusting him or his actions.

"I know you just came from a walk, but do you mind going for another one?"

"How do you know that?"

"I stopped by your house first. Your mom told me."

"She what?" Rachael stepped away from the doorframe, dropping her hands to her sides. "My mother wouldn't tell you that unless you lied to her too. What did you tell her?"

"The truth."

Rachael snorted. "Which is?"

"That I was an ass for withholding information from you and that I wanted to talk to you. Tell you everything."

Softening, she relaxed her shoulders before spinning around and heading out the door. Jake took that as a positive sign and followed her down the steps. They walked in silence toward the center of town and didn't stop until they reached the park. Finding a secluded granite bench, they sat, Rachael facing forward and ignoring him.

Jake lowered himself on the bench, keeping a safe distance between them. "Ross Noles is my parole officer. I've been meeting him at the diner every Friday at three o'clock for the past three years. I have five weeks left before I'm done serving and will be a free man. So to speak."

"You were in jail other than juvenile hall?"

"Yes."

"For how long?"

"Two years. Aggravated assault. A Class B crime."

Rachael's hands clenched, her knuckles turning white. Jake studied her profile as she gritted her teeth, her breathing becoming more labored.

"Yet you teach women self-defense moves. Is this to protect them against men like you?"

"Rachael." He placed his hand on her arm and she flinched, jumping to the edge of the bench.

"Don't touch me."

Jake dropped his head into his hands and sighed. "It's not what you think."

"Like I haven't heard that one before. You lay in bed listening to me tell you about my abuse and acted sympathetic and caring and understanding. Little did I know you were just as bad."

"Don't clump me in the same category as your asshole ex-boyfriend."

"You think you're better?"

"Yes. No. Dammit, Rachael. It's not the same thing."

"I'm sure your next line is going to be that he or she deserved it. That's what he used to say to me."

Jake jumped to his feet, pissed that Rachael could even imagine that about him. "He. I'd never hit a woman." Tucking his hands into his pockets so he wouldn't be as tempted to reach out and touch her, he paced back and forth.

"That night. The night Julia left with Snake, she crashed her car. I told you that part but I left the rest out. They found signs of a struggle. Drugs in her body. But no one knew what had happened other than she'd wrapped her car around a tree. When I saw her lying in the hospital, hooked up to a thousand machines, my family hoping and praying she'd survive, I lost it. I blamed myself for not going after her earlier. I blamed my punk ass friends for getting me ripshit drunk and unable to protect her. I blamed the asshole she left with for doing this to her." Jake stopped pacing and faced Rachael, his eyes fixed on the gazebo behind her.

"For six days my parents and I didn't leave the hospital. We waited while test after test was done, praying Julia would come out of her coma. I needed to be by her side when she woke. I looked for any sign of life. When the doctors said she'd survive but had brain damage, I knew someone had to pay. I couldn't find the asshole who'd hurt her—he'd packed up and moved away before I could get my hands on him—so I hunted down someone else."

Jake paced again, curling his fingers in his pockets. The rage had built up inside him again as he relived that night. The anger, the fear, the evil that had taken over his body and released itself into his victim.

"Wolf. He knew more than he would say, so I tried to beat it out of him." The police said she'd done some drugs and that was the cause of her accident, but Jake knew better. Julia would never touch drugs; she barely drank even after she turned twenty-one. He fought for his sister's name and reputation, but it got him nowhere. "I found our group of thugs on the streets of Portland and I jumped Wolf. I kicked him in the head. Broke his ribs, and beat the living shit out of him for protecting the guy who ruined my sister."

Jake returned to the bench and rested his elbows on his thighs, dropping his head down to his chest. "I wanted someone to pay. At that point I didn't care who. Wolf had a reputation for hurting women so I let him know what it felt like." Rachael slid closer, still not touching him. He'd completely lose it, cry like a little girl if she did. "The police showed up and yanked me off his limp body and arrested me. Since I had a list of priors longer than my attitude, the judge went pretty hard on me. I served my time and got out early for good behavior. Wolf, he's got a permanently crippled leg and his vision out of his left eye will never be the same. He won't hurt another woman, but I still don't know what happened to Julia that night."

Rachael sniffed and he looked up into her lovely eyes. Moisture gleamed in them.

"Don't cry. I didn't mean to make you cry. I don't know how to deal with tears."

She wiped them away with her sleeve and shook her head. "I don't know what to say. I'm sorry—"

"Don't."

"This time I need to. Jake, I'm sorry I jumped to conclusions. I did that with your texts from Julia. I should have learned then. I know you. The Jake Morgan I know would never hurt a woman, or a man. An innocent man. I'm sorry I reacted so terribly."

"You're too quick to apologize and to forgive. Rach, I'm sorry for snapping at you. I was surprised to see you and... ashamed that you saw me with Noles. I only have a few more weeks of parole and it's not something I'm proud of. Not something I wanted to dump on you."

"It's not dumping." Rachael placed her hand on his forearm and squeezed. "It's what people do when they're in a relationship. They share. They communicate. They vent. I... care about you and want to help you get through your pain."

"You turning shrink on me?" He winked at her, needing to lighten the mood. "I'll never forgive myself for shrugging you off like I did. I wish you would've called me on it. Put me in my place. No one deserves to be treated that way. And for that, I'm really, really sorry." Jake placed his hands on her cheeks, relieved she didn't jump or pull away. "Can I kiss you now?"

"I hear make up sex is supposed to be phenomenal." Jake paused halfway to her mouth. "And I have my own private room just a half mile down the road."

"Babe," he growled before crushing his mouth to hers.

CHAPTER TWELVE

"Why didn't we do this after our other fight?" Jake's weight nearly crushed her, and she didn't care. Make up sex totally lived up to its reputation. Rachael could tell he wasn't letting himself rest completely on top of her, still, the man was solid.

"Good things come to those who wait."

"Hell, I've been waiting twenty-nine years for you. No wonder it's so good."

Rachael's heart squeezed so hard little droplets of tears appeared in her eyes. She knew with all her heart that she loved Jake Morgan. He was everything her father would have wanted for her.

Keith and Doreen had raised all their kids to see good in people. Not to judge on past behaviors or circumstances. Being young and naïve, she'd looked past Dylan's problems to find the good in him, but she found herself making more excuses for him than ever finding any redeemable qualities.

Jake, however, had a warehouse full of them. He didn't use his past transgressions as an excuse for his behavior. Instead, he learned from them and worked hard to rectify himself.

"Can I ask you something?"

"Anything." He rolled off her and turned to his side, pulling Rachael's body into his in spoon fashion. There fingers interlocked and she cuddled their joined hands to her chest.

"Teaching the self-defense classes, was that part of your probation?" Jake's body stilled behind her. "I'm not asking to judge. I'm curious."

"Yeah. I had to put in three hundred hours of community service before my parole was up."

"Did they make you teach the class?"

"Actually." He laughed. "I had to convince Noles to let me. I'd picked up martial arts in prison and thought I could use my new skill for good."

"How many hours do you have left?"

"Uh, none."

"That's great. Was my class your last one?"

Jake draped his leg over hers and sighed. "You really want to know?" He sounded unsure of himself. Maybe a bit insecure.

"I do."

"I've more than tripled my quota. I like teaching the classes, seeing the transformation in people, the strength and confidence grow by the end of the course, so I continued doing it."

"And the money students pay for your classes goes to women's shelters and domestic abuse programs." She felt him shrug. Rachael dislodged their hands and rolled over to caress his face, lingering her fingers over his mouth. "You're a good man, Jake Morgan."

"I have a lot of sins to atone for."

"I think you've done that already." His sad smile and downcast eyes made him appear vulnerable, despite the radical tattoo on his chest and shoulder. "Will you ever forgive yourself? Even though Julia's accident wasn't your fault, you're still carrying an enormous weight on your shoulders. You have to forgive yourself, Jake."

He kissed her fingers and his dark eyes stared back at her. Their color and expression changed from mournful to... something more. Jake shifted closer and, draping her leg over his hip, ran his hand up and down her thigh.

"I love you. You're too good for me, but I can't help it. I'm in love. With you." He tucked a lock of hair behind her ear and sipped her lips. "I don't know what it means to be in love with a woman, it's never happened before. But what I feel in here," he placed a hand over his tattoo, "has to be love."

Tears rolled down her cheeks, mixing with their kiss. "I love you too, Jake. So, so much."

• • • •

SHE WOKE IN A TANGLE of sheets, and Jake. Purring with content, Rachael snuggled deeper into his arms and thought about how far she'd come. From the beaten girl who Luke had to come rescue, to the independent breakfast cook at the Rocky Harbor Inn who had her own apartment and the sexiest boyfriend in the world.

Unfortunately, being a responsible adult meant she needed to get up and start working. Ellie had said muffins and scones were fine for this weekend and they'd break out the new breakfast menu next Friday. Rachael also had orders to bake for Coast & Roast. Sliding out of Jake's warm embrace, she slipped out of bed and crept to her closet.

Not one for showering in the morning—she woke too early and got too messy anyway—Rachael grabbed the first thing she could find in her dresser and crept to the bathroom to change. After brushing her teeth and running a brush through her hair, she turned off the light, careful not to wake Jake, and tiptoed to the door.

"No kiss goodbye?" The bed creaked as he stirred under the sheets.

"I didn't want to wake you."

"We've talked about this before."

"I'm not allowed to apologize, am I?"

Jake furrowed his brows at her. "You can apologize in a different way."

"Oh yeah? And how do you propose I beg you for forgiveness?" She meandered her way to the bed.

"For starters, you'll need to be naked." Jake lifted the hem of Rachael's T-shirt, skimming his hands up her ribs and cupping her breasts.

"I'm not apologizing now. I have to work. I'll make it up to you. Promise." She placed a chaste kiss on his lips before she slipped away, ignoring his pleas, and giggled as she left her room.

Rachael couldn't help but grin as she replayed their evening. Jake loved her. She felt carefree and weightless. No stress on her shoulders, no pit in her stomach. They were in love and in an open, honest relationship. Life was amazing.

As she took her fourth batch of muffins out of the oven at Coast & Roast Rachael checked the clock. Almost six. She'd need to take inventory of the kitchen at the Inn and cart all of her supplies over to her new workspace.

"You work too hard." Mackenzie strolled into the kitchen and snatched up a cranberry-orange muffin, breaking off the top and shoving half of it in her mouth. "Not that I'm complaining."

"Pot calling the kettle. Do you ever take a day off?"

"I think we've had this discussion before. Besides, I'm not leaving a hot guy in my bed every morning. If I had Sexy Six-pack in my bed you can bet your ass I wouldn't be here at four in the morning."

"I'm sure that's not entirely true. You've had quite a few dates since I've been working here."

"All duds. No one I'm bringing back to my place. You're lucky. Jake seems like a good guy."

"He is."

"Wow. That look says it all. You're totally in love, aren't you? Mags had that same expression on her face when she fell for Graham."

"I'm happy."

"And in love." Rachael nodded. "Good for you."

"Really? I pegged you as the type to guffaw at the notion of love."

"Just because I haven't found my forever guy doesn't mean I don't believe in it. I'm happy for my friends when they find the right guy. If Mr. Right doesn't come walking into my life in the near future I'm cool with that. I'm not ready to settle and I don't want to deal with the hassle of trying to make someone else happy."

"I admire you." Mackenzie snorted. "Seriously. You're a strong, beautiful, independent woman who has a successful business, good friends, and an amazing baker."

Laughing, Mackenzie tossed the muffin wrapper in the trash. "That I do. Now get back to work before I fire your ass."

Beaming with pride, Rachael whipped up a triple batch of oatmeal butterscotch chip cookies then cleaned up for the day.

· · · ·

IT DIDN'T TAKE LONG for them to work out a schedule. Rachael would sleep at Jake's house Monday and Tuesday nights and he'd go into work late. Not that eight was late, but compared to the four and five o'clock alarms that they'd been used to, it felt like heaven cuddling or rolling around in bed for a few extra hours.

Jake stayed at Rachael's place on the weekends, and they spent the other nights apart, talking to each other on the phone until they went to sleep. In a few weeks the summer people would leave, lightening the baking load. Jake's work schedule would keep him busy until the snow fell, and then he'd spend more time at The Warehouse, teaching classes, and designing landscape ideas to pitch to businesses in the spring.

He'd gone car shopping with her earlier in the week, helping her pick out a solid Volkswagen sedan.

Rachael had just finished bringing in her bags from the grocery store when her cell phone beeped. She continued to empty the bags, stocking the cabinets and fridge while she answered.

"Hey, Blondie."

Her face lit up. Hearing Jake's voice would never get old. "Are you on your lunch break?"

"I'm working through lunch today since I have to head out soon."

It was Friday. Jake had one more session with his parole officer and then he'd be free and clear.

"I thought I'd grill some salmon tonight. How does that sound?"

"Perfect. Listen, I, uh. I wanted to ask you something."

The serious tone in his voice caused her to pause. "Sure. Anything."

"Are you busy?"

"No. Not at all. What is it, Jake?"

"Would you, uh…would you want to come to the diner with me this afternoon? At, uh, three."

Her heart swelled with emotion. Sniffing back tears, she whispered, "I'd love to." She knew how hard this was for Jake—to show her his vulnerable side, to show her the scars from his past—and she was honored that he wanted to share it with her.

"Thank you."

"No, Jake. Thank *you*."

· · · ·

"ROSS, THIS IS RACHAEL. Rachael, Ross Noles, my parole officer."

Rachael chuckled as she stuck out her hand. "Did you ever watch *Friends*?"

Jake furrowed his brow and regarded Noles and Rachael, both laughing at some inside joke.

"I did. My wife and I wanted to name our daughter Emma, but Rachael named her girl Emma we had to ditch it. Pretty soon Emma was the most popular on the girl's list. My wife's name is Jennifer and was one of a hundred Jennys, Jens, and Jennifers growing up."

"I've actually never met a Jennifer. Can you believe it?" Rachael practically ignored Jake as she made small talk, making herself comfortable in his usual spot in their booth.

Jake should be irritated at being forgotten, but he slid in next to Rachael, draping his arm on the back of the bench, so proud that she was his. No, she didn't belong to him. He didn't own her and would never possess her, but she chose him out of the billions of people in the world to let her guard down and love.

That made Jake feel pretty damn special. He tried to focus on the conversation, Noles lighting up when Rachael asked about his wife and kids. They shared stories he'd heard over the years about Noles' kids and appreciated Rachael's honest interest.

"Your family sounds lovely. You must be pretty busy keeping up with your children's activities."

"I am, and I wouldn't have it any other way. And it sounds like you've been keeping Jake busy as well."

For the first time since meeting Noles, Rachael turned her sapphire eyes Jake's way, her smile bringing out tiny lines around her eyes. Jake's head, heart, and groin filled with pride. "I'm doing my best to keep him out of trouble," she teased. Realizing what she may have implied, she stuttered and faced Noles again. "I mean, it's not that Jake has been in any trouble. Not that I know of. He's a wonderful man. Kind to his employees, an amazing instructor, wonderful with—"

"Easy, Blondie. Noles doesn't need you to defend me. That's not why I brought you here." He ran his hand through her hair, happy to see it down and free-falling around her shoulders. He especially enjoyed when she was on top of him and her hair fell into his face. Or brushed against his stomach and thighs as she... Yeah. The last thing he needed was a raging hard on.

"I'm sorry. I..." Rachael bit her lip and looked between Jake and Noles.

"No need. Ross has given me a clean bill of health." He winked, continuing to play with her hair. "He's been an integral part of my recovery and I wanted to show you off. I mean, if I can land a girl like you, I must be fixed, right?"

Rachael cocked her head and shook it. "Has he always been so humble?"

Ross laughed. "Humble is not a word I'd use for Jake Morgan."

Jake wasn't offended. He knew Ross and Rachael were enjoying giving him a hard time.

"You're right. He can be quite arrogant at times, but when serious matters arise, Jake tends to save the day, taking ownership for his faults and praising others for their strength."

"Now you're making me sound like a pansy. All I wanted to do was show off my hot girlfriend."

Thankfully Noles picked up on Jake's embarrassment and changed the subject. "Jake tells me you're quite the chef."

"I wouldn't call myself a chef." Rachael blushed. "I enjoy cooking. And baking. Pretty much anything involving food. Jake graciously samples everything I make."

And then some. Rachael and Noles continued their idle chatter about food while Jake sat back and studied Rachael's profile. Her eyes grew large with excitement when she talked about a favorite recipe. When describing a taste, she closed her eyes and moaned, almost as loudly as she did in bed. The woman who he'd met a few months ago in his class was nothing like the one sitting next to him today.

And he was nothing like the man he'd been a few years ago. He supposed if she could make such a drastic transformation in a few weeks, he could admit he'd done a pretty decent job over the past few years as well.

Maybe it was time to forgive himself like Rachael said. Let himself love and be loved. She had the perfect amount of softness and curves yet her brutal honesty made her strong and feisty. Rachael wouldn't be walked over again, and damn if he didn't love and respect her more and more with every look. Every touch.

Needing to be alone with Rachael, he grabbed her hand and pulled her out of the booth, interrupting Noles' idea of the perfect French toast recipe.

"We're good, right?"

"Sure." Noles' eyes shone with amusement. "It was nice meeting you, Rachael." He slid out of the booth as well, standing and holding out his hand to her.

"Oh, I enjoyed meeting you too, Ross. Please let me know if you want me to write down the recipe for the German potato salad."

"Sounds good." He stuck his hand out and Jake shook it before placing his hand around Rachael's hip, guiding her out of the diner.

"What's the hurry?"

Jake unlocked his truck and helped her up. "Babe."

"Oh," she gasped in realization and looked down at the crotch of his jeans. "Oh."

CHAPTER THIRTEEN

R achael's brothers' cars were already in the driveway when she stopped by her mother's house the following day. Luke had called a family meeting and fearing something was wrong with her mother, she raced up the front steps and stormed through the front door.

"Mom?"

She found Graham, Luke, Lucy, Maggie, Sage, and her mother standing around the kitchen island, somber faced and red-eyed.

"What's wrong? Somebody tell me what's wrong. Why didn't anybody call me? What's going on? Mom?" Doreen's health had never been an issue before, but her face was pale and her body slouched as if she were a frail old lady.

Maggie set her coffee down and put her arm around Rachael's shoulders. "Your mother is fine. Everyone here is okay. It's...Colton."

"No." A weight so heavy she thought she'd fall to her feet dropped in her gut, bringing tears to her eyes. "He's not..."

"He's okay. He's better and he's home."

"Home? As in here?" Rachael spun around the room, looking for signs of her brother.

Luke rounded the counter and hugged Rachael. "He's kept us all out of the loop. Blake called me late last night. He'd been working near the vet hospital where Colton's been and stopped in—barged through security and nearly got kicked out—but Colton vouched for him when he saw Blake's temper. Apparently our brother hasn't wanted us to know how bad things are for him and has wanted to deal with things his own way."

"How bad is he?"

"Blake says he's got some major PTSD going on and that's primarily what's keeping him away from the family. Colton doesn't want us to see him like that."

"And his leg?" When their mother received the call on Christmas that Colton's Humvee had been attacked and everyone but Colton was killed, the entire family went into shock and prayer mode. He'd been in a hospital in Germany for a few months before coming back to the States and being honorably and medically discharged.

"He lost his left leg, just below the knee. Blake says he got a prosthetic about a month ago and has been working with a therapist. Colton wanted to be able to walk out of the hospital on his own before coming home."

"And he's here now? And he hasn't stopped by? Where is he staying?" Rachael loved her brothers more than life itself. While Colton's visits were sparse and short over the years, when she was in Maine she spent every second with him. It pained her when she was in California and couldn't see him.

Luke and Graham had been with her from the beginning, but there was always something sad inside Colton that she wanted to fix. He needed her more than the others, whether he'd admit it or not. Maybe it was the loneliness in him that reminded her so much of her childhood.

"That's what we are trying to figure out," Graham said, leaning across the island. "Blake received a text from Colton last night. Says it looked like a drunk text, but it sounded like he was in Maine."

"What did it say?"

Graham and Luke looked at their mother with apologetic eyes. "We were waiting for you to come home before we said anything else."

"You sure took your sweet-ass time today, sis."

"Lucy."

"It's okay, Mom. Had I known you were all waiting for me, that this was about Colton, I would have come home hours ago."

"I told them not to bother you. You had a late night and are working so hard to get your new business afloat." Doreen stroked Rachael's hair and held on to her hand. "We are all so proud of how far you've come."

"Mom, this isn't about me right now. It's about Colton. Guys, what did he tell Blake?"

"Let's sit down in the living room," Luke suggested.

"No, Luke. We're all here. No more stalling. Just tell us." Lucy crossed her arms and lifted her chin.

"I won't quote him exactly, as the texts Blake forwarded to us aren't exactly coherent, but he's pretty pissed with the world and doesn't want a pity party. Especially from the girls. Mom, Rach, even Lucy. He said he'll leave again with no contact if you—if any of us smother him or give him pity. He wants to be treated as anyone else."

Doreen sniffed and Sage passed her a paper towel. Rachael put her arm around her mother and held tight.

"Got it. No welcome home parade or any of that shi—crap." Lucy scowled. "Why the secrecy? Why couldn't he tell us this?"

Graham stood behind Maggie and rested his hands on her shoulders. "I guess Blake told him about Luke and Sage, Rach and Jake, and me and Maggie. It's hard for him to see us moving on with our lives when his...when his was almost cut short."

"But it's not. He's alive." Rachael squeezed her mother's hand.

"He thinks of himself as broken. He has no job. No place to live. No friends. You know Colton. He's always been... somewhat mysterious." Luke hugged Sage a little tighter. "Our family has grown, but he hasn't been a part of it."

"And it's been his choice." Always the negative one, they wouldn't have to worry about Lucy giving Colton pity stares. Granted, she didn't know Colton very well. He'd been over-seas before she was adopted, and they'd only met during the few short stays he'd had over the years.

"Maybe." Luke nodded. "He needs our support now. You know Colton, never one to ask for favors, never one to di-vulge any more info than necessary. It's always been pulling teeth trying to figure out what's going on in that thick skull of his. He threw us all for a loop when he told us he enlisted and shipped out the next day."

"We will support your brother in any way he wishes. If he needs us to give him privacy, we'll do it." Doreen regarded each of her children with eyes only a mother of six could do. They nodded in agreement.

"So now what?" Lucy asked.

"He knows how to find us. We wait for him to come to us. I don't want to hear about any of you badgering him."

"We couldn't if we wanted. Blake didn't even know where Colton was staying." Graham shoved his hands in his pockets and rocked on his heels.

"It's a small town, but if he doesn't want to be found, he won't be. Respect his privacy, boys. And girls." Doreen glowered at Lucy.

"What? Don't look at my like that."

"You've always been fascinated with him, Luce, probably because you barely know him. And you're a snoop. If anyone can hunt down Colton it'd be you." Graham winked.

"Don't you encourage her," Doreen scolded.

• • • •

LATER THAT NIGHT WHILE snuggled up with Jake, Rachael told him about the news of her brother.

"Your mother must be devastated."

"She is. She's strong, though, and will make sure we all keep our word and let Colton have his privacy. We'd all be searching the woods for him, blowing up his cell phone with texts and calls, putting out an APB on him if it wasn't for Mom. She's never pushed us to do anything we weren't comfortable with, letting us figure out our own lives in our own time but always there for us to pick us up when we fell, or to celebrate our successes."

"Which is why she didn't kick me to the curb."

"You're too charming to get kicked. Speaking of, after your class tomorrow we're invited to Luke and Sage's. They're throwing a Jack and Jill shower for Maggie and Graham."

"Another opportunity for your brothers to try out their intimidation act on me. Sounds like fun."

"I've got your back."

"And I've got your front."

· · · ·

MAGGIE REFUSED TO LET Rachael cater the wedding—wanting her to have fun, not work—so Rachael took advantage and cooked for the Jack and Jill party. After leaving the Inn, she stopped at the store and went straight to Luke's to prepare. Her brothers thought paper products would be fine but since Sage had access to stemware, plates, and utensils, they'd be celebrating in style.

Lucy stopped by a few hours before the party to decorate the large white tent Graham had set up with lights and flowers while the boys went out to stock up on beer and wine. It wasn't going to be a large affair, thirty or so people—half of them family.

Giving herself twenty minutes to get ready, she lowered the temperature on the Crock-Pots, checked the mini quiches in the oven, and scurried off to get changed. The tangerine halter dress shone bright against her sun-kissed skin. She and Jake spent many of his lunch breaks picnicking on his tailgate in the sun and walked the beach on weekend afternoons.

An hour later, the party was in full swing and Jake arrived fashionably late, since his class didn't get over until seven. "You're gorgeous." He kissed her hello under the twinkling lights. "Nice set up." The sun hovered over the horizon, the sky streaked with dark orange and pink clouds.

"I'll introduce you to Sage's sisters. They're the ones who've helped me with my Kids in the Kitchen parties." They'd been slow, not real moneymakers, but a fun little side job to put some extra cash in Rachael's pocket. "Jake, this is Grayson Montgomery. He's married to Thyme, the youngest sister, and is an architect. His office happens to be across the hall from Maggie's practice."

The men shook hands, and Rachael introduced Sage's other sister, Rayne, and her husband, Trent.

"Your girlfriend is giving me some serious competition," Trent teased.

"You own the bakery in Portland. Sweet Spot, right?"

Rachael's heart warmed. Jake had listened to her the other night when she rambled off the names of everyone he'd be meeting at the party. The men bonded over beer and meatballs, plowing through the plethora of appetizers and finger foods. When the food ran low, Rachael went inside to bring out the tray of desserts. She opened the fridge and heard heavy footsteps on the other side of the open door. "Perfect timing. I can use some help bringing these out."

Lifting the long tray laden with dessert bars, mini eclairs, and cream puffs, Rachael turned and closed the door with her hip and shrieked.

"Colton!" She dropped the tray and stood in shock. Wanting to jump into his arms but respecting his need for some space, she squatted and picked up the mess she'd made, her heart hammering away in her chest.

Most of the desserts had stayed in the tray, only a few casualties falling on the floor, so she busied herself making the arrangement look pretty again while she regained her composure. Was it okay to hug him? To ask him how he was do-ing? She had no idea.

"I didn't mean to scare you." She watched out of the corner of her eye as he tried to lower himself to the floor.

Knowing his leg must be causing him a lot of pain and squatting couldn't be comfortable with a prosthetic, she wanted to tell him to stop, but didn't want to damage his pride either. When he finally made it to his knees, she allowed him to pick up the tray for her. Seeing the struggle in his eyes as he started to stand, she took the tray from him and placed it on the counter.

"They still look edible."

"You still like to cook, huh?"

"I do. I'm actually the chef, well, breakfast cook really, at the Rocky Harbor Inn. And I bake for Coast & Roast. It's an amazing coffee shop in town. And I offer cooking classes and parties for kids. I've only had a few of those parties, but they're really fun," she babbled.

"That's good."

"I'm glad you're here, Colton. I've missed you. I know you want your space and you hate any sort of emotion, but I really need a hug. It's not for you. It's for me. Give me a second to hold you and then you can push me away. Okay?"

His body tensed when she touched him and she slowly put her arms around his back, resting her head on his chest. It had been too long since she'd been in his arms. When Colton left ten years ago he'd been a fit and rugged twenty-year-old. Rachael had seen him a handful of times in the beginning when he'd be home for his short stop-overs, but during her five years in California she'd missed all his visits.

"It's been nearly six years since I've seen you." She sniffed. Finally, his massive arms—arms that could easily compete with Luke's—came around her. They held each other in silence, the only sound coming from his quiet heart.

"Am I interrupting something?"

Rachael jumped out of Colton's embrace and wiped her eyes. "Jake." She bit her lip and eyed Colton. She didn't want to overwhelm her brother by announcing him to the whole party, but she wanted him to meet her boyfriend. "This is my brother. Colton."

Jake's face softened with understanding. "Nice to finally meet you. And FYI, your brothers have already given me hell and guaranteed a slow and painful death if I hurt Rachael." He stuck out his hand and waited patiently until Colton offered his as well.

"Good to know."

"I came in to refill the beer cooler, but that was before I knew you had éclairs." Jake snatched one off the platter and popped it in his mouth. "These are the best," he said when he'd finished chewing. Colton's hard face showed signs of a possible quirk of his lips trying to work its way out.

"If you took time to actually chew it you'd enjoy it more." Rachael elbowed Jake in the ribs and gave him an affectionate smile for trying to make things less awkward for Colton.

Jake grinned before grabbing another. "Can I buy you a beer?"

Colton's brief show of amusement instantly shut down. "No… thanks," he added haphazardly.

"No problem. I'm going back out. Is there anything you want me to get for you?"

Colton glanced back at Rachael and shook his head. "I'm good. I'm leaving anyway."

"Please stay a little longer?" Rachael pleaded as Jake slipped out, giving them some privacy. "I won't tell the others that you're here if you don't want." Colton's gaze moved to the back door. "And Jake won't either."

"So you've talked about me."

"Of course. We care about you and missed you like crazy."

"This Jake. He's treating you better than the asshole in California?"

"There's no comparison. I think you'll like him. He's a lot like Graham and Luke rolled into one. With a little bit of Blake and a splash of you mixed in."

"Me? I hope not."

Rachael led him toward the living room, where they wouldn't be spotted if someone came inside to use the bathroom. "He's got some badass in him as well."

"I'm not badass, Rach."

"Oh, yes, you are." She laughed and sat on the couch, hoping he'd join her. "Can I ask where you're staying?"

"Only if you promise to bring me one of your blueberry pies." He lowered himself to the lazy boy chair, wincing through the pain.

"I'll start baking one the second I get home tonight."

"And only if you promise not to stop by without calling. And not to tell anyone else where I live."

Rachael moved to the coffee table, sitting across from him, wanting to place her hand on his leg but unsure how her touch would be received. He wore jeans and work boots, his prosthetic undetected. Only the grimace of pain Colton made when getting up and lowering himself gave away any indication that there was something wrong.

"Colton. We all love you and want to support you."

"You can support me by not smothering me." Rachael leaned back and nodded, holding back her tears. "Dammit. See, this is not what I wanted."

"I'm sorry. I didn't mean to smother you."

"Hell. You're not smothering me. It's those damn tears. I don't want to see them. I don't want pity."

"Well screw you, Colton Riley. These aren't pity tears. These are tears of joy because I haven't seen one of the most important people in my life in six years—and he wants nothing to do with me. You're the one having the pity party. Not me."

"Rachael." Graham's deep growl startled her. "Leave him alone."

"Oh don't worry." She stood and walked away from Colton. "I will. Colton's made it loud and clear he wants nothing to do with me."

"Aw shit." Colton spewed out another string of curses as he pushed himself out of the chair. "That's not what I said and you know it. Christ. What happened to the girl who worshiped her brothers and did everything they told her to do?"

"You've been gone a long time, man. Rach doesn't listen to any of us. Neither does Maggie. Or Sage. They all think they're right and the hell of it is, they usually are. Hell, we've chosen women like Mom."

Though inwardly softening, Rachael kept her arms crossed and her scowl deep. "What's that supposed to mean?"

"Oh, little sis." Graham put her in a gentle headlock. "You've got a lot to learn about men."

"Jake is the only man I know."

"And she's feisty too. I like this new Rachael. Text me when the pie is ready and I'll send you the address." Colton nodded to Graham and limped out the front door.

"That went well." Rachael said as she pushed her hair out of her eyes. "I don't even have his number."

CHAPTER FOURTEEN

Colton had been true to his word and texted Rachael his address the following day. She'd plugged it into her GPS and followed the directions out to a rusted out trailer situated on a big open field just a few miles past their mom's house.

He'd greeted her stonily on the rotting doorstep, didn't invite her inside but thanked her for the pie. They exchanged short texts off and on for a few days, and when she invited him to a family barbeque a week later, he surprisingly agreed. From what she'd heard, Colton had stopped in to see Doreen twice and showed up at Luke's doorstep a few nights after the party. Other than that, he'd stayed recluse.

Every night Jake worked hard to comfort Rachael, wrapping her in a warm embrace and covering her with kisses. He was an excellent distraction at night, but she worried about her brother during the day while she baked in solitude of her kitchens.

Rachael climbed out of bed and got dressed for work. She hated leaving Jake's arms so early in the morning. Sitting on the bed and letting out a loud sigh and pouted. "Our work schedules don't exactly mesh, do they?"

"We have some afternoons and evenings. I'll take it."

"I love having Mondays and Tuesdays off, but I'd rather have a day with you. It would be nice to have an entire day together. To stay out late, sleep in, and do something fun."

"And what would you plan on doing with said day off?" Jake toyed with the strings to her apron. "Because I'm having plenty of fun during the night with you."

Rachael slapped his hand away from her thigh. "I need to go."

"You didn't answer my question."

"That's because you turned it into something sexual."

"What's wrong with that?" Jake scooted to a sitting position, his back resting against the headboard.

"You're relentless." She leaned in and kissed his nose. "Dinner at my mom's tonight. Be there at six. Colton is supposed to come."

"I still don't know why I can't come with you earlier."

"I already told you, my mom and I are making dinner and you'll be a distraction. I can't cook with you hovering and touching me."

"Your mom will be our chaperone. I'll be good. Promise."

Rolling her eyes, Rachael stood and shook her head. "You have my mom wrapped around your finger as well. No. I'll see you at six."

"As well? Does that mean I have you wrapped around my finger too?" he asked, wiggling his eyebrows.

Biting back a smile, Rachael crossed her arms, ignoring his question. "Graham will probably still aggravate you and Luke will drill you with ruthless questions as well. Colton will be...well, you were great with him last time."

"Your brother doesn't aggravate me, and Luke was cool to me at the party. Colton isn't going to bark at me unless

I bark first. Besides, the women will be there to keep your brothers in line, right?"

"They will, which will mean more chatter, more distractions, and Luke and Graham will take the opportunities to make you uncomfortable."

"They didn't do this with Dylan the dickhead?"

"I take that back. You fit in perfectly with them." Rachael gathered her hair and tugged it back into a ponytail. "As for Dylan, they never got a chance. I kept him a secret and then took off for California. You can bet they won't let you or anyone else slip through the cracks."

His face hardened and he jumped out of bed, backing Rachael to the wall, her hand trapped in her hair. "Just me, Rachael. No one else."

"I didn't mean... I..." Rachael lowered her head, and he tilted her chin until her eyes met his. She wasn't scared of his sudden movement or being trapped. Jake's gaze held her hostage, but it was the cloud of doubt and insecurity in them that had her softening.

"Shit. I didn't mean to sound so territorial." Jake lowered his hands and rested them on her hips. "I don't like thinking of any man coming after me. I love you. I have promises I want to make to you. Not now. Not when you're rushing off to work or I'm hurrying to a class or a job site. When we have those long, leisurely days we've been talking about, I'll share those promises with you. I may not be perfect, but I'm a man of my word."

"I've never doubted you, Jake." She settled her palms on his chest and placed a kiss over his heart.

"Yes, you have, and I gave you good reason to. When I make you promises I don't want you to have any trace of doubt in your eyes. Or in your heart. When you're ready, I'll make them to you."

Jake kissed the top of her head and drew her into his arms, holding her so tight she could feel their hearts beat as one. Heat and passion and calmness rushed through her simultaneously. That's what Jake did to her. Caused a mess of emotions, mostly good, yet sometimes confusing. She'd never felt so loved, so complete, so satisfied, as if all the crazy, windy roads she'd taken over the past few years finally came together into one direct path.

To Jake.

"I need to go," she said with regret. "The strata isn't going to make itself."

"I know. I'll see you tonight. I'll make you proud. That, I can promise."

"I have no doubt."

· · · ·

THE HUM OF A MOTORCYCLE brought a grin as wide as the Atlantic to Rachael's face.

"Boyfriend's here," Lucy stated the obvious.

"Go greet him. I'll keep an eye on the pies." Doreen waved her away with a dishtowel and lightly swatted Lucy's backside with it. "Shush, you. We don't want to scare the poor man away."

"Oh, she's tried, trust me, Mom. Jake can handle Lucy. It's your sons I'm worried about." They had been on their best behavior at Maggie and Graham's shower, but tonight was a more casual gathering. At least, that was the intent.

Tonight, however, she was more concerned about Colton than Jake.

"Imagine if Blake were here as well." Lucy, a fan of family arguments, grinned.

Rolling her eyes, Rachael hurried to the front door, hoping to catch Jake before her brothers came through the house. She stepped out on to the front porch just as Luke, Graham, Sage, and Maggie rounded the corner from the backyard.

"Nice bike." Luke brushed his hand across the handlebars, giving them a closer inspection. "You customized it?" He gave the bike a thorough once-over before making eye contact with Jake.

"Yeah, it's sort of customized, but that's only because I used whatever parts I could get my hands on."

He had told Rachael the story of the bike, how it had belonged to his grandfather who rode it every Sunday until his arthritis got too bad. When he died Jake was still in prison and the bike had been left in the rain and neglected. It gave Jake a purpose when he got out. Rebuild the bike, work with his hands, keep himself out of trouble.

"You're not getting a bike, Luke," Sage warned.

"You'd look hot on the back of one. I know you'd love it once you went for a ride." Luke grinned.

"Want to take her for a ride?" Jake held out the keys.

Luke's excitement was contagious and Sage had to laugh. "Fine. But only up and down the road. And no wheelies or anything stupid."

"Think that toy can hold you?" Graham teased.

Jake tossed Luke the keys and handed his helmet to Sage. "Sorry. I didn't bring another helmet. You'll need to wear this."

"Damn straight I am." She shoved the helmet over her head and strapped it on.

"Definitely hot." Luke kissed her before jumping on the bike.

Jake opened up the pouch on the back of the bike and withdrew a beautiful bouquet of wildflowers before they took off.

"Don't get any ideas," Maggie warned Graham. "You have your toys in the sky. Let Luke and Jake have theirs on the ground."

"I've got you, Mags. What else could I possibly need?"

"Oh, gag me," Lucy whined behind them.

Once Luke and Sage were out of the driveway, Jake turned to Rachael. "Well, hello." He kissed her briefly, and tastefully, before turning to the others. "Nice to see you all again."

"Nice trick there, buying my brother's approval by letting him take your bike for a spin." Graham tried to come off as abrasive, but the shine in his eyes gave him away.

"Works every time."

Rachael swatted at him playfully and he pinned her arms behind her back before kissing her again.

"Enough with the lip-lock. This is a family establishment. Now give me those flowers before you crush them to death." Lucy huffed before stomping back in the house.

"They're for your mother," Jake called after her.

"She needs to get laid."

"Graham!" Maggie reprimanded and pushed him away.

"I'm talking about Lucy, not Mom. That's gross." Graham jogged away before Maggie could slap some manners into him.

"Come on, Rachael. Let's go inside and let the guys be... guys."

The evening couldn't have gone better if Rachael had scripted out the scene. Granted, Colton remained aloof, but he was there sitting in a camp chair around the fire with his brothers. The men made sure there were no chili or cornbread leftovers before cleaning the kitchen.

Proving his mother did raise him right, Jake offered to help in the kitchen, but Doreen wouldn't hear of it. "You're our guest. And you brought me beautiful flowers."

"You always told me flowers were a waste of money," Graham whined.

"That's because you would send me some ostentatious display instead of coming to visit me. Besides, you know me better than that. Simple is best. The wildflowers Jake picked out are perfect."

"Kiss ass," Graham mumbled.

And just like that, Jake fit in to the realm of the Riley family. Jokes, sarcasm, support, and friendship. When the last dish was dried and put away, Rachael opened the oven and retrieved the tray of pies keeping warm. Maggie found the vanilla ice cream in the freezer while Sage grabbed a pile of paper plates and forks from the pantry.

This was one of Rachael's favorite memories growing up. Having a fire and hanging out in the backyard. On special occasions they'd roast marshmallows and even set up their tents during warm summer nights.

"Remember that time we had the baseball team over and camped out here?" Graham started after tossing his dirty plate into the fire. "We must have had six tents and three or four people in each. Rach was so mad that she couldn't camp with us." At the time she'd been the only girl in the house; Lucy hadn't been adopted until Rachael graduated and by then the boys had moved on to college, the military, or work.

"I don't see what the big deal was." Rachael nestled into Jake's lap, his arms cocooning her tight.

"Colton found her in Brad's tent and nearly shit a brick."

"These stories are better told without me. I'm going to head in for the night." Doreen got up from her chair and everyone stood.

"Thank you for having me and for the wonderful dinner." Jake stood, plopping Rachael on her feet, and Doreen drew him in for a hug. Rachael watched his body relax in her mother's arms and her heart glowed.

"Rachael deserves the thanks for dinner. All I did was provide the table. You're welcome any time, Jake." She passed around hugs and kisses to everyone before heading inside. Colton didn't get any special treatment from Doreen, just the same five-second hug and kiss on both cheeks as everyone else.

"So tell me about this Brad guy," Jake said once Rachael was cozy on his lap again.

"That's not necessary. Let's hear about the time Colton hid a snake in Blake's bed or the time Graham got caught with two girls. Twins."

"Graham Riley!" Maggie scolded.

"Rach. You really want to go there?"

Smug that she had the upper hand, she twisted her body sideways so she could see the fire and Jake while she listened to Graham stumble over the story. It really wasn't as bad as it sounded. He'd been dating Emily Bishop, but she wanted to date Colton, so she asked her sister Molly to pretend to be her. Molly had been crushing on Graham forever so it was no hardship for her, but when Colton turned Emily down she went back to Graham. And then he found he had his hands full. The Bishop girls had no problem sharing him, but he wasn't into the ménage thing, thus breaking the hearts of both of them.

"Sounds like the Riley siblings have a lot of stories to tell."

"How about you, Morgan? Got any skeletons in your closet you'd like to share with us?"

Jake tensed and surveyed Rachael for a clue. "I haven't told them anything," she said softly, only for his ears. "I swear."

She read the struggle in his face. He could laugh it off as if he didn't have any stories to hide, or he could open up and let her family see where he'd come from and how he'd changed. Just as all of them had dug themselves out of some dark, hopeless hole.

"Actually, as of three o'clock yesterday, I'm a free man." He chuckled, trying to lighten the mood. Rachael stroked his face, his ear, his neck, turning him toward her.

"You don't have to do this," she said into his mouth.

Jake kissed her back and pulled away with a sad smile. "Yeah, I do." He laced his fingers with Rachael's and kept his gaze on the fire, avoiding eye contact with her brothers and sister.

"When I was a teen I was a punk. A total loser."

"Join the club, man," Graham called out.

Jake nodded. "I got myself into some serious shit. Drugs. Alcohol. Theft. You name it. I dropped out of high school. Anyway, Julia, my twin sister, she went off to college and I stuck around here working odd jobs, never holding one down for too long. Bosses tend to get pissy when you don't show up to work on time, or show up drunk. Or hungover."

"Been there, done that too. Although I think Blake may hold the record for most jobs lost," Graham said. Blake and Colton had gotten into the most trouble as teens, nothing too serious, but enough to keep the police at the Rileys' doorstep almost weekly.

"I was high or drunk for pretty much the entire time my sister was away at college and grad school. On the night of her graduation..." Oh, Rachael's heart swelled with pride. With sorrow. With love. "I took off to go to a bar with Squeek, Snake, and Wolf."

"What?" Colton leaned forward with his elbows resting on his knees.

"Sorry." Jake squirmed in his seat, tightening his hold on Rachael's hand. "The crowd I ran with. We didn't use names. I honestly don't know if we actually knew each other's real names. Didn't care."

"What was your nickname?" Lucy asked, just as intrigued as everyone else. Rachael was as well; this was part of the story she hadn't heard.

"Spider. I was quick. Good at climbing fences, walls. Escaping the police." Letting out a deep sigh, he continued. "Julia just wanted to hang out with her brother. She thought she could save me, you know? She followed us to a bar in Portland and I yelled at her for dancing with Snake. Next thing I know he slithers out of there with her. Too pissed off to care, I drank nearly a fifth of Jim Beam."

Rachael could relate to Julia, just wanting to fit in and spend time with her brothers; they were connected in so many ways.

"Next thing I know, I'm waking up from my hangover and my phone has blown up with messages from my parents. They'd been at the hospital all night. Julia had been in an accident. I stayed by her side for nearly a week. When she came to from her coma and was diagnosed with brain damage, I went looking for Snake. He'd been the last one to see her. She had traces of opiates in her blood. Julia didn't do drugs. Ever. Next thing I hear, Snake's moved outta state with his bimbo girlfriend, so I took my anger out on the next best thing. Wolf happened to be there. He was an asshole anyway. I caused some permanent damage to him and did time for aggravated assault. Since it wasn't my first time, the judge went pretty harsh on me. But I can honestly say, I've been sober and non-violent ever since."

Rachael smoothed her hand up and down his arm, doing her best to ease out the tension in his body.

"However, if I ever see Snake again..."

Colton let out a string of curses and shoved awkwardly to his feet. She didn't like the rage she saw in his eyes. "What is it, Colton?"

"Nothing."

The tension in the air, not from Jake's story but from Colton's rapid breathing and flaring nostrils, scared her.

"Hey, girls. Why don't you go inside and get those pies? I could go for another slice." Graham patted Maggie's thigh and she nodded.

Lucy balked. "Get it yourself."

"It's okay, Lucy. I think the boys want to talk." Sage followed behind Maggie and yanked Lucy out of her chair as she walked by.

"I'm not going inside. What is it?" Rachael glared at Colton.

She, Luke, and Graham eyed Colton, then Jake, who squeezed her hand even tighter.

"Go inside," Colton growled at Rachael.

If Colton was going to berate Jake, judge him for his past mistakes, or toss him out, then he'd have to go through her first. "You're not so clean and innocent yourself. Don't you dare—"

"How much do you know about this guy?" Colton's stare pierced, through her, scaring her. "*Spider.*"

"She can stay." Jake, as if oblivious to Colton's mood, rubbed his free hand up and down her back.

Colton glared at Jake. "What do you know about *Snake*?"

"Not much. Rich prick from what I gathered. He liked to show off his money, but when it came to any major theft he'd pass it on to Wolf or me. Snake was just that. Slimy. No one trusted him. Don't know why he hung out with us, but we figured home life must have sucked and he wanted an escape."

Even though his home life had been loving and nurturing for Jake, he chose a path of self-destruction, which confused and saddened Rachael. Yet his parents treated him with love and respect, just as Doreen and Keith had to their kids when they screwed up.

"What did he look like?" Colton asked.

"Why, do you know him? Think you can tell me where he is?" Jake's body stiffened.

"Blond. Blue eyes. Probably a little shy of six feet. Maybe one-seventy? A scar by his left eye?"

Startled, Rachael whipped her head toward her brother. He'd just described Dylan. The scar had been from a car accident when he was ten. Or at least that was what he'd said.

"Sounds about right," Jake said.

"Oh my God." Time stood still as Rachael's heart stopped. She thought her near-death beating was the worst moment in her life. Then when Jake crushed her heart she didn't think she could move on. But neither of those events had been as horrifying and permanent as this.

The date of Julia's accident. The timeline. It was too much a coincidence. It couldn't be. But she knew. It was why Dylan was in such a hurry to leave Maine. Her throat constricted and her stomach spasmed.

It was her fault. She'd caused Jake and his family the most horrific pain and suffering one could possibly imagine. There'd be no forgiveness for what she did. For what she didn't do. All this time, the guilt of that one night had been pushed aside as she'd focused on her own pain, forgetting about the girl...

Her head swam and her eyes went fuzzy as if she was about to faint. Her body went limp as she released Jake's hand and slid to the ground, pulling her knees to her chest and lowering her head.

Rocking. Crying. Nearly hyperventilating.

No.

• • • •

JAKE LOOKED AT RACHAEL'S brothers for an explanation. Graham's head hung low, resting in his hands, and Luke came over to sit on the ground with Rachael, cradling her in his arms. If something was wrong with her, it should be Jake providing comfort. He dropped to his knees in front of her. "Rachael? Honey, what is it?"

She'd heard the story before, with more graphic detail. He hadn't even told her siblings about Julia's condition. So why was Rachael a crying mess? He usually didn't do tears, but they were Rachael's and he loved her unconditionally.

Waiting for a signal, a sign, a break in her sobs, Jake sat back on his heels and stroked her ankles, the only part of Rachael not being enveloped by her gigantic brother. When her breathing leveled and only faint sniffles could be heard, Graham moved over two seats so they were closer together. Jake still couldn't interpret the signs the brothers gave to each other, and every passing minute made him more and more anxious.

Colton remained aloof, the tension in his face not giving off the warm and fuzzies.

Finally, Rachael lifted her head. Her eyes were red, wet, and swollen, and wouldn't reach his. "Rachael?" She scooted out of Luke's lap and lifted herself into a camp chair. Jake stayed on the ground by her feet.

"What was the date?"

Puzzled, Jake hunted her brothers' regretful faces for a clue. "The date of what?"

"Your sister's accident."

The worst night of his life. The night he'd killed his sister, or killed any chance at her having the life she deserved. That night would be etched in his brain forever. Some stupid pop song blared too loudly from the dance floor of the bar while beer flowed freely from the tap and into the mouths of twenty-somethings looking for a good time.

When he saw Julia leave with Snake, Jake had switched to the hard stuff. Anything to distract from the waste of a life he'd created for himself. He didn't want Julia in it. She was a constant reminder of how much he'd screwed up. And sweet, sweet Julia was hell bent on helping him get on the right path. To prove a point, she'd gone to the seedy bar and even tried to befriend the losers he'd hung out with. She had no idea. No freaking idea how bad he was.

The smell of stale beer and vomit woke him on May fourteenth. After hurling the rest of his insides, he'd brushed his teeth and scavenged through his cabinets for something to eat. Nothing. Opening the fridge, he'd found twelve beers, leftover pizza, and a carton of eggs. The freezer housed four half-drunk bottles of whiskey.

Needing coffee, he'd headed out of his seedy apartment and to the Dunkin Donuts that was only a block to the right. His favorite bar was a block to the left. Location. Location. Location. The sun shone bright and warm for mid-May in Maine. Wishing he'd had his sunglasses to block the sun from intensifying his hangover, he'd squinted and trekked toward DD. Shoving his hands in his jeans, hoping to find a few dollars in his pocket, he'd pulled out his cell phone instead. Nine messages from his mother. Sixteen texts. Not wanting to hear her disappointed voice, he clicked on the texts first.

A car honked at him as he paused in the middle of the street reading the first text.

Mom: Julia's been in an accident. We are at Maine Med.

And then the next.

Mom: It's not good. She might not make it. Please, Jake. Call me. I love you. Be safe.

He couldn't read on. Forgoing the coffee and forgetting the hangover, he sprinted like an Olympic athlete two miles across town to the hospital.

"Six years ago. May thirteenth. The accident happened around eleven-thirty that night."

"Oh, God."

"Rachael?"

"It was Dylan. He blew me off that night as he often did." She sniffed and wiped her eyes with her sleeve. "I thought it was something I did and wanted to make it up to him. I was working at the ice cream stand in town and drove to his place after work. Around eleven. He was… he was in a car in front of his apartment… with another girl."

Jake tried to swallow but the lump in his throat prevented it. "Who was she?"

Rachael shook her head. "I don't know. I didn't know. I went up to the car. He… he had her pinned down and she was pushing him away. I was… so hurt to find him with another woman."

"What kind of car was it?" he asked, his voice brittle.

Shaking her head again, she choked, "I don't know. I didn't care about the car or the girl. Dylan was… he was cheating on me."

"What color car was it?" he asked more forcefully, sitting taller on his knees and gripping her legs with his hands.

Rachael squeezed her eyes shut. "Light colored. Beige." She didn't open her eyes when she continued. "Dylan yelled at me. Told me to leave. That I was always ruining things for him. I was so hurt that I didn't stick around. I ran to my car and drove away. When I looked in my rear view mirror, I saw him get out of the passenger side of her car and slam it shut. He kicked the door and yelled something before storming into his apartment."

"Who was the girl, Rachael?" Jake's voice was thick with fury as he gripped her ankle. The heaviness of guilt weighted down with a rush of rage and confusion.

"I'd never seen her before."

"What did she look like?" Jake knew the answer but needed to hear it from Rachael. His throat tightened and he breathing turned into quick, short rasps.

"I didn't get a good look. She had... she had long dark hair."

"Was she wearing a red tank top?" Rachael nodded, opening her tear-filled eyes.

She reached down where his fingers dug into her flesh and covered them with hers, stroking the back of his hands. "Dylan used to try to slip drugs into my mouth when we were kissing. Said it would loosen me up. He probably did that to Julia right before... before he left."

The burning in his veins clawed its way to his chest and up his neck until he thought his head would explode. "You knew that and you left her there to suffer at the hands of a monster? Left her to get raped? No, to wrap herself around a tree and never be whole again?"

Gasping, Rachael's eyes rounded. "I didn't... I didn't know."

Jake raked his hands through his hair and clenched his fists at the back of his neck. He jumped to his feet and paced in front of the fire.

"Jake, I'm sorry about your sister but you can't blame Rachael for—"

Jake shoved Luke out of his way with a force he couldn't restrain and Colton, the guy who could barely walk, grew super human powers. He leaped across the lawn, reaching Jake in two quick paces. "Don't you ever lay a hand on my family."

"Woah. It's okay. Let's everyone chill." Graham stood between Jake and Colton, warding off a brawl.

Not caring who he pissed off, Jake spat out at Graham, "She could have prevented the whole thing. What would a good Samaritan have done? She'd have gone to the struggling woman in the car and made sure she was okay." He turned to Rachael, his finger pointing firmly at her. When she flinched and retreated into Luke's chest, he didn't back down. Julia didn't have him to defend her six years ago, but she did today. "Didn't you learn anything in class?"

Some part of his brain registered she hadn't taken his class back then and he sure the hell wasn't teaching it, yet he couldn't stop the tirade in him.

"You don't walk away from someone in need. Dammit, you could have saved Julia's life. Screamed for help. Called 911. Instead all you cared about was yourself. And then what, you forgave the asshole who was just cheating on you and move across the country with him to continue being abused?"

Spitting out a string of curses, showing more ways of using the F-bomb then Jake had ever heard during his years on the street, Colton broke free of Graham's hold and grabbed Jake by the collar. He wasn't scared. He didn't give a shit what kind of damage the Marine did to him. He hadn't been whole for a shit long time. There wasn't much he could do or say to Jake that he hadn't already thought or said himself.

"You ever talk to my sister like that again I'll mince you into so many pieces your mama won't be able to differentiate between you and the ashes in this fire."

"Jake. I realize you've been given a sudden blow, but don't go blaming Rachael for what happened. She was just as much a victim as your sister," Luke said calmly, prying Jake's shirt out of Colton's fists.

"Bullshit." Filled with rage and afraid he'd resort to his old ways a day after being off parole, he swore again and stormed off.

Colton's eyes had raged with fury. The eyes of a man who'd seen pain and suffering, just as Jake had. Eyes of a man who wanted revenge. Just like Jake. Hell, is this what he looked like just now as he accused Rachael of hurting Julia?

Her body shook with fright as if she feared he'd hurt her. Like her ex had. Hell. He'd hurt her, like he promised he wouldn't.

Jake jumped on his bike, the guilt and shame in his chest weighing down heavily, and took off without putting his helmet on. It would serve him right if he got into an accident and cracked his skull open. He was a first class shit who didn't deserve any of the happiness that had been handed to him.

• • • •

SATURDAY AND SUNDAY night were especially lonely. Those were the nights when Jake would sleep at the inn with her. Instead, Rachael cried into her pillow, not only for herself, but for Jake and Julia and the Morgan family.

If only. If only Rachael had protected the woman she'd seen in the car. At the time, and up until Saturday night, she'd never thought about that woman as a victim. She'd been the one responsible for spreading doubt in Rachael's mind. Or at least that's what Dylan had told her.

He'd promised never to stray again. Blamed it on too much alcohol and suggested they move cross-country. His dad had a job and apartment lined up for him in California.

They could start over. It would be just the two of them. No one to come in between them again.

It meant Rachael would have to transfer colleges. There were so many to choose from in Southern California that she hadn't thought twice about it. Only, when they got there, Dylan didn't want her hanging out on campus. She'd be too tempted by college guys, he'd said.

So Dylan got her job as a secretary at a software company down the block from their apartment. He'd supported them with his job and kept the finances in his name. Since her work was so close, she hadn't needed a car. They were saving for a nicer place, he'd said.

And stupid, stupid Rachael fell for it all, never thinking about the dark-haired girl in the car until the other night.

Had Julia seen her? Did she recognize Rachael from that night? Jake swore Julia's mental state was fairly sharp and that she could hear and process just fine, and that it was just her motor skills holding her back. Rachael needed to talk with her. Maybe Rachael could help put the pieces of the night together. Not that it would matter. Jake hated her and she didn't blame him.

They'd probably never have enough evidence to charge Dylan for anything unless Julia could speak and tell the judge what Rachael believed to be true. That Dylan White attacked Julia and when she fought back, he slipped her a drug, causing her to get into an accident, which resulted in anoxic brain injury.

Rachael made a large breakfast for the inn's guest before heading out to the Morgans' place in Westbrook. She hoped

Jake wasn't there; he probably wouldn't allow Rachael to talk to his sister if he was.

Pulling to a stop in front of his childhood home, Rachael mourned the sweet boy the Morgans raised. Her brothers' bad behavior stemmed from their biological parents and up-bringing, but Jake had a solid, sturdy home, proving parents can only protect their children so much. People made choices and were responsible for their actions.

She made her way to the front door, clutching a bakery box of brownies in front of her, and rang the doorbell.

"Rachael? What a nice surprise. I thought you and Jake went away for a few days. Come on in."

She must not have gotten the memo that her son be-lieved her to be guilty for Julia's condition and had dumped Rachael. Granted, he hadn't told Rachael they were done ei-ther. He'd ignored her one text. She wouldn't chase after him and his message the other night was heard loud and clear.

He blamed her for Julia's accident.

"I have something for Julia."

"Are those your brownies I smell? She's sitting on the pa-tio. Let's go out back." Rachael followed Lesley through the house. Julia stood in the grass, a field hockey stick in hand and an orange ball near her feet. "She was an amazing athlete in high school and college. I came across her stick the other day and Julia started making all sorts of sounds. I could bare-ly make out her words, but I think this is what she wants. I'm so proud."

Julia looked up at them and rocked back and forth, her mouth opening and closing as if she was babbling a mile a minute. "Are you happy to see me or the brownies?" Rachael teased. Still holding the stick, Julia dragged her feet across the lawn. "Ah, brownies win every time."

Lesley put the box on the table and placed one on a napkin for Julia and one for Rachael. "I'm going to finish the laundry. You girls better save me at least one brownie, though." She squeezed Rachael's shoulder with a knowing smile before going inside.

"Your brother told me you were some hot shot field hockey player in high school," Rachael said, breaking off a piece of her brownie before tossing it in her mouth. "I've never played. If you go easy on me, I'd love to learn. Do you have another stick or should I pick one up for the next time I come over?"

Julia opened her mouth, taking the time to formulate her words. "I... have... fow."

"Four sticks? Great. I'll ask my sisters-in-law to come over as well. I'd ask my sister, Lucy, but she'd show no mercy on me."

"Ja... Jake?" Julia looked over Rachael's shoulder, most likely expecting to see him emerge from inside.

"Don't tell your mom, but Jake and I aren't exactly talking right now. He can be a stubborn ass, you know." Julia nodded and Rachael laughed. "I suppose you would know. Some day I'd love to hear some of your favorite childhood stories. He had to have had some cute years before he turned into a surly teen."

Nodding vigorously, Julia picked up another chunk of brownie and slowly brought it to her mouth.

"Look at you, shoving food down your throat. Your brother would be proud, but your mom's going to be mad if you don't save her any," she teased.

Rachael continued to make small talk while they ate. Normally Jake swallowed the brownie in one bite; eating with Julia took a bit longer. When she was finished and Rachael had swept the crumbs into a napkin, she turned toward her, taking Julia's hands in hers. "I'd like to talk to you about the night of your accident." Julia's face dropped in hopeless despair.

"Have you ever seen me before? Before Jake introduced us?" Julia's head lifted and she studied Rachael, blinking rapidly. Rachael closed her eyes and swallowed before continuing. "The night of your accident... when you were in the car with Dylan... Snake. I'm not sure what he called himself. Do you remember me?" She opened her eyes and watched Julia's reaction. "I was the girl who yelled at him. I was his girlfriend."

Her eyes rounded, her mouth forming a perfect O. Unintelligible noises came from her lungs. Her hands started shaking, her body rocking back and forth in the chair.

"Shh, it's okay, Julia. I'm not here to hurt you. I'm here to apologize. I didn't make the connection until the other night. Jake told me about you leaving with... Snake. I didn't know Dylan went by that name with his... friends. He'd never introduced me to any of them. He and I were... he was my boyfriend." She stammered, wanting to get to the apology before Julia went into a panic attack. "When I saw him in the car with another woman, well, you heard me. I didn't stop and look at the situation objectively. I looked at it with only my best interests, or what I thought those were, anyway. I'm so, so sorry." Rachael wiped her eyes with her hands and returned them to hold Julia's. "I wish I had done something to help you. Stayed around to make sure you were okay."

Julia's body shook as she rocked back and forth, but she didn't pull her hands from Rachael's.

"I suffered for five years living with him. He beat me up mentally and physically until my brother's rescued me. But he hurt you so much worse than he hurt me. If I had stopped to think about someone else, about you, the innocent victim in the car, I could have saved both of us. I'm so, so sorry, Julia."

The woman was a pillar of beauty and innocence, her life taken from her in one brief moment. A moment Rachael could have prevented had she not been so self-centered. Remorse, guilt, anger, and waves of sadness crashed over her as tears flooded down her cheeks.

"Had I not been so selfish, I could have protected you." She was repeating herself, but she needed to make sure Julia heard her. That she understood Rachael's involvement, her guilt. "I should have stayed to make sure you were okay. That you were able to drive. I didn't think about it at the time, but he used to slip drugs to me through his mouth as well. I never wanted them and he thought they'd lighten me up. My God, Julia. I'm sorry I didn't protect you from that monster."

She replayed Jake's hurtful words from the other night. Words that were true, but that he had no right to say to her. Rachael lowered her head to the table and sobbed.

Julia released her hands and stood. Not knowing what to do, Rachael stood as well and was welcomed with the sweetest, warmest hug she'd ever received. They embraced and cried, soaking each other's backs with tears, which then turned to laughter.

"He... hurt... you... too."

Rachael nodded. "My scars are hidden where yours are visible. In the end, I'm the one who had it easy. He stole five years of my life, but I've been rid of him for over a year. He can't hurt me anymore. You, though, Julia." Rachael stroked her long, dark hair and smiled sadly into gorgeous chocolate eyes that mirrored Jake's. "He stole more than one night or a few years. I could have—"

"Sh." With a force she hadn't seen or felt before, Julia pulled Rachael back into her arms and held her as they shed more tears.

A turbulent wave of emotions tore through her body. Her core shook with rage, and her head throbbed with guilt while her arms squeezed Julia's in hope of forgiveness. When their bodies relaxed and Rachael feared Julia's legs would tire, she pulled back. "Your shirt's a mess. I'm sorry."

"What have I told you about pointless apologies?" The deep growl from behind startled them both.

Afraid to turn around, Rachael kept her back to Jake and focused on Julia. "I should go." Julia shook her head. "I'll be back though, okay? I promise." Julia hugged her one more time before nodding to Jake and stepping away to find her field hockey stick.

"When did she learn to hold her stick again?" he asked, his voice hoarse.

"This past weekend," she said softly.

"You helped her?" Jake came up next to Rachael, standing shoulder to shoulder, but she avoided his stare, keeping her gaze on Julia.

"No. She told your mom she wanted to play. I'll leave so you and Julia can talk." Not wanting to see his beautiful and devastated face, she kept her eyes lowered as she brushed past him. She raced around the side of the house instead of going through the kitchen and risking bumping into Lesley.

Angry at herself for taking flight instead of calling Jake out on his out-of-line and out-of-character words the other day, she paused at her car, hoping he'd chase after her so she could read him the riot act. How dare he put the burden of Julia's accident on her shoulders.

Could she have possibly prevented the accident? Maybe. Who knows, they could have had words. Julia could have said she was fine to drive and the drug wouldn't have kicked in until later. She was ten miles from Dylan's apartment when she crashed. If Rachael had delayed her she could have crashed into another car, killing innocent people. Or Julia could have been killed.

One thing Rachael learned from her time in therapy was that you can't repeat the past. Living every day thinking *if only* was not healthy. Instead of berating yourself for your mistakes, you had to prove yourself with your current actions.

That was something Doreen and Keith had instilled in all six kids. Maggie reiterated the sentiment, as did Rachael's other therapist. And she thought Jake believed in the mantra as well. He'd spoken those words during his self-defense classes. Many times.

Jake started and ended each class with a feel-good message, making sure the women didn't blame themselves for any trauma they'd experienced in the past, and took control of their lives by making the best of their futures.

Hypocrite. Rachael got into her Jetta, still smelling like new car and Jake, and drove back to the inn. Once in the safety of her room, she changed into running clothes and jogged down to the beach. Most tourists had packed up and headed home to get their kids ready for back to school shopping, with only a few diehards still in Maine. Mostly elderly couples who didn't have young children. Rachael looked forward to the slower, more leisurely tourist season coming up. Leaf peepers would come in mid-October and head north or inland toward the mountains.

The coast would be beautiful with the gold and red leaves as well, but people came to see the mountains and the leaves reflecting off the rivers and lakes. Still, Rocky Harbor kept busy. Often travelers would stop and stay on the coast to break up the ride or for lobsters and clam chowder.

Pushing her legs faster than they'd run in months, if not years, Rachael worked on clearing her mind of the crap Jake put her through. No, that wasn't fair to him. She knew him better than that. It was a knee-jerk reaction to finding out Rachael's connection to his sister's accident. She would be furious too if the situation was reversed.

Julia's response, her immediate forgiveness gave Rachael the strength to fight for her integrity. She needed to confront Jake, to see what this would mean for their future. If they had one.

Luke had called her Sunday and said the same thing. He was mad at Jake for blaming Rachael, but Luke said he would have reacted the same way had he been in Jake's shoes. If Rachael was the one hurt, she knew her brothers would fight until the end for her. Jake had been an ass, there was no question about it, but he spoke out of hurt and love for his sister. Jake was hurting. While he had said some cruel things to her, he didn't say anything that wasn't true.

Rachael had hoped he'd come apologizing by now, begging for forgiveness and telling her how much he loved her. She'd read the troubled look in his eyes and the flicker of guilt when she'd backed away from him. It was instinct. A loud, angry man directing his harsh words at her usually resulted in a blow to the head or a kick to the stomach. Jake wouldn't have hurt her physically; she never feared for her safety, but she couldn't help her body's reaction.

Slowing her pace as she approached the Inn, Rachael thought back to her therapy sessions. She wouldn't let another man dictate her fate and make decisions for her. If they were going to break up, Rachael would be in on the conversation as well. She and Jake had a mature, loving relationship that had hit a rocky patch, that was all, and they'd get through it. How they got through would be the challenging part.

CHAPTER FIFTEEN

The next morning Rachael ran errands, did the grocery shopping for the week, and gathered her thoughts and courage. She picked out one of her favorite T-shirts her brothers gave her, hoping Jake would appreciate it. The cloud cover lowered the temperature for the day, so she tugged on jeans instead of her usual shorts, and laced up her running sneakers.

Jake wouldn't want the distraction of a serious discussion at work. When she'd stopped by before it was for a surprise picnic lunch or a quick visit, and that was when he couldn't keep his hands off her. If yesterday was any indication as to his feelings toward her, he'd be keeping those strong, callused hands to himself. Unfortunately.

Not knowing when he'd call it a day, she packed her cooler with the food she'd prepared and drove out to his house. She brought a book and attempted to read on his front steps. Even though she had a key, she didn't know how he'd receive her using it now.

When the wind picked up and rain started to fall, she ran back to her car and passed the time by playing games on her phone and watching stupid videos. She flipped through the pictures, pausing at the one of her and Jake at Pemaquid Lighthouse. Their bodies fit so perfectly together; their smiles genuine, as was their love. If only it was enough to heal their broken hearts.

It had to be.

Another hour past and the sun began to set. Still no Jake. Maybe she should have texted him? No, he would have avoided her. Checking her phone for the zillionth time, she jumped when it vibrated in her hands.

Jake: Where are you?

No, *Hi, Rachael. I've missed you and still love you.* Just a plain 'ol *Where are you?*

Fuming, she texted back: ***Right here***

After she hit send, she realized he could interpret her text as playful and she was in anything but a playful mood.

Jake: Where exactly is that?

He should be the one kissing her butt, yet here she was sitting in his driveway for three freaking hours with a thoughtful dinner in the backseat, and he wanted her to answer his questions? Bring it on.

Rachael: In the comfort of my bed. Alone. Exactly how I want to be.

She tossed her phone on the passenger seat and started up the car. The rain came down in buckets. She couldn't see a damn thing and would have to wait it out before trying to back out of Jake's driveway. Her phone dinged again.

Jake: No you're not.

Annoyed that he was right, she huffed and fired off another text.

Rachael: How do you know?

She didn't have to wait long for Jake's reply.

Jake: Because I've been sitting on it for the past two hours waiting for you.

Goosebumps—from the cold? From Jake? —covered her flesh. Rachael wanted to run to him. To jump in his arms and feel the warmth and solidness of his chest and his heart beating against her skin. No, she was still mad at him. He owed her an apology and an explanation. And then he texted her again.

Jake: Where are you? I'll come to you.

Nibbling on her bottom lip, she counted to ten. Then to twenty, not wanting to seem too eager to see him again. Another ten count for good measure before she replied.

Rachael: I'll meet you at your house.

He replied immediately.

Jake: On my way.

Rachael's heart beat erratically as if she'd just finished her morning sprints. It took twenty minutes to get to Jake's house from the Inn on a good day. Tonight, with the howling wind and torrential downpours, it would take at least a half hour. She hoped he would drive safe. The last thing she needed on her conscious was another accident.

Nineteen minutes later, headlights flashed in her rear view mirror, blinding her momentarily. Unable to hear anything with the pouring rain, she shrieked when her car door flew open and a pair of familiar hands hauled her out, pinning her against the car. Lips she'd memorized months ago and had longed to touch again crushed against hers.

"Damn, I've missed you." Jake ran his hands up her arms and into her wet hair, pushing it back out of her face. "You taste so good."

Sick with worry, she hadn't eaten anything since lunch and had chewed off all of her strawberry lip gloss. "Jake." She didn't know what to say. What to do. They stood in the pouring rain, soaked to the core, not caring about anything but being in each other's arms.

Jake separated their lips with a loud slurp and leaned his forehead against hers. They stood toe-to-toe, chest-to-chest while they caught their breath.

"Can we go inside?" she asked when she started to shiver.

"Hell. Of course." Jake eyed her from head to toe, stopping where her wet white T-shirt was stuck to her chest. "Nice shirt."

"I thought you'd like it."

"It's white and it's wet and it's on you. What's not to like?" Jake picked her up, tossing her over his shoulder, and bounded the steps to his front door. Fumbling in his pocket for his key, he finally opened the door and shoved his way inside. When he kicked the front door shut, he put Rachael down, allowing her body to slide along his, and pinned her to the door, nibbling on her ear. "Bacon is the duct tape of the kitchen. Really?"

"Blake sent it to me. I wasn't sure how you'd react when you saw me, so I went for funny."

"Babe."

Recognizing the deep undercut of his voice, Rachael ducked under his arm and headed toward the kitchen. Toeing her wet sneakers off by the back door, she turned with a sigh. "We can't jump into bed right now." They needed to talk and Jake naked would be a distraction. It always was.

"How about the shower?"

She couldn't help but laugh. "No. We're talking. I brought dinner. Oh." She pulled out a chair and began lacing up her sneakers again. "I left it in the car."

"You're not going back out there. I'll get it." Before she could argue, he'd banged the front door open and shut and fled.

Kicking off her shoes again, she peeled off her wet socks and unstuck her shirt from her boobs. She could only imagine what her hair looked like. And to think about how much time she put into ironing all the frizz out.

"This thing weighs a ton." Jake huffed as he set the cooler on the counter.

"I packed a lot of ice. I wasn't sure what time you'd be home."

Jake peeked in the cooler and shut the lid quickly. "You've been waiting here all night?"

Damn. She didn't want him to know that. "Sort of." She shrugged.

Rounding the island, he braced his hands on the arms of her chair and lowered his head so he was level with her. "You've been waiting for me to come home?" That devilish grin that got him out of so many jams appeared and her girly parts quivered.

"Maybe. And only because I'm mad as hell at you."

"Babe. You can't swear at me and not expect me to get turned on."

"Seriously." She huffed. "Is everything always about sex with you?" She knew it wasn't. Jake had never pressured her into anything and the crushed expression on his face told her she'd hurt him.

Jake turned serious and righted himself to a standing position. "I've never pushed you into anything, Rachael."

"I know that." She followed his retreating back down the hall to his bedroom. He reached behind his neck and pulled his wet shirt over his head, tossing it in the corner by his laundry basket.

"I need a shower. I've been working all day. I'll be out in a few." Gone was the playful Jake.

Annoyed that she'd turned their light moment into something more serious, Rachael stomped back to the kitchen and unloaded the cooler. It wasn't anything fancy. Caprese salad, spinach lasagna, and garlic bread. Turning the oven on to preheat, she kicked herself for being so stupid. Tonight was supposed to be about them having a grown up conversation about their pasts.

About their connected pasts. She believed Jake had started to forgive himself for Julia's accident, but if he thought she was responsible, they'd have no relationship. Ever. Rachael needed to hear from Jake whether he truly believed she could have prevented the unstoppable.

She put the food in the oven to warm and set the table. After she poured two glasses of red wine, Jake emerged, his hair still wet from his shower. The rest of him was dry in a snug pair of jeans that did incredible things to his already incredible ass, and a forest green shirt that had his company's logo on it.

"I put a dry shirt and pair of sweats in the bathroom if you want to change."

Rachael had packed an overnight bag—just in case—but she didn't want to bring it up. "Thanks." It felt good to strip out of her wet jeans and shirt. Soaked to her bra, she took that off as well and hung it over the shower rod. Jake's shirt hung loosely on her. Maybe he wouldn't notice she'd gone braless. The sweats were big and comfy as well. She rolled the top a few times and pulled the drawstrings as tight as she could make them.

Wishing for an elastic, she ran her fingers through her hair, doing her best to get out the biggest tangles. This would have to do.

The moment she stepped into the kitchen, Jake's eyes zeroed in on her braless chest. Quickly crossing her arms to cover up the evidence of her chilled body—or turned on body, it was hard to tell—she nodded toward the oven.

"Dinner should be ready in about twenty minutes."

"Thanks for dinner. You didn't have to do that."

"I know."

A smile escaped his lips before he had time to push it back. Rachael liked that Jake appreciated her snarkiness. If he wanted a submissive girl who would cater to his every demand and not speak her mind, he would have to look elsewhere.

Jake picked up a wine glass and handed her one. "I'm assuming these are for us."

"Are you expecting company?"

Once again he smiled at her snip. It didn't take much to turn the man on. He'd told her once before that it was only Rachael who could do that to him. She wondered if that was a classic line he'd used on other women or if it was true.

Wanting to still believe in Jake's honor and integrity, she tucked it away as a lovely compliment.

"I'm glad you're here," he said. "I was worried when you didn't show up at your place. Ellie swore she didn't know where you were. I even grilled her kid."

"CJ? He's a good kid."

"Yeah. Seems so. You're avoiding this."

"What?"

"Talking."

"I'm talking. I believe you were the one avoiding this discussion for the past four days."

"Not avoiding. Processing."

"Really? Because not returning a text classifies as avoiding in my book. Not coming over Saturday night when that had been our night at the Inn is avoiding."

"Saturday was rough for both of us. Sunday is our usual day. And Mondays you come over here. So it looks like you were the one avoiding."

"Really? Are we going to play this game? You're avoiding having this serious conversation by bringing up stupid stuff. I need to know, Jake." Rachael set her wine glass down on the counter without taking a single sip and cocked her head at him. "Do you believe I am responsible for Julia's accident?"

He remained where he was, leaning casually against the counter, unmoving. Not a single muscle in his body or face ticked. A chill ran down her spine, freezing her heart and stabbing her eyes.

"Well then. I don't think there's anything left to say. Goodbye, Jake." She crossed the house to the front door, yanking it open to the pouring rain, forgetting she didn't have sneakers or her keys. No, she'd left her keys in the car. She took one step on the front porch before Jake's strong arms wrapped around her waist, yanking her back into the house. "Let me go, Jake. We have nothing left to say."

"We haven't even started. I didn't think you were the type to run away from a fight."

"Yeah? You also told me you didn't think I was the type to walk away from a person in need. I guess you were wrong on both accounts."

"I never should have said that."

"It seems to be a habit of yours, doesn't it? Saying things you should never have said? Am I supposed to keep forgiving you? Keep letting you bully me? Walk all over me? Third time's a charm, right?" She shoved at his chest and he stumbled back.

"Is that how you feel?" he asked, shame filling his face.

"Yes." No. She didn't feel bullied by him. Hurt, mostly. He had hurt her three times. Once was out of pride, too self-conscious of his meetings with Noles. The other two times were about protecting his sister. She could understand and respect family coming first in his life, but she needed to know where she placed. A distant or close second? And his pride needed to come much, much later than his feelings for her.

Jake closed his eyes and sank to the couch. She should let him suffer in guilt until his heart was twisted and as broken as hers. "No." She wasn't that type of person, and neither was Jake.

"Once again, I screwed up. Big time. I lost it, Rachael. When you told me Dylan, the asshole who hurt you, is the same guy who hurt my sister... I... I needed someone to lash out to and you were there. It was wrong of me." The overhead light revealed shimmering tears in Jake's dark eyes.

Rachael sat next to him and scrunched her face, holding back tears. "I'd never once thought about the girl in the car other than how much I hated her for causing Dylan to stray. She was someone I wanted to forget. Learning she was your sister, that I could have... that I didn't..."

"Shit." Jake pulled Rachael on to his lap and cradled her like Luke had the other night. "I don't blame you. Not at all. I said those words out of shock. Hell, I still am, and I was processing. Which doesn't make it okay. I'm still new at all of this. Not that it's an excuse to treat you the way I did. I needed time to absorb the news but you were there crying, your family supporting you, and I had no one. I... took my anger out at you and your brothers when none of this is your or their fault."

He cradled her head into his neck. She breathed in the scent of rain and integrity and Jake.

"You're not to blame for any of this. Nor is Julia. I'm the one who let that snake into my life. If I hadn't tried to ditch Julia that night, if I'd been a better brother—"

Rachael placed her finger over his lips. "We can't keep doing the *If only* thing. What's done is done, Jake. We need to forgive ourselves. To forgive others."

"I can't make any promises that I'll act like the mature responsible adult if I ever see Dylan the Snake, though."

"I'll beat you to it. I had this incredible self-defense trainer. He taught me all sorts of moves." She sniffed and cuddled into his warmth.

"I'm sorry, Rachael. I'm sorry you got brainwashed by that asshole. And I'm sorry that I was an asshole to you as well. I can't promise I won't be an idiot again, but I promise I'll work as hard as hell to be good for you. To you."

"I can't believe I was so weak and naïve for so many years."

"There's a reason we called him the snake. He manipulated my sister as well. No way in hell would she have offered to give him a ride home if she thought he was sketchy. She thought he was my friend, so she trusted him. That's the kind of woman Julia was. Is. That's the kind of woman you are and were as well. It's not your fault that you have a kind heart. I really, really, really like your heart."

"Yeah? You sure it's not just the lumps of fat and skin covering my heart?"

Jake cupped her breast and nibbled on her earlobe. "Lumps of fat and skin? Babe. I can think of plenty other ways to describe these glorious globes over your heart."

"Mmm. Like what?" The oven timer went off and they both moaned in frustration.

"That's probably a good thing. I'm starving. And the growling I've been hearing from your stomach tells me you're just as hungry. Mind if we take a rain check on the euphemisms?"

"You can say them over dinner."

"Babe. I cannot. I won't be able to eat, and then I'll lose all respect making you think I only think about sex. With you, of course, but still."

"Nice save, Six Pack."

"Six pack?"

"It's what Mackenzie calls you."

"You girls talk about my body when I'm not around?"

Rachael laughed. "You've heard Lucy and Mackenzie. They talk about your body when you are around."

"The only one I care about is you."

"Well then. Yes, I talk about your body too."

Jake's pearly whites gleamed against his tanned skin. "Babe."

They turned the oven off and had their dinner later. Much, much later.

CHAPTER SIXTEEN

Loving the warmth of Jake's body, Rachael didn't want to move, but her bladder felt like a biscuit in a can—not that she'd ever buy or serve them—ready to burst. Rubbing her eyes against Jake's bicep to scratch out her sleepy seeds, she rolled her shoulders and braced herself for the cool air.

They'd opened his window sometime in the night, their bodies dripping with sweat after a long bout of lovemaking, but the morning air was chilly. A pleasant change from the hot summer. Labor Day was right around the corner with another Riley wedding on tap.

Rachael loved the fall. Not only because of the natural beauty Maine showcased so well, because it meant she wouldn't sweat so much in front of her oven. While summer smells were flowers, ocean breeze, and barbeques, fall and winter begged to be scented with foods from the kitchen.

Hopping out of bed, she raced to Jake's bathroom, did her business, and when she returned to his room, noticed the clock. Rachael gasped and bounced on the bed, startling sleeping beauty.

"Jake! Wake up. You're going to be late for work." Keeping his eyes closed and groaning, he blindly reached for her and pulled her body on top of his. "It's nine-seventeen. Wake up, honey."

Opening his eyes with a smile, he tugged her body closer to his and rolled them over, pinning her to the mattress. "You called me honey."

"Yes. And you're late."

"You've never called me anything but Jake before."

"Oh, I've called you other things, just not to your face."

Laughing, he dusted her neck with kisses, spending extra time on the sensitive area behind her neck.

"Jake—"

"Say it again."

"Jake?"

"No. Honey." He turned her over and continued nibbling his way across her shoulder, making a zig-zag pattern from her left side to her right.

The man knew how to distract her from any and all coherent thoughts. Her body, exhausted from their late night antics, buzzed with need, her core aching for him as if he hadn't just loved her a few hours ago.

"Jake," she moaned.

He stopped as he neared her breast and picked his head up. "What happened to *honey*? I kinda like that. Makes us sound like an old married couple."

"Seriously?" She couldn't believe they were having this conversation right now. She could feel his desire against her leg and was impressed with his control. He'd always impressed her in bed. Whether it was his sensitivity, his dedication to her body, or his willpower, he always put her needs first. Even when she could feel the tenseness in his body, he held back for her.

"Jake. Honey. Please don't stop."

"Now you're talking."

"Wait!" She pushed at his shoulders before his mouth came down on her breast. "Work. I can't let you fall behind because...well, I don't want to distract you from your job."

"Babe. You distract me from everything. And I wouldn't have it any other way." He lowered his mouth to her aching body, stopping a fraction of an inch away from where she wanted him most. "Besides, I texted the boys a few hours ago telling them I was taking the day off."

There was no more talking after that, just moaning, begging, and some excited yelling.

• • • •

"WHAT DO YOU WANT TO do with your day off?" Rachael asked as she loaded the dishwasher with their breakfast dishes.

"I'm happy being naked in bed with you for the day." Jake brushed her hair aside and kissed the nape of her neck. "Mmm. Salty. You taste like you had quite the workout last night. And this morning. Let's go shower."

"Stop." She giggled. "You're relentless. We can't spend the entire day in bed."

"Why not?"

Turning, she faced him, and he set his hands on the counter, drilling her with his stare and his body. "I'd like to think there's more between us besides amazing sex."

"Rachael, you don't think—"

"No. I know there is." She placed her palms on his cheeks and stared deeply into his eyes. Eyes that could melt her with one look. Eyes that spoke of so much pain and hurt. And love and compassion. Jake may not realize it, but his eyes never hid what he was feeling and she loved knowing how to read him. "I love you, and"—she continued talking even when he opened his mouth to speak—"and I know you love me. I have no doubts," she said before placing a gentle kiss on his lips.

They held each other in the kitchen, breathing in each other's air, soaking up the warmth from each other's bodies. At last she said, "Let's go visit your sister."

"You want to spend our first day off together in months with my sister?"

"Is that okay?"

Jake's adoring eyes turned soft, the corner of his lip stretched into an amused and bewildered smirk. "You amaze me, Rachael Riley. Every freaking day. You amaze me."

They showered together—to conserve water—and toweled each other off. "I need to get my bag from the car."

"Why didn't you tell me you packed a bag? I would have gotten it for you last night."

"I wasn't sure at first if I'd be invited to stay the night and then when I was invited, I didn't really need anything. Clothing seemed to be optional."

"Always is. However, my mom and Julia would probably appreciate it if we were dressed. Stay naked for a few more minutes. I'll go get your bag."

Back in record time, Jake watched her with predator eyes as she dressed. Rachael packed the raspberry linzer bars they didn't get to last night as Jake locked up the house.

"Mind if we take your car? My truck is a mess. I wasn't expecting company."

"Sure, but I don't mind your truck either. Your tools and work gear don't bother me."

"It's not that." He stopped with the car door partway open, obviously remembering what she had said about needing to drive her own car rather than being a passenger. "It's a mess. I've eaten a lot of take out over the past few days. Sort of slumming it."

His kitchen had been spotless last night. No sign of Jake making any meals. The coffee cup she had used last week still sat in his sink until she loaded it during their midnight dinner break. Touched that he'd been too much of a wreck to cook or eat at home, she handed him the keys.

"You can drive."

"No. It's your new car. I don't want to be all alpha on you. Isn't that what you said?"

Rachael picked up his hand and kissed his knuckles. "Driving was something...something that was stripped from me. Another piece of my independence. I know that if you drive my car it's not because you're trying to control me. It's okay."

"I love you." He kissed her before walking to the passenger side and opening the door for her. "And while I appreciate your desire to be independent and free from someone's hold, I'm still going to treat you like a lady. Do the chivalrous thing. My mom worked hard for nearly thirty years teaching me my manners. It's about time I show her I've been listening."

"She's proud of you and loves you. And so do I." Rachael slid into the passenger seat and buckled up while Jake rounded the hood.

They held hands as he drove to his parents' house. Rachael said, "Julia said she has extra field hockey sticks. I'm thinking we could bring her down to the park and play pass. Or whatever they call it."

"She'd like that."

Julia was more than excited to go out with them. Rachael followed her to the basement and opened a large tote marked *Sports*. In it she found an assortment of cleats, shin guards, goggles, and balls.

"Want to wear these or just sneakers?" Rachael asked, holding up a pair of black and pink cleats.

"Sneaker... an... shin guard. You... wear too," Julia said.

"Absolutely." Rachael found two matching pair, closed up the tote, and led Julia back up the stairs.

Staggering to the living room couch, Julia finally made it and plopped herself down. Jake rushed to her side. "Hey, Jules. You okay? If not we can do something else."

"Not a... in-va-lid."

Julia slipped one foot into her sneaker and picked up her laces, not moving her fingers to tie them. Jake and Rachael waited patiently while Julia stared at her feet. Jake had said she often forgot the sequence of events and would get extra irritable when she realized she'd done something out of order.

Realizing she hadn't put on her shin guards yet, Rachael casually sat next to Julia. "So, I've never been an athlete. More of a spectator. Can you tell me how to put these things on?" She could have figured it out on her own, but Rachael wanted Julia's confidence to build by helping others. And for her to realize on her own she'd forgotten to put on her shin guards.

Her tactic worked. Before Julia started tying her shoes, she slipped them off and reached for her guards. "This." She modeled how to put them on and Rachael copied her actions. When they both had the protective gear on, they simultaneously put on their shoes.

Rachael slowly tied her laces, making sure Julia was watching so she could see the order in the loops. Soon Julia mimicked the motion and tied her own shoes. Jake let out a sigh and a smile.

The adventure at the park went better than they could have hoped for. While Julia had a hard time driving the ball very far, she'd gained control of the stick and worked on dribbling. Rachael remembered her brothers talking about dribbling with basketball and didn't know it was a field hockey term as well.

Jake played too, forgoing the protective gear and having fun teasing the girls with his long distance drives. When one of his balls almost took out an elderly couple walking in the park, he piped down his competitive nature and kept his swings short and soft.

They went to the deli across the street for lunch and Julia ordered her own sub, remembering everything she liked on it. In the short time Rachael had known Julia she'd seen major improvements. Maybe she'd make a nearly full recovery after all.

Later in the afternoon they dropped Julia off at home, visited with Jake's parents, and drove back to the Inn so Rachael could get another set of clean clothes.

"These are really unnecessary." Jake held up a pair of panties and a bra she'd thrown on her bed to pack.

"You want me to go out in public sans underwear, do you? And braless?"

"Well, no. Just around my house."

"You're working tomorrow and I have errands to run. I'm wearing these." She snatched her lingerie from his hands and tossed them in her bag.

"Or we can stay here. However, I don't have a change of clothes so I'll have to lay around naked. That okay?"

Rachael shook her head and laughed. "I like being at your house. It gets me away from work for a little bit."

"So you're using me for my house?"

"And your body," she teased.

"That's more like it." Jake twirled his keys around his fingers. "Actually, if you don't mind, I'd like to stop at Lowes to price out a few things. My kitchen needs a serious renovation and I'd love your opinion."

"A kitchen remodel? You haven't mentioned this before." Rachael shoved a pair of jeans and a T-shirt in her bag.

"I was lacking motivation." He smacked her butt lightly. "Let's get a move on. I can't watch you fly around your room holding silk underwear and not toss you on your bed. You have less than thirty seconds to get out of here before we rumple your sheets."

• • • •

WHILE JAKE WAS AT WORK on Wednesday, Rachael met Lucy for lunch. The invitation surprised her, Lucy not being much for a lunch date kind of girl. Drinks. Coffee. Donuts. But not lunch.

Dressed in a black slacks and a funky patterned top, her sister did not resemble the pierced punk rocker look she'd donned for the first five years as a Riley. Working for Sage had helped her clean up her attitude and her look, without losing her artistic style.

"I'm glad you invited me to lunch, Luce. This is nice." They'd met at a local Subway shop, so Lucy had to know the *nice* wasn't a reference to the fine dining, but the time together.

"Yeah, yeah, yeah. Here. I did some research. This is all I could gather in such a short time, but I'm still working on it." Lucy slid a manila folder across the table. Rachael eyed it with confusion.

"What is it?"

"Open it." Lucy waved her sandwich in the air before chomping down and chewing loudly. "I'm decorating this hot shot lawyer's office downtown. Haven't met him yet, but his secretary is cool. At first I thought Scotty was hitting on me, asking me out all the time, but he's gay. And totally hot. Too bad. Anyway, he's kind of like a personal assistant to Gary Shepherd—"

"I've heard of him before."

"Yeah. He does a lot of high profile cases. Not that we have many in Maine, but when we do, he's on it. Anyway, Scotty does research for Mr. Shepherd and said he'd do some digging. Looks like the statute of limitations for a car accident is six years. You said Julia Morgan's accident was six years ago?"

"Almost six and a half. Seven in May."

"Yeah, so the Morgans are technically out of time. Or close to it."

"I'm not seeing how this is helpful."

"*Technically*. Scotty is familiar with dickhead Dylan's family. Class act snobs. His Daddy's some well-known tech dude. They won't want their name or reputation tarnished in any way."

"Still not following you."

"We get Shepherd to file a case, fighting the six year law, go to the media, put some pressure on the Whites. Play the pity card with Julia. No offense, but she hasn't been able to communicate much, you said, right? Now that she is and she can communicate what happened that night, the Morgans could have a case."

"Isn't that blackmail?"

"Yeah. So. You gotta play dirty sometimes."

Rachael thumbed through the thick stack of reports. It was too much to read now but she'd take it to Jake tonight. "This was really nice of you. To help Julia, but the law seems pretty cut and dried."

"Shepherd is good. If it's high profile, he'll want it. He can do the *cold case* angle. New evidence and all. At least, that's what Scotty says. I dunno. I'm just the messenger."

"You've spent a lot of time with this Scotty guy to help Jake's sister." Touched at Lucy's actions, Rachael held a fist to her mouth to stop the tears.

Lucy shrugged and finished her sub. "Not a big deal. Like I said, I'm at the office a lot and Scotty and I have been hanging out at night. I told him about Julia's case. I didn't use her name or anything, but told him the situation. He wants dickhead Dylan to pay as well. Like I said, he knows his family and says they're a bunch of pretentious pricks."

Dylan had never introduced her to his family. All she knew was they were wealthy and not involved with their son's life, with the exception of sending him money at his beck and call.

Eager to share the news with Jake, she hugged her sister when they parted and sent a quick text asking him to come home early if possible.

"Hey, Blondie. I thought you'd be naked on the kitchen table by now." Jake kissed her and she gently pushed him away.

"Later. First, look at this." She handed him the file and poured them both a glass of wine.

"What is it?"

Rachael filled him in on Lucy's connection and waited while he thumbed through the papers. She'd spent the afternoon highlighting certain paragraphs and data that connected more closely to Julia's case. She tapped her feet in excitement. Finally, Dylan would pay and Julia could have the medical treatment her family couldn't afford.

"Holy shit." Jake swallowed his wine in one gulp and continued to flip through the pages. When he set them down again he had tears in his eyes. "We contacted a lawyer after her accident, but he couldn't do anything since the police reported the cause to be the driver's fault. It's been so long. I don't know how we can prove Dylan White had anything to do with it."

"I dug into the White family and made some discoveries of my own. The whole family is shady. If this Shepherd guy is as good as they say, he may be able to make them squirm."

"Blondie." Jake pulled her on to his lap. "I appreciate what you and your sister are doing, and I want the snake to pay for the rest of his life, but my family doesn't have the kind of money to hire a lawyer like Gary Shepherd. The medical bills are so massive they've nearly lost the house. Twice. It was practically paid for before the accident and they refinanced. Took a second mortgage. They're tapped out. And so am I."

"I'll find a way to help as well."

Jake lifted her hand and kissed her fingers. "You've already done so much. Julia's made great progress since meeting you. She blew me away the other day at the park."

"I want to help. It's the least I can do."

"Hey." He turned Rachael's body so she straddled him, taking her face in his hands. "You don't owe us anything. I'm an ass and will never forgive myself for making you feel any of this was your fault. I didn't believe it when I said it. Those were angry words and I took my frustration out at you because you were closest to me. You being here with me, spending time with Julia, is more than I can ever ask for."

She cherished his words but still wanted to move forward. "Do you mind if Lucy pushes this with Scotty? He's Shepherd's secretary and is the one who provided her with this info. She didn't disclose any personal information, just described the situation. It can't hurt to ask, can it?"

"I love you for fighting for my sister."

"She's a big part of your life, so that makes her important to me as well. I like her and have fun with her."

"Wait until she gets her competitive streak back. You won't be saying that any longer."

"I look forward to it." Rachael rested her forehead against his shoulder. "This could be a huge break for your parents as well."

"Okay, Blondie. Let's do it."

• • • •

IN LESS THAN THREE weeks, the amazing Gary Shepherd rounded up enough evidence, much of it circumstantial, to bring the case against Dylan White before a judge. With his father's status as one of the top CEOs in a technology firm, the last thing he wanted was a family scandal. Between Julia's toxicology report, the numerous eyewitnesses who saw Dylan leave with Julia on May thirteenth, Rachael's eyewitness account, and the police report she filed last year, Shepherd was able to stretch a few things and put the fear of God in the Whites and their attorney, settling quickly and quietly out of court.

The only thing the Morgans asked for was help with the medical bills. Shepherd wanted to sue for at least a million over the cost of past, present, and future bills, but Jake's parents weren't after a profit. They just wanted to make ends meet and get the best care possible for Julia.

Thankfully Rachael never had to face Dylan. He hadn't even come to Maine, his father and family's attorney taking care of everything, wanting to sweep the incident under the rug before the media got a hold of it.

The Morgans and Rileys celebrated with a family gathering at the Rocky Harbor Inn, potluck style. All of Rachael's family, except for Colton and Blake, came to celebrate as well.

"You're an angel," Lesley said to Rachael for the umpteenth time.

"I wish winning the case meant Julia would recover faster."

"She's made great strides the past few months, even with us having to cut back on some of her therapies. Now she's able to work with all the specialists she should have been seeing all along. They don't think she'll recover completely, but we're thankful for every day we have with her."

"She has a wonderful support system at home. I'm sure that's worth more than the best specialists you can hire."

"I couldn't agree more."

"Mind if I steal my...girlfriend away?" Jake looped his arm around Rachael's neck placing a kiss to her head.

He led her to the edge of the lawn overlooking the ocean. The foliage had peaked, the trees on the islands across the bay making a beautiful backdrop to the bright blue sky and gentle waves. Dressed in jeans and a thick sweater, Rachael shivered as the ocean breeze blew cool air across her face.

"Have I told you lately how much I love you?"

"Isn't that a song or something?" Rachael teased.

"No, it's a Jake Morgan original."

"Right." Smiling, she faced the love of her life, studying her reflection in his adoring eyes. "And I love you right back."

"You better." Jake nuzzled her neck, keeping his hands clasped around her waist and resting slightly above her butt, their bodies rubbing but not X-rated. Yet.

Aware of their possible audience on the grass a ways behind them, she wiggled seductively into his groin.

"Babe."

"Yes?" she asked innocently.

"This isn't how I had planned on doing it. I didn't want to have a raging hard on in my pants. I'm a little more tactful than that. A little."

"Well how else do you plan on *doing it*?"

"Babe," he growled before plunging his tongue into her mouth and tasting her like a starved child. When she needed air, he withdrew, panting wildly. "I didn't bring you out here to grope you."

"No? What did you plan on doing, then?"

"This." Jake dropped to one knee in front of her, holding her left hand. "Rachael. God, you're breath-taking. I don't know how I got so lucky."

Gasping, she brought her free hand to her mouth, tears already streaming down her face and over her fingers. She'd never seen anyone or anything so beautiful as Jake on his bended knee in front of her.

"Blondie, don't cry. You know I don't do well with tears." He closed his eyes tight and breathed slowly. Taking his free hand to rub the corner of his eye, he huffed out another breath before looking up. "I've done nothing in life to deserve you. You're kind, strong, confident, independent, intelligent, and can cook as well as you make love. You're as sweet as a summer strawberry and I'm as dark as... dark chocolate? I don't know what I'm even saying right now. I had it all planned out. Thought up a bunch of food analogies but I'm drawing a blank. You do that to me. I look into those fascinating, caring blue eyes and I'm lost."

Jake stuck his hand in his pocket and pulled out a square cut diamond. "Get lost with me every day, Rachael. Marry me? Please?"

"Oh, Jake." Rachael nodded and wiggled her finger as he slipped the ring over her knuckle. "Yes. Yes I'll marry you. And you're not lost. We found each other. We'll never be lost again."

She leaned into kiss him and he stood, keeping their lips locked until he started laughing. "What's so funny?" Rachael pulled back and studied his face.

"That sounded like a cheesy soap opera. *Get lost with me*? That wasn't in my original script."

"It was perfect. You're perfect. I don't care how cheesy you sound. I love you and am never letting you go." Rachael grabbed on to his hair and yanked him in for a rough kiss.

"Oh lordy. They're at it again. Get a freaking room!" Lucy yelled across the lawn.

"I take it she said yes?" Graham called out.

"You told them?"

"Nope." Jake smirked. "I asked them. They all gave their blessing. All six of them."

Rachael did the math. "Five?"

"Your mom, brothers, and sister."

"You talked to Colton? And Blake?"

"I needed to make sure they wouldn't beat me up at the wedding. They even promised to show up in monkey suits and everything."

"You're going to wear a monkey suit for me?"

"I'll wear anything for you."

"I prefer you naked."

"Babe."

"**I** want my wedding to be just like Maggie and Graham's." Rachael scrolled through the photographs from her brother's wedding, making notes of the flowers and simple, elegant touches Maggie and Sage had incorporated. Blake had flown in the day before and left the day after, but had enough time to form a strong bond with Jake. It was the perfect day.

The love and laughter in the room warmed her heart. This was what she always wanted. To be surrounded by girlfriends. Family. Love. Something she always dreamed about as a little girl.

"I'm sorry I missed it. CJ's been sick a lot lately." Ellie opened another bottle of wine and placed it on the table.

Mackenzie was the first to reach for it, filling her glass then topping off Maggie, Rachael, Ellie, Sage, and Lucy's. The women had formed a close bond over the past months.

"Hey, Ellie. What do you think about opening up the inn as a wedding site?"

"That sounds like a lot of work."

"You have a beautiful view. I could have your backyard booked all summer long." Sage tapped her top lip with her perfectly manicured finger and went to the kitchen window. "A white tent in case it rains or to keep the bright sun from frying the bride. Once the gazebo is fixed up it would be the perfect place for the vows. I like it."

"Woah, woah, woah. That sounds like a lot of work. I can't even make breakfast for my guests."

"You have Rachael for that," Lucy said, refilling her wine glass.

"Jake's and my wedding can be a trial run. Of course I'll have to run it by him first. I don't think he'll mind."

"Men typically don't want much to do with the planning. I'd say it's a safe bet." Sage pulled out her phone and typed in notes.

"I don't know." Ellie paced the kitchen, shaking her head.

"You won't have to do a thing. All you're doing is offering up your backyard and a powder room. The weddings will be catered, all the dishes rented. It's a win-win for you. A great business deal."

"You think?" Ellie twirled a strand of hair around her finger.

"I love the idea." Rachael hopped out of her chair and squeezed Sage in a quick hug before taking Ellie's hands in hers. "I'd be honored to have my wedding here. And think of the business you'll rake in by hosting other weddings and events. Oh, Ellie, this is going to be so much fun!"

"Okay, I'm game. I'm not sure how much help I'll be. Booking and cleaning rooms seems all I'm good at."

"Bullshit."

"Lucy," Rachael reprimanded.

"I may be new to the interior decorating world, but I know talent when I see it. You've done a hell of a job with your room makeovers. I was hoping to talk you into letting me have a hand at redesigning some of the guest rooms, but they look fab. I wouldn't change a thing. The place needed upgrading and you did that all on your own."

Lucy was not the kind of girl who doled out compliments, so this litany of accolades was extremely out of character. Sage's lips twisted in a sly grin and Rachael's heart raced with happiness. Her sister-in-law had helped Lucy grow into a beautiful young woman. Not a term anyone would have used to describe her punk rocker sister a few years ago.

The rest of the night, the women pitched ideas for Rachael's wedding as well as ways to promote the Inn in a different capacity. Her life had done a one-eighty. Who would have thought in less than a year that she'd come out of hiding, fall in love with a tenderhearted badass tattooed biker, and be planning her wedding with a bunch of girlfriends?

Watching Luke and Sage's love story and then Graham and Maggie's made Rachael believe in love again. And, of course, having Jake rescue her was the icing on the cake. She wanted all her friends to experience the euphoric sensation of love.

Lucy was still young and Rachael didn't think Mackenzie was ready to settle down yet. Ellie, on the other hand, had a longing in her eye as she *ooh* and *ahhed* over the wedding details. No one knew the details of CJ's father, if Ellie had been married, widowed, divorced, or always a single mom. While they all wanted to know, respecting boundaries was what made a Riley a Riley.

If Ellie wanted to talk, she knew the girls would listen. Rachael spent the most time with her, using her kitchen to bake for local shops and host her Kids in the Kitchen classes. In the past few months Ellie never once alluded to a man in her life, just that Rocky Harbor held a special place in her heart. There was a story there.

While she may not be able to cook, Ellie had a gentle side to her, most likely from being a single parent to an adorable little boy who was sick a lot. There was spunk and compassion and a realness to her that made her an instant friend to all the women.

There was a love story buried inside and Rachael was set on bringing it out. Maybe she couldn't connect Ellie to a long lost love, but she had a brother who needed a woman's touch. Colton came back a shattered man and he needed someone to help bring out his humor and personality that got lost in battle.

And Ellie might be the perfect person for the job.

THE END

• • • •

ACKNOWLEDGEMENTS

WRITING IS A SOLITARY event. Sometimes. Well, except when you jump back and forth from Facebook to Instagram to Twitter every time you've written a few hundred words. For this social butterfly, I am truly grateful for my friends, followers and fans whom I've never met, but rely on as a source of entertainment and ideas on a daily basis.

Thank you especially to my Ricecakes who support and pimp me regularly: Rebecca, Amy, Chloe, Brenda, Anne, Amy, Denise, Stephanie, Suszet and Mary.

And of course, thank you to my family, especially Princess who is completely mortified that teenagers in her high school are reading her mother's books.

Happy reading, friends.

I hope you fell in love with the Riley family as much as I did! If you enjoyed Rachael and Jake's story, please leave a review wherever you purchased the book.

I love hearing from my readers. You can find me all over social media or you can drop me an email! And if you're looking for more of my books, they can be found on my website: www.mariannerice.com[1] On my website, you'll also find a link to sign up for my newsletter.

---

1. http://www.mariannerice.com

About the Author

Marianne Rice writes contemporary romantic fiction set in small New England towns. She loves high heels, reading romance, scarfing down dark chocolate, gulping wine, and Chris Hemsworth. Oh, and her husband and three children. You can follow her all over social media, and keep up to tabs with her latest releases on her website: www.mariannerice.com

9 798736 873999